THE
INCIDENT
AT
PARKSIDE AVE

TED FINK

THE INCIDENT AT PARKSIDE

by
Ted Fink

Edited by Kim Grenfeld
Cover and formatting by John Gibson

Dedicated to: My three fabulous grandchildren –
Sammy, Zevi and Emanuel.

FOREWORD

I said "Yes".

Without any hesitation, when my old friend Ted Fink asked me to write an introduction to his new book, The Incident at Parkside, I said "yes". I had just finished reading the manuscript, and I was blown away.

Ted is a multi-talented artist. For many years he has enriched my life by being a live story-teller. He tells his original adult tales with great dramatic flair to spell-bound audiences. Now he has written another book that his fans can read and savor.

The Incident at Parkside, is a well-written, complex story told from the heart. Through the main character, Melvin Kappernick, Ted probes the desire of a retired older Jewish man to leave the comfort of gliding to the end of his life in the relaxed security of his son's home in order to reconnect with some of the vigor and passions of his younger life. He doesn't ask permission—he departs without any particular agenda. He simply wants to leave the blandness of a too-snug existence and seek to enrich the quality of his declining years. Without notice or fanfare, he returns to live in his childhood home. There is only one problem—everything has changed.

This book is not a contemplative reflection on aging. From its unlikely premise it evolves into a tale of modern life—replete with crime, drugs, danger, race, old and new loyalties, love, politics, courage and values. Melvin Kappernick does not leave to seek adventure, but he does not flinch from life and its modern complexities when they confront him. He engages the new challenges by invoking the values of a well-lived past.

I congratulate Ted on writing this book, and I want to celebrate the experience of reading it with all those who I know will enjoy it.

Joel M. Levin, Ph.D.
President, Escotek, Inc.

DAY 1

MELVIN KAPPERNICK was going home, maybe to die. He wasn't sure.

In his mind, home was not the house he'd been living in for the last two years. That was his son, Bruce's home, although Bruce, the high-powered attorney, was never there. And it was the home of his daughter-in-law, Barbara, who was always there eating bonbons and talking on the phone to some of the silliest women Kappernick had ever met. And it was the home of his two grandkids who really didn't care about anything other than playing video games. The move he'd made to live in his son's house had been a mistake; he wasn't sure why he'd done it. He'd tried to adjust, but it never felt right.

When he made the decision to go home, the place he'd been born, the place he'd been raised, he packed a small overnight bag and waved to Barbara, who absentmindedly asked where he was going and didn't get it or even care when he said "away." "Okay," she replied, not looking at him. He smiled, shook his head, and opened the front door that led out to the tree-lined street. *You could play professional football on my son's manicured lawn*, thought Kappernick.

Once outside, he turned around and looked at the magnificent structure he was leaving, the one made of Philadelphia fieldstone, with its bay windows, six bedrooms, five baths, and Italian red slate roof. It *was* truly magnificent, but it was not for him. It held no memories. So, he smiled that wide Kappernick smile, walked down to his car, and drove out of the posh Lower Merion suburb into Philadelphia.

Kappernick had grown up in West Philadelphia on a tiny commercial street packed with small, struggling mom-and-pop businesses, dilapidated stores above which the owners and their families often lived. A shoemaker's, a dress shop, a drugstore, a deli, a cleaners—these were just some of the merchants who eked out a living on 42nd Street, and Kappernick, as a kid, had known them all.

His grandparents had owned Teabloom's, a rundown fruit-and-vegetable shop that also specialized in live jumbo carp that swam in a dark tank at the back of the store, waiting to be yanked out, beheaded, and gutted for some Jewish housewife who wanted to make gefilte fish. His grandparents' entire family lived above the store.

Kappernick could talk volumes about his old neighborhood: "I mean," he'd say, "you opened your door, and there were kids *everywhere*. And everybody knew who you were; you were one of the guys. Fairmount Park was one block away. That's where I learned to ride. There was no TV, no Nintendo, no cell phones; there were no restaurants, no order-in pizzas." When Kappernick went into one of his rants, people would just nod and stop listening. But the few friends he had left would cry, "Enough already with the old neighborhood! We're trying to play pinochle, here. When's the last time you were back there, eh? Have you seen what that place has become?"

Yes, he knew what *that* place had become. He still owned his grandparents' old store, and for a song had bought up the four buildings to either side of it. Now, on that once-busy little street, just a few of the structures were left standing. Except for a bar on the corner where the deli used to be and a Spanish-owned convenience store that stayed open until four in the morning, everything had been boarded up or torn down years before.

Kappernick pulled up in front of Teabloom's, where he could still make out the name on the window, despite its faded lettering. He carried his bags to the door that led to the second floor, then schlepped them up the long flight of stairs.

After his grandmother had died, Kappernick had, against his wife's wishes, secured the place, closed off the third floor, kept the electricity on, and although no one had lived there in over a decade, he'd had the rooms cleaned twice a year. Nancy, his wife, would bitch and moan and shake her head. "What are you doing there?" she'd say. "You got a mistress or something? You drag her to that dirty neighborhood for a little on the side? What, I don't do you good enough?" He'd would shake his head and give her that Kappernick smile, one that reminded people of the old comedian, Joe E. Brown. Tight-lipped, this smile almost ran from ear to ear. "No?" Nancy would say. "Then get rid of it already; sell and repent!"

"What do you care what I do with it?"

"You could make a little money."

"What, you don't have enough? When I die you can sell it."

"Believe me, the minute you go, it'll be gone, as well."

But Nancy had died first, and that's when his son had almost reluctantly convinced him to move in with them. "It's no good to be alone, Dad," was his argument. But Bruce's house was, for all intents and purposes, just like living alone—no one talked, and for the last two years, nothing had excited him.

Other than Nancy, whom he'd loved with all his heart, his only pleasure was Dutchman, his gelding he rode three to four times a week. He'd owned Dutchman for close to twenty-five years, had stabled him up above Chestnut Hill, and together they'd ridden through the myriad of trails that made up Fairmount Park. As long as he was on the Dutchman, Kappernick was content, and they were a sight to see, because it was easy to discern the affection they held for each other. Kappernick, in his beat-up cowboy hat and boots, jeans-jacket in the fall, mackinaw in the winter; and Dutchman always with his head held high, a pure white mane, and dark patch over his eye. Kappernick had mourned the passing of Dutchman like he'd lost a child. And maybe that's what had precipitated his moving out of his son's house. Or maybe it was the passing of Nancy *and* Dutchman that had made him realize for the first time just how lonely he was, and how he didn't want to die there in his son's house. If he got sick, he knew they'd send him to a nursing home, where the constant smell of stale urine would be worse than the thing really killing him. He didn't want to sit in a chair and stare into the empty eyes of those about to die. No, he didn't want to die where nothing was happening. The week before he moved, Kappernick had a sophisticated alarm-and-camera system installed at the entrance to the store and in the apartment. The same company had put new lighting in the hall and in the living room. He unpacked his bag and, after putting his dungarees and shirts into his grandmother's old bureau, he lay down on the bed and napped. When he woke an hour later, his body told him he needed a new mattress.

At three that afternoon, he left the apartment and went to the Open-Til-Four convenience store to buy food. The storekeep was an Asian man with two front teeth missing. Kappernick started to tell him that his store once belonged to Olsen the shoemaker, but he soon realized the man who was profusely shaking his head had no idea what he was talking about. When he left the store, three Black guys in their twenties were standing on the sidewalk, looking up the street. One guy was huge, had to be six-nine. Kappernick nodded to them, smiled, and said "Gentlemen" as he walked by. The three men eyed him suspiciously as he crossed the street. Just when Kappernick had reached the other side, five kids—they couldn't have been more than eleven or twelve years old—riding on small bikes came pedaling down the street, almost simultaneously doing wheelies and other tricks as they passed him, and as they passed the guys standing in front of the convenience store, the tall guy slapped the hand of one of the bikers. Later that day, looking out through his shaded front window, Kappernick saw the bikers come down the street from the other direction, and one of the bikers slapped the hand of another man in front of the store. This time, he saw one of the riders was a girl. Kappernick thought nothing of it.

That night, he watched the six o'clock news, made himself a can of Campbell's tomato soup, and read the newspaper. Things were not good in the world. Isis was blowing up artifacts and ancient monuments, and this annoyed Kappernick to an extreme. There was no reason for it, no sense to it. Structures that had been standing for thousands of years were now no longer there.

Unable to watch any more, he turned off the TV. It was close to nine o'clock. The house seemed incredibly silent, until he thought he heard something upstairs on the third floor. He wasn't sure. Could have been outside. He told himself he'd have to check it out in the morning. He picked up a walking stick—which he didn't need, but enjoyed carrying—opened his apartment door, walked down the stairs and out into the street. The night was black; only two street lamps were on. And no one was out. He walked up to the bar on the corner.

The place was called Springer's—Springer's Spot Lite. A name that was a joke unto itself. A red-and-yellow-lit jukebox in the corner sang the blues, and for good reason—the place was sad and in need of a face-lift. Four or five guys sat at the tired bar, and of the ten tables haphazardly situated, only two were taken.

Everything stopped momentarily when Kappernick walked in. He strode up to the bar, where the bartender eyed him suspiciously as he wiped a shot glass. Kappernick smiled.

The barkeep was wrinkled, Black, tall, thin, and sharp-tongued. "Can I help you?"

Kappernick ignored his attitude. "What you got on tap? Anything dark?"

"Everythin's dark in this place, mister," he growled.

"How about a dark ale?"

"You bein' funny?"

"No," Kappernick snapped. "All I'm tryin' to do is get something to drink."

The barkeep softened. "We ain't got no ale."

"Okay. How about a Rolling Rock?"

"Now you talking what we got." The barkeep walked up the bar, flipped open a cooler, pulled out a bottle, then sauntered back down and placed the beer in front of Kappernick. "That'll be five dollars."

Kappernick blinked. "Five dollars? For a Rolling Rock!"

The barkeep *tsk*ed. "That's what it is."

Kappernick stared at him coldly. Then, taking a five-dollar bill out of his pocket, he said, "Well, like my daddy used to say, 'even a thief needs to make a living.'"

The barkeep stiffened, then grinned, snatched up the five and, as he walked away, said, "Enjoy your beer, honky."

Kappernick watched him as he talked to the other people at the bar. Then he saw the snippety bartender put the five into the till and come back down to place three dollars by the half-drunk bottle. "It was only two dollars," he said. "I was just tryin' to see what you were made of."

Kappernick nodded. "I'm made of the same crap you are, only a different color."

The barkeep laughed. "Awright, I hear ya. This is my place. My name's Jesse, Jesse Springer."

Kappernick smiled. "Melvin," he said. "Melvin Kappernick."

Springer's mouth dropped open. "What? You the same Mel Kappernick that use to live right down the street? You old lady Teabloom's son?"

"Grandson."

Springer shook his head in disbelief. "You Mel Kappernick!"

"Same guy, only sixty years older."

"Yeah, it do fly." Springer stuck out his hand. "Slap me five. It's good seeing you."

"It wasn't five minutes ago."

"That was then, this is now. Man, what you doin' here?"

"I just moved back in."

A sympathetic look ran across Springer's face. "What? You go bust?"

"No."

"You go crazy!"

"Nah, I just wanted to come back."

"Back? There ain't no back. Even I don't live here."

Somebody up the bar needed Springer, so he walked away, shaking his head. Moments later, he returned, looked at Kappernick, and laughed. "I don't know what you're doin', but you're welcome here anytime. What kinda dark ale you like, 'cause I'll stock it just for you."

Kappernick left the bar at ten o'clock and noticed the

street was basically empty. Of course, the same guys who'd been there that day were still in front of Open-Til-Four, milling around. But then he saw someone standing by his car, looking in. The guy was just about to touch the door handle, when Kappernick pushed the alarm button on the keyring in his pocket, setting off a mini-siren, and the guy's hand froze momentarily just short of the car handle before he quickly walked away. The loiterers in front of the convenience store also disappeared.

Kappernick smiled, turned off the alarm, and went into house. In the bedroom, he turned down the covers to the bed, and read for about an hour, and just before falling off to sleep, he thought he heard something upstairs and reminded himself to check it out the next morning.

DAY 2

USUALLY, MELVIN KAPPERNICK'S eyes opened at 7 a.m. Didn't matter how many hours he'd slept the night before. He was a man of routine.

His eyes opened and, like the soldier he once was, Kappernick hopped out of bed, did thirty squats and then twenty push-ups. These days, the count had fallen to fifteen, and then ten. These days, he was panting after the routine. There was a time … Shit, to hell with that "there was a time" crap. Nobody cared what he'd been. Nobody could look now and see what he was.

He sat on the bed and swallowed hard. His arms and legs ached. He ran his hands through a head full of thick, white hair, forced himself up and marched to the bathroom where he took two Tylenol, showered, and brushed his teeth. Back in the bedroom, he made his bed. At his son's house, he always made his own bed. In fact, before leaving yesterday, he'd stripped the queen-size bed, folded the dirty sheets, and left a note that read:

THANKS FOR EVERYTHING—MELVIN

17

While he was scrambling a couple of eggs, he thought he heard the noise again and he looked up at the ceiling, listening hard, but heard nothing. After he ate, he examined the door that led to the third floor. Years ago, the carpenters he'd hired had installed a steel door with a heavy-duty lock. Kappernick had the key, but he'd left it in the car with some other things he'd packed. He told himself he'd get it after taking his constitutional walk and, taking his cane, he left the building. He planned to go into the park to look at Memorial Hall, and as he walked up the street, he saw the same hoods again standing in front of Open-Til-Four. He knew they were watching him, so he stopped as if making a decision and then, looking at them, Kappernick smiled and walked across the street. One of the hoods was so tall, Kappernick had to strain his neck to look up at him, and he figured this one was in charge, because he stood his ground, staring at him as he approached.

"You the boss?" Kappernick asked, looking up.

"I just might be," the big man answered in a Jamaican accent.

The other two started to come over to see what was happening, but Kappernick stopped them with, "Hey, I'm talking to this man. This is a private conversation."

The two guys stopped, and the big man laughed. "You one crazy son of a bitch," he said. "What you want?"

Kappernick smiled. "What's your name?"

"They call me Too-Tall."

"Great name. Okay, here's the deal: I got a job for you, and it pays twenty dollars a week."

"Heh. Twenty dollars ain't shit."

"Well this is an 'ain't shit' job. It requires no physical work, and it's gonna help you."

The big man's eyebrows knitted together and a smirk spread across his face. "How it gonna help me?"

"Okay, here's the deal: You see that car over there? That's my car. If somebody tries to open it or fuck with it, an alarm goes off automatically. It's like a siren. Sirens can draw fire engines, and cop cars, and people that some don't want to—"

Too-Tall laughed. "I get you, man. I like you. You one crazy son of a bitch, but I like you. What's your name?"

The big man held out his huge hand, and Kappernick slapped it. "You can call me Mel. Now, introduce me to your friends."

Too-Tall waved his friends over, then wrapped an arm around each. The guy on his left he called "Sweets," and the guy on his right he called "Rollins." "Rollins," he said, "he be bad." And Too-Tall winked.

Kappernick stuck his fist out to Rollins, who touched it with his own. "I'm glad you're bad, Rollins, and I want you to be bad with anyone who fucks with my car."

Too-Tall laughed again. "I love this, Melvin. When payday be?"

"You get paid at the end of the week. Deal?"

As Kappernick began to walk to the park, he heard Too-Tall say with delightful sarcasm, "Hey, boys, I got me a job!" and they all started to laugh. The walk to the park was short. Three football fields away stood the picturesque Memorial Hall, now the Please Touch Museum, built for the centennial celebration of 1876. At that time, Parkside Avenue, the street he now crossed to enter the park, had been one of the city's posh neighborhoods, and rightfully so, for the magnificent brownstones that lined the street and overlooked the park were truly beautiful in every way. But time had taken its toll. Once the brownstones had been converted from single-family mansions into apartments, the landlords had failed in their upkeep. Now the buildings were shabby remnants of better times, and Kappernick winced at their long-standing disrepair.

To the right of Memorial Hall stood the Smith Memorial Arch, a beautiful structure with towering statues, also built for the centennial celebration as the entrance to the park. Locals called it The Whispering Walls, and that's where Kappernick headed. He crossed over to where the kids used to play football and capture-the-flag—a good twenty-minute walk through mowed fields—then sat on the stone benches that surrounded the walls and caught his breath. He leaned back against the cool stones and reflected as an adult how wondrous the monument was. At least no one had graffitied the stonework; the masonry and statuary were wonderful. Kappernick shut his eyes and thought of his youth: the way the kids had played, the games they'd made up—wire-ball, hose-ball, wall-ball, step-ball, half-ball—how they'd kept score in stickball, how they'd chosen up sides for tackle football played without pads, not twenty yards away from where he sat. He saw Nancy as a young girl with her hair down around her shoulders, promising to wait for him when he returned from Vietnam. Nam. *If* he returned?

Flashes of night-fire fights filled the air. An explosion— *BAM!* A crash. "Get the fuck down!" Arms flying, legs ripped off. *CRASH!*

Kappernick's eyelids flew open, and he was momentarily disoriented. His eyes darted. No one else was in the pavilion, but the sound had been so real! He focused on where it'd come from—not fifty feet away, a metal can had been knocked over. And now he saw what had occurred: a huge dog had toppled over a heavy, wire trash container and was rummaging for food. Kappernick watched as the animal backed its way out of the bin, then gasped at the size of the beast.

"Jesus!"

But just like the crash of the tipped-over can, the cold, stone walls amplified his voice, and the dog looked up. Man and beast stared at each other, neither able to avert his eyes. Kappernick didn't know what it was thinking. All he could think about was the stature of the brute—easily the size of a small pony a kid could ride—and it was obvious the dog was starving. You could see his ribs.

"Hiya, big boy," Kappernick said without moving. The dog lifted his upper lip and let out a slow growl. Kappernick didn't know what to do. He had his cane, but even with the animal's emaciated condition, he knew he'd be no match for the beast. In his pocket lay two biscuits he'd made that morning—things to nibble on in case he got hungry on his walk. Carefully, he extracted them, and just as carefully, he tossed one underhanded to the approaching hound. The big dog sniffed it, then swallowed it in one gulp. He kept coming.

"Did you like that, big boy?" Kappernick asked, still not moving while the animal cautiously approached. Kappernick held out the second biscuit, which the dog ate from his hand then sniffed to see if any more was to be had. Kappernick kept talking, not making any quick movements, and the dog seemed to listen until the brute finally turned, almost reluctantly, and left the monument. Kappernick watched him cross the road, walk through a wedge of woods the kids in the old days used to call "Horse Chestnut Island," and disappear.

That afternoon, Kappernick put off his plans to examine the third floor, and instead, drove to a library in the Wynnfield section of the city. He was fascinated by the dog, knew it was a purebred, but not one he'd ever seen before. It looked like an exotic golden retriever, though bigger, taller, sleeker, and black—a deep, shiny black with a curly, wiry coat. At the library he found a book on dog breeds, and sure enough, there it was: a curly-coated retriever. Rare. Loyal. Smart. Kappernick stopped at a supermarket on the way home to pick up several large cans of Alpo dog food, then he parked in front of his building, waved to the guys standing in front of Open-Til-Four, ate an early dinner, watched Jeopardy, and fell asleep reading *The Storied Life of A.J. Fikering*. He slept soundly and woke at exactly 7 a.m.

DAY 3

DESPITE WAKING AT HIS USUAL HOUR, Kappernick got a late start. He did his exercises, made himself breakfast, then planned to open the door leading to the third floor. But the key didn't work; he couldn't get it completely into the lock. He called Ajax, the company that had installed the door, and they suggested he use graphite or WD40. If that didn't work, they'd set up an appointment.

But he'd heard the noise again while making his eggs and wanted to find out what it was, so he drove up to a hardware store on 52nd Street and bought both lubricants the company had suggested. When he returned, though, he didn't try to open the door immediately. Instead, he took a can of Alpo dog food, a dish, and a can opener, put them into a plastic bag, and took his walk.

As he'd done the day before, he crossed Parkside Avenue and went to The Whispering Walls. A nice breeze was blowing through the monument, blowing toward Horse Chestnut Island. He opened the can and emptied the contents into the bowl, then placed the bowl in front of him and waited.

Once again, he closed his eyes and thought of the past— as Springer had said, "It do fly."—and when he opened his eyes again, the dog was there, not more than five feet away, looking at him, studying him. He wore no collar.

"Hey, big boy," Kappernick said, "this is for you." The dog seemed to understand, but was hesitant, so Kappernick inched the bowl forward with his foot. "Don't be afraid. I'm not gonna hurt you. I can see you're hungry."

Slowly, softly, Kappernick spoke to the dog, spoke to him like he used to talk to Dutchman. Finally, the dog ate—gobbled it down, finishing it in a matter of seconds. Then he moved closer to Kappernick and sniffed him up and down. Kappernick didn't try to touch him, and just as the dog had done the day before, he turned and left through Horse Chestnut Island and back into the woods.

When Kappernick got home, it was close to three o'clock, and he again tried the key to the security door. It'd been years since it'd been installed. The door was heavy, and it took some strength to swing open. To the right of the entryway was a light switch, which Kappernick tried, but it failed to turn anything on, so he grabbed a large flashlight. As far as he knew, the third floor had no electricity.

From where he stood, the place was dark, almost black. Slowly, cautiously, he climbed the stairs, unable to imagine what was up there. He knew there were two small rooms— one where he and his brother, Isaac, had once slept in bunk beds; the other, toward the front of the house, was where his parents had slept in a double bed. He checked that room first. Filthy, grimy, once-white shades now covered two darkened, dirty windows, their glass panes caked with years of grime. Decades before, every stitch of furniture had been removed from the third floor, and just as he'd thought, the room was completely empty.

He first checked the tiny closet and the locks on the windows—all secure. Then he shined his light on the floor. The dust was thick, but he smiled when he thought of his parents sleeping in that room, and the smile broadened when he recalled how, as a little boy, he'd go in when he was scared and ask if he could sleep with them.

Absently, he left the front room and walked over to the smaller one where he and Isaac had bedded down. This room should have been empty like his parents' room, but it wasn't. On the floor near the single window lay a pallet. Someone was living there! Well, if not living, at least sleeping there. This discovery so startled him, he took a protective stance, jerking the flashlight around as if he might find the intruder. Yet the room was empty. Still, this wasn't what he'd expected. What had he expected? A mouse, a squirrel, a raccoon? Anything else, but certainly not a person! How … ?

He looked in the closet—nothing. He checked the window—filthy, like those in the front room, and it was nailed shut. So how were they getting in?

"How the fuck?" he whispered aloud. This was the third floor! Impossible!

He re-examined the bedding, which looked like a couple of army blankets set atop a thin piece of foam, but it was enough to alarm Kappernick. And unlike the front room, this back room had been swept. In the corner stood a broom, near which rested a small pile of dust and debris.

Once again, Kappernick moved his flashlight around the walls, which were gritty and covered with torn, rose-colored, flowered wallpaper, but they were solid. How, then?

Slowly, he backed out of the room, went back down the stairs, and locked the door. He made himself a cup of coffee and, sitting in his easy chair, contemplated the problem. He didn't believe in ghosts, but the possibility crossed his mind.

That night, Kappernick went to Springer's Spot Lite and took a seat at the end of the bar. Springer smiled, greeting him with a bottle of Raison d'Etre, a dark ale, at which

Kappernick smiled.

"It's supposed to be pretty good," said Springer. "From Dogfish Breweries."

"I've heard of it. Thanks."

"Unfortunately, that there'll cost you five."

"That's okay."

"How's it going? Enjoyin'?"

"Aw, not bad…"

Springer read the concerned look on Kappernick's face. "What?" he said.

"I think I got something crawling around in my third floor. It makes noises, but I can't figure out how it gets in."

"Oh, is that all? For a minute there, I thought you had some real problems. Did you check the crawlspace?"

"The crawlspace?"

"Yeah, all these old buildings have a crawlspace, like three or four feet, between the third floor ceiling and the actual roof. When I first bought this place, I had to have my electric guy go up there to disconnect the old knob-an'-tube wiring."

"Really? How'd he get up there? Did he have to cut open a hole?"

"Nah, nottin' like that. Usually, dare's a hatch. I think he found mine in the ceiling of a closet."

Kappernick smiled. Sure, he checked the closet in the back room, but not its ceiling.

Springer, seeing the smile on Kappernick's face, was pleased. "Did I help you?"

"Yeah, man, thanks."

DAY 4

KAPPERNICK WANTED to be at The Whispering Walls early so he could see where the big dog came from. This time, he brought two cans of food and opened both, put them in the bowl and waited. This time, he didn't close his eyes. It didn't take long. As if the big dog had been waiting, he emerged from the woods that bordered Horse Chestnut Island and, before crossing, he stopped at the road that separated the island from the monument to make sure no vehicles were coming. When he entered The Whispering Walls and saw Kappernick, there was no hesitation. This time, the bowl of food sat at Kappernick's feet. Kappernick stood totally still, hands by his sides, and started to talk softly as the dog ate. The food was gone in a matter of minutes.

After licking the bowl clean, the big dog did something strange: he nudged his head under Kappernick's hand as if needing to feel the warmth of another living being, and Kappernick stroked the dog's head. It was certainly the big dog's way of thanking the man for being a friend. Though that bit of affection lasted less than a minute, it filled Kappernick's heart all the same, and it was as important to him as it was for the dog. Then the dog retreated, leaving Kappernick all alone again.

Suddenly, Kappernick felt as cold as the statues that towered above him. He stood there for a couple of minutes before heading back toward 42nd Street and the Teabloom building. He'd just crossed Parkside Avenue when he saw them coming—the bicycle gang; the same set of kids he'd seen before. They turned in unison onto 42nd and actually passed him, when the lead kid, dressed in a short leather jacket with a ratty fur collar, skidded to a stop, turned around, and went back to where Kappernick was walking. The rest followed.

"Where you goin', white-eye?" the kid asked. He was only eleven, maybe twelve, at most. "What you doin' here?"

"Just walking, is all. Going home."

"Jus' walkin'?" He snickered. "Goin' home? You live down here? Who say you can live down here?" The other kids started to laugh, but Kappernick kept walking.

"Hey, I'm talking to you, muthafucka! You tryin' to be smart with me?"

Kappernick stopped, turned, and smiled. "No, I'm not trying to be smart. Why don't you go pick on someone your own age?"

The kid bit down on his lower lip, a la Muhammad Ali. "What dat? What you say, bitch?" With his left hand on the handlebars, he shoved Kappernick in the chest with a flat open palm, a blow that pushed Kappernick back a step or two.

The kid came at him again. "Give me your fuckin' money, bitch…" He leaned forward, planning to hit him again in the chest. This time, though, as the kid's hand touched him, Kappernick, with the speed of a much younger man, caught three of the kid's extended fingers and pulled him off of the bike.

The kid fell to his knees, screaming, as Kappernick bent his fingers back. Another kid started to get off of his bike, but Kappernick whacked him hard on his thigh with his cane, and that kid fell back into the street. The rest stood frozen on their bikes. One of them was a girl, and her eyes widened when she saw her leader begging and crying, "Let me go! Let me go!"

Kappernick stood above the kid, whose face was contorted in pain, while his own wrinkled one was contorted with rage. "If you don't shut the fuck up, I'm gonna stick this cane down your fucking throat. YOU DON'T THINK I WILL!"

"Please, please …" The kid's voice was barely audible.

"Oh, now you're pleasin' me?" Kappernick said sarcastically, quickly scanning the others' faces. "I could break these three fingers right now, but I'm not gonna. I'm gonna let you go, but I want an apology first."

After the kid whined out an apology, Kappernick released his fingers, and the gang all fled up the street, stopping in front of the convenience store to tell Too-Tall and his homies what had just occurred. They pointed down the street toward Kappernick, who continued walking at his usual pace.

Too-Tall shoved his hands onto his hips and bent down, yelling at them. Kappernick, of course, couldn't hear the big man, but he could imagine he was saying: "You motherfuckers tryin' to kill my biz?"

The gang rode away, glaring at Kappernick as he came up the street. Too-Tall crossed over to meet him.

"You one tough ol' bird."

"I just want to be left alone. I don't like being intimidated."

"Dat one who's hand you almost broke got a mean old man."

"Oooh, I'm scared. Should I start carrying my gun?"

"Nah, I'll take care of it. He won't be botherin' you, and neither will those other kids."

"Thanks."

Too-Tall laughed. "I gots to protect my boss. Where you learn to be so tough?"

"Right here, these very streets, and … the Marines. 'Nam, baby!"

"Yeah. Awright!" Too-Tall extended his hand and wiggled his fingers, and Kappernick extended his until the tips of their fingers met.

When Kappernick entered the building, he shut the front door and leaned against it, out of breath. He was exhausted. He climbed the stairs and fell face-first into his bed. Shit, being tough was hard and a lot of work. But so far, it was a hell of a lot better than sitting around watching, *As The World Turns*. There were a lot of things to think about.

His eyes shut, and he slept for a good hour and a half.

On each side of the four buildings Kappernick owned stood empty lots; huge cavities where several stores used to be. The city had bulldozed the lots flat, and four times a year, crews were sent to clean up the accumulated debris. No question this part of 42nd Street was a wasteland, and Kappernick had a hard time understanding why. Why hadn't developers come in and rebuilt? This area was so close to the fabulous Fairmount Park, to Memorial Hall, The Whispering Walls, Old Lake, the Dell Music Center, Concourse Lake, The Horticultural Center, and all of the other buildings that had been erected for the centennial celebration of 1876. At one time, this neighborhood had been so vibrant! Parkside Avenue had been so beautiful. He could remember, as a boy of only six, the day the second world war had ended and Nazi Germany had surrendered, how the whole neighborhood had celebrated with huge bonfires right on the corner of 42nd and Viola, ones that roared into the sky and had lasted all night.

Now, as he stepped over the debris of the empty lot that used to be Singer's Cleaners & Repair, he examined what was once the demolished stores' backyards to determine how anyone could gain access to the roofs of his buildings since these buildings had no fire escapes. Years before, he'd replaced the broken-down wooden fence with a chain-link one, and as he walked alongside this fence, he immediately saw the problem. Where he walked, the grass and the weeds were high but for a narrow path that led to several heavy-duty milk crates stacked like stairs to facilitate climbing over the fence. On the other side rested a plank that led down into the yard of what used to be Murray's Soda Fountain, and not four feet away from the foot of the board stood a gigantic weed-like tree that gently leaned against the old building.

It was so obvious. Somebody, like Jack in *Jack and the Beanstalk*, had been climbing over the milk crates, down the plank, then up the tree to get to the roof. Shaking his head, Kappernick grinned. Well, he'd put an end to that. At least now he knew for sure it wasn't a ghost.

So they were coming in from the roof, which meant some things had to be done immediately. *Tomorrow*, Kappernick thought as he walked back through the empty lot, *I'll have to call a tree surgeon to cut down that tree. Then I'll have to get a roofer up there to close up the hatch, or door, or whatever it is they're opening to get in.* Having never been up there, he had no idea what it was.

Grimly, he emerged from the lot and walked to his car, where inside the trunk was a toolbox that contained a power drill and Phillips-head wood screws. He put a half-dozen two-inch screws and the drill into a tote bag, then went into the house and into the bedroom. From the nightstand next to his bed, he removed a .38 revolver stored in a hip-holster, and snapped the holster onto his belt. In the kitchen, he retrieved the large flashlight, unlocked the security door to the third floor, and went up the stairs.

Cautiously, he entered the room with the pallet, but no one was there. In the closet, he checked out the ceiling, and yes, there it was, just as Springer had said: a hatch to the crawlspace. He intended to secure the closet door with the screws, but standing there, he started to think that might be a bad idea. Suppose the person came in, but couldn't get out because the door was screwed shut?

For a couple of seconds, Kappernick vacillated about securing the door or just leaving it alone, when suddenly he heard noises up on the roof. Footsteps, followed by the roof hatch/door being lifted. He flicked off his flashlight and stepped behind the closet door, his heart pounding, when the hatch in the closet ceiling opened, immediately filling the closet with light. The interloper had a flashlight!

Kappernick silently removed his pistol from his hip holster. The trespasser obviously used the closet shelf as a step, then almost silently jumped down and into the middle of the room. That's when Kappernick flicked on his own light and kicked the closet door shut. "Don't fucking move or I'll blow your fucking brains out!"

The break-in artist froze.

"Turn around—slowly," said Kappernick. "Don't do anything stupid."

"Please…"

"Shut up and do what I tell you."

Slowly, the person turned around, and when Kappernick saw who it was, his mouth fell open. It was a kid! One of the kid bikers, and unbelievably—it was the girl!

Kappernick gasped. "What the fuck … ?"

"I'm sorry … please …"

Kappernick looked down at the .38 in his shaking hand. "Jesus Christ, I could have shot you," he said. "You're just a kid. What the fuck are you doing here?"

"Please … just let me go. Don't hurt me."

Suddenly it was Vietnam. A village. Straw huts. A girl—ten, eleven—walking toward the man on point. Malley, the point man did something stupid. He should have shouted for her to stop. She kept coming. "Shoot her, Malley!" someone yelled. "She's just a fucking kid!" Malley shouted back over his shoulder. "Get down, Malley!" Her face was dirty, with tears running down her face. "Shoot her! Get down!" "She's just a…"

"Please … just let me go. Don't hurt me."

"What are you doing here?"

"I just wanted to sleep here."

"What? Why? Go home!"

"I'm afraid."

"Afraid?"

She was caramel-colored, wide-eyed, oval-faced. Under her baseball cap, her hair was pitch-black, long and wavy. She was beautiful. He remembered riding up from North Carolina on old Route 13. It was 1980, and there'd been a twenty-four-hour fast food chain restaurant called, believe it or not, Sambo's. Yes, Sambo's as in "Little Black Sambo." And their logo was everywhere—the paintings on the walls and on the menus were of what the company thought Little Black Sambo looked like: a Black kid with White features. This little girl looked just like that image.

"How old are you?" he asked. "Don't lie."

"I'll be twelve in six months."

"What are you afraid of?"

"Ice Man. He been after me."

"After you?"

"Yeah, you know…" She looked at the floor and bit her

lower lip. "He be wantin' me. I can see it in his eyes. He gonna make me one of his. But I don't want it. I don't wanna be like them others. I just wanna be left alone."

"What about your parents?"

"Ain't got none. They say my daddy got killed when I was real young, and my mom been in prison for the last five years."

"What's your name?"

"Tiffany."

"Tiffany."

Kappernick let out a short laugh, and Tiffany became indignant.

"What you laughing at?"

"Nothing. All right, here's what we're gonna do. We're gonna go downstairs where we can talk."

"You gonna hurt me? I seen what you done to Spokes. Almost broke his hand."

"No. I'm not gonna hurt you. Just don't do anything stupid."

"I won't."

"Give me your word."

"I swear." She let out a big sigh of relief.

"You hungry?"

"I can eat."

"All right, let's go. I got a package of hot dogs downstairs."

Tiffany gobbled down three hot dogs like she hadn't eaten in weeks, then she slowly began to relax and tell him an unimaginable story.

She began with things she wasn't quite sure about. She believed, through whispers and innuendo, that her father was killed in a gunfight, trying to protect her mom. According to her grandmother, who'd taken her in when her mom went to prison, the death of Tiffany's father, a good man, sent her mother into a deep depression that spawned a drug dependency, and trying to pay for the drugs made her do things that had sent her to prison. Three months ago, a hit-and-run driver had killed Tiffany's grandmother, and Tiffany moved in with Renee, her mother's younger sister, who belonged to Ice Man. Renee worked for him, and supposedly she tried to protect Tiffany, set her niece up in a little room of her own, but told her someday she'd have to do things to help out.

"She never said what things, but I knew," Tiffany said. "I knew, because sometimes, late at night, Ice would come into my room and touch me and stuff. He'd get in bed with me, and hold me, and touch me, and say things like, 'You gonna be mine.' Said he was saving me for someone special. Made me do some things he said older girls like to do, and sometime soon he'd be trainin' me to be his angel."

Kappernick held up a hand to stop her, not wanting to hear any more. It was all too fantastic, too unreal. Was she making it all up? But, really, who'd make up such a tale? What would make a girl—a mere kid—climb up a tree to sleep in a dirty, empty room?

He blew out an exasperated puff of air. "Listen, kid, er … Tiffany. I admire you. I think you got a lot of guts, climbing up the tree and all. But all that's gonna end. Tomorrow, I'm cutting down that tree."

The corners of her mouth turned down, like the girl from La Strada, and her eyes teared up. "Can't you just let me stay up there? What difference does it make to you?"

"Suppose you fell off that tree and got hurt?"

"Please."

"No. You can't stay. I'm an old White man. People will

think stupid things. I could get arrested. You're eleven!"

"I'll be twelve soon."

"No. It's not gonna work."

"Can I just stay here tonight? Please. I got nowhere else to go now. If I go back tonight, he'll get me, for sure."

"Look, I can call the police—"

"No." Tiffany jumped up. "Please don't do that. I'll go. I won't bother you no more."

This was becoming too much for Kappernick. "Jesus, what—"

"Listen, there was another girl, Aminna. She went to the police, but they didn't believe her, so they took her back, and when Ice found out about her, he nearly killed her. Beat her bad every night. She barely talks now. How do I get out of here? Just let me go. I won't be back." Yet she didn't move, like she was frozen in her spot.

"All right. Here's what we're gonna do." Kappernick paused, unsure of what to say, then blew out another puff of air. "I'm gonna let you stay here tonight. No cops. There's another small bedroom on this floor with a single bed and a pillow. You can stay there, but just for the night, understand? Just for the night."

He led her to the tiny room behind the kitchen, telling her the only way out was through the front door and he'd have to let her out the next morning because the door was key-locked and he had the only key.

Her eyes lit up when she saw room—clean, painted, bright. Kappernick left her there, locked the door leading up to the third floor, then went into the front bedroom. He locked his own bedroom door and placed his gun into the drawer of the night table.

For a long time, he lay in bed, thinking. What the fuck was he doing? He should have put her out—*Shoot her,*

Malley!—but he couldn't do it. He thought of his grandchildren, unable to imagine them climbing up a tree. Normally, they were chauffeured everywhere, and they were overweight because of it. If you get driven everywhere, and sit around and play computer games all day, that's what happens. This girl, this Tiffany, looked sweet, but was tough, hard. At eleven, if she were telling the truth, she'd been through a lot and had, so far, endured.

Shoot her, Malley!

He prayed his grandkids, as much as he didn't like them, would never have to go through what this girl was. And it pained him to admit he didn't like his grandkids. But that's the way it was. They had everything, and because of that, they had nothing. He once told Nancy how he felt, and her face had dropped. "That's ridiculous," she'd said. "They're your grandkids. They love you."

"No, they don't. They don't care about me."

"They're kids! And if they don't care about you, then maybe it's your fault!"

And maybe she was right. He hadn't tried. But he didn't think he'd needed to try. That wasn't his job. Hey, maybe his son and daughter-in-law should have done their job, said to them, "This is your granddad. Put down that crap and go have a catch. We owe everything we got to him. He did his job with his own kids!" Or had he? He'd been a good dad, hadn't he? Now he wasn't so sure. Maybe he was too messed up after 'nam.

Kappernick shut his eyes, and shortly, he was back in 'nam. Things he couldn't stop envisioning appeared like an endless movie reel—almost-real glimpses that clicked by: flashes of the company bivouacking, the streets of Saigon, the fight of Hue, the patrols, the helicopters, the weapons, the blown-up bodies … but it always returned to the girl coming out of the dilapidated hut, staggering toward Malley, tears running down her dirty face.

DAY 5

WHEN KAPPERNICK WOKE, Tiffany was standing outside his room. "I washed up and used a towel that was in there," she said as he opened the door. "I just wanted you to know."

"Did you eat? Are you hungry?"

"No. I didn't want to touch anything that wasn't mine."

"Do you want something?"

"No. I just got to leave."

Kappernick nodded, and Tiffany started to walk to the locked door leading to the third floor stairs.

"No. Not that way," he said. "Out the front."

Tiffany started to protest, but after seeing the hard set look on his face, gave up. Kappernick opened the door to the small foyer, and then the one leading out to the street.

Standing in the archway, Tiffany glanced up and down the sidewalk, then bolted away. "Thanks!" she called back without turning around.

Kappernick breathed a sigh of relief. In a way, this was like slapping his hands as if to say, "Well, that's done." He went in and made himself some breakfast—toast and coffee. While nursing the coffee, he called a tree cutting service who said they could remove the tree that day, after which he called a roofing company who said they'd get somebody out there that afternoon to check out the roof.

Then, as usual, he put two cans of dog food into a plastic bag and headed for the park. This time, the big dog had been waiting for him, and this time, after he ate, he sat next to Kappernick and listened as the old man softly talked to him.

"Well, big boy, how's it feel to have a friend?" Kappernick sat on the long, circular stone bench which could have easily held a hundred people. But he was alone—just himself and the dog. The dog lay his massive head on Kappernick's thigh and seemed to be listening as Kappernick said, "You know, you and I have a lot in common. We're both loners. Hey, maybe that's what I should call you. Loner. What do you think? Nah, I'll come up with something else."

Kappernick must have talked for a half-hour when the cold, hard stone bench started to put an ache in his legs. He got up, joints cracking, and stretched.

"Okay, buddy, I'll see you tomorrow," he said. But the dog started to follow him.

Kappernick stopped. "Wait a minute ... you want to come with me? No, I don't think that's good idea." The dog put his snout against Kappernick's gut. "Aw, you just like being petted. All right, here's what we'll do: I'll buy a leash and a collar, and tomorrow, if you still want to, I'll take you home. I promise. No, I can't take you home without a leash. There's cars and trucks and people. Suppose you see someone you want to bite? And living in a house requires responsibilities. You need to be cleaned and checked out; you got to go to a veterinarian. No. It won't work. Today is out. Go ahead"—Kappernick pointed—"go back home."

As Kappernick turned and walked away, the dog still stood there, but when he turned back, the dog was gone.

Damned dog is smarter than I am, Kappernick thought, and he was still ruminating when a guy emerged from behind a bush not ten yards away. Even though it was a mild day, he wore a long raincoat and a gray fedora, and it looked like he had a gun in his pocket. He was dark-skinned, with eyes sunken into his long, bearded face.

Kappernick was almost halfway between The Whispering Walls and Parkside Avenue. He had his cane with him, but that wouldn't do much against a gun. As the man approached in long strides, Kappernick thought he looked like a crack-head who'd been cracked on the head more than a couple of times. His eyes crazily darted left and right.

"Stop right there!" Kappernick yelled.

The man stopped momentarily, then smirked. "Fuckin', motherfucker, piece of shit, give me everything. GIVE IT TO ME! GIVE ME EVERYTHING!"

Kappernick stared at the crazy son of a bitch, stalling for time, trying to figure a way out. Could he hit the asshole with his cane before he shot? If he gave him everything, would the guy shoot him anyway?

"You got a gun in there, or a finger?" Kappernick asked.

"I got a motherfuckin' gun, bitch!"

"All right. Take it easy. Just asking."

And that's when he heard it: almost a heavy gallop. The guy turned as the big dog came galloping like a racehorse across the green, and he tried to remove his hand from his raincoat pocket, but Kappernick whacked the hand with his cane. At the same moment, the dog leapt into the air, sailing like a log coming off a sluice, and hit the guy in the chest, landing on top of him, snarling in the bandit's face.

"Off! Get back!" Kappernick shouted, and as if he understood, the dog backed off. Kappernick stepped on the guy's left hand and thrust the tip of his cane at the thief's Adam's apple. "Now you listen very carefully. Remove what you got in your coat pocket. Just use two fingers to do it."

"It ain't got no ammo."

"Just do as I tell you and don't be stupid."

The dog growled as the guy extracted, with his thumb and forefinger, a .22 target pistol. Kappernick told him to toss it, and when the guy was back on his feet, Kappernick ordered him to take off his belt and drop it on the ground. The guy tried to protest, but Kappernick cane-whacked him across the thigh. Then he took the guy's picture with his cell phone and told him to beat it. The guy limped off.

Kappernick looked down at the dog who'd just saved his life, and smirked. "What the hell took you so long, soldier?" He picked up the guy's discarded belt and wrapped it around the dog's neck. "Well, that's one way to get you a leash. But I owe you a better one, and we'll get that this afternoon."

Then Kappernick picked up the dropped weapon, which had a single bullet in its chamber—just enough to kill a man. He put it into his pocket and talked to the dog as they both headed for Parkside Avenue.

"Man, what a day, eh, Soldier? Yeah, that's what we'll call you. Soldier. Soldier, between me and you, this is like fighting in a goddamned war!"

That afternoon, the first company to show up was Landmark Tree Service, and Kappernick immediately put them to work. They'd taken the tree down in less than two hours. An hour later the roofers came, and in less than twenty minutes they'd secured the hatch that Tiffany had been using. While all of this work was being done, Kappernick called Dr. Jacob Harriman, the veterinarian that had taken care of Dutchman. Dr. Harriman was pleased to hear Kappernick's voice. "What'd you do, get another horse, Mel?"

Kappernick laughed. "Well, he's almost as big as one. But no, he's a dog. Could you see him later on this afternoon?"

"I could see him at four thirty, but only because it's you."

"There's just one other thing, doc." Kappernick didn't wait for Harriman to ask what it was. "He needs a bath—bad."

"Better make it at four o'clock, then."

Soldier took all of his shots like a real trooper, practically standing at attention as the vet gave him the required injections. "It's like this dog understands English," said Harriman. "He's smart—real smart."

"He saved my life, doc." And Kappernick told him the whole story.

"Then this is only fitting. You owe him."

Soldier was just as obedient when Harriman's assistant bathed him. In fact, the big dog licked the young lady's face, and when she was finished, Soldier looked like a different dog. He was actually handsome!

On the way home, Soldier stood in the back of the car with his head out the window, relishing the wind blowing in his face, and Kappernick wondered what had happened to make him go it alone. Harriman had estimated the animal to be young, at least not more than four, and his breed was rare and valuable, so Soldier was definitely not a dog people would just give up on. Kappernick had bought him a strong chain collar and a leather leash. He'd keep Soldier as long as the big dog wanted to stay.

Just as they got back to 42nd Street, Kappernick's cell phone rang. "Hello?" he said, opening the front door, then the foyer door, leading Soldier up the stairs.

"Dad?" the caller's voice replied.

"Who's this?"

"It's your son, Bruce. Who else calls you 'Dad'?"

"Oh. I didn't recognize your voice. It's been such a long

time since I'd spoken to you."

"Dad, are you trying to lay on a guilt trip?"

"No, I'm just telling the truth. When's the last time we had a conversation?"

A long silence followed, and then: "You're right, it's been a long time." Kappernick didn't say anything. "Listen, Dad, I'm worried about you. Concerned. Where are you?"

"Home."

"In Overbrook Park?"

"No, you made me sell Overbrook Park after your mom died."

"Then where?"

Again, Kappernick didn't answer.

"Wait a minute ... not Forty-Second Street? Tell me you didn't go back to Forty-Second Street. Dad, are you insane?"

Kappernick hung up.

Bruce called right back. "We must have gotten disconnected," he said.

"No, we didn't get disconnected. I hung up. Do I call you crazy? Listen, Bruce, let me ask you a question: Do you think I was a good father? Did I ever beat you? I paid your way through law school, didn't I? And every once in a while, I took you to baseball games and things like that when you were a kid, right?"

"Yes."

"Then why in God's name did it take you five days to figure out I was no longer living in that place you call a home?"

Another long silence followed. "I don't know, Dad."

"Well, when you figure it out, give me a call back and we'll talk."

When Kappernick snapped off his phone, he felt heartsick, as though he'd lost his son. He didn't want to lose him, but what could he do? Bruce wasn't a bad kid, but he was busy, had a family of his own, and a life—his own life—he had to lead. And that's exactly what Kappernick wanted him to do. Still, he found it disconcerting that Bruce treated him like a memory, even while he was still alive! Like he, Kappernick, already sat in the nursing home, vacantly drooling out from the side of his mouth. Shit, that would come soon enough. Kappernick had long-since decided he wouldn't wait until the last minute to let go, and he sure as hell wasn't gonna sit in some urine-smelling nursing home with spittle running down his chin.

A half-hour later, the phone rang again. It was Bruce. "Dad, don't hang up. Please, give me a break. Can we have lunch?"

Kappernick's voice lost its sharpness. "Yeah, sure."

"Can you come up to my office? How's Friday? At noon."

"I'll be there."

"Thanks."

Kappernick ended the call, then studied Soldier. The big dog, after he'd checked out the entire second floor, had found himself a place in the kitchen. The curly was obviously content and seemed thankful to now have a home. Kappernick sensed he was ready to trust and knew instantly he was safe with his new friend, who was obviously tired of being alone, too.

Kappernick made a cup of coffee and sat in one of the living room chairs. Soldier came in from the kitchen, stretched out at Kappernick's feet, and together they watched the evening news.

That night, Kappernick and Soldier went for a walk around the empty streets of the neighborhood. Man and dog both seemed at peace. At nine o'clock, on the way back from the walk, Kappernick peeked into Springer's bar. Springer saw him and waved him on in. It was early and the place was basically deserted.

"I got a dog with me," Kappernick said.

"Not to worry. Bring him in." But when Springer saw Soldier, he gasped. "Holy Toledo! What the hell is that?" he said, opening a bottle of Kappernick's favorite ale.

"Yeah, he's big, ain't he?"

Springer looked over the counter. "That is the biggest, coolest … wait a minute, I heard about a huge dog that's been seen roaming in the park. People call him 'the Ghost.' Where'd you get him?"

Kappernick told him the story.

Springer grinned from ear to ear. "Hey, everybody, lookie here," he announced to the few bar patrons, "Melvin Kappernick has caught and tamed the Ghost!"

Not too many knew what Springer was talking about, but there was a murmur, and one wise guy yelled back, "That deserves a round of drinks! Is he buying?" Everyone, including Kappernick, laughed.

Moments later, an older man approached Kappernick. Soldier was immediately on alert, but Kappernick calmed him.

"Excuse me, sir…" The man was bent over, shabbily dressed, and looked like he'd been through hard times. "Is you Lieutenant Kappernick?"

"At one time…"

"In 'nam?"

Kappernick stared at him. "Yes."

"First Marine Regiment. Da Nang, September of '68?"

"Yes, I was there."

"Lieutenant, it's me, Perkins. Darnell Perkins."

Kappernick would never have recognized D.P., as they called him back then. The man had aged considerably, and it'd been almost fifty years since Da Nang. But obviously

Perkins knew him, remembered him.

"Perkins." Kappernick smiled, nodded. "Hey, it's good to see you." What could he say?

Perkins took a step back and, standing up as straight as he could, saluted.

"At ease, soldier. Sit down and have a drink."

"If you say so, sir."

"I say so."

DAY 6

JUST AFTER DINNER came a frantic pounding on the door. Then the bell started ringing. Soldier stood, senses on alert, though he didn't make a sound. Kappernick went to the intercom and saw through the installed camera system that it was the girl. She was holding her small bike.

Kappernick held down the switch. "What's going on?"

"I'm in trouble. I need to come in. Can I please come in?"

"Wait a minute." He led Soldier by the collar into the bedroom. "Quiet," he said. "Be good."

Then he went back to the intercom. Even though he knew perfectly well she was alone, he asked her anyway. "Are you alone?"

"Yes. Please."

Reluctantly, he rang her in, and the foyer camera took over. "Leave your bike there and I'll buzz you in," he said

Tiffany stomped up the stairs, and when she reached the top, she yelled angrily, "You took down the tree!"

"I told you I would."

"Now I got no place to escape to." Her thin lower lip was drawn back, quivering.

Kappernick was about to say, "What the hell are you talking about?" when he saw her face—the whole left side of her jaw was swollen and bruised. "What the hell happened to you? Did you fall off your bike?"

"No."

"Then what happened?"

"It was Ice Man. He did it."

"What?"

"He beat me! So I ran. Now, he's looking for me and I got no place to go, no place to hide."

Kappernick was aghast. He sat down on a kitchen chair. "He beat you?"

"Yes, he beat me. He beat me bad." She pulled up her shirt to reveal bruises in several places where someone had punched her hard. "See?"

Kappernick went into the bathroom and, after returning with a bottle of peroxide and a box of cotton swabs, he gritted his teeth, told her to sit down, and she did—hard. Then he drew a chair up across from her and tried to dab at her face. Tiffany slapped away his hand.

"Don't you dare touch me!"

Kappernick pushed back his chair and jumped to his feet. "What are you, crazy? You came here for help, and I'm trying to help you, and you're yelling at me! Slapping me! Apologize immediately, or get the hell out. I don't need your bullshit!"

Tiffany began to sob—*Shoot her, Malley!*—tears streaking down her face. "I'm sorry. Please."

Kappernick softened. "All right, all right, calm down. Let's talk quietly and calmly," he said, stressing the word *calmly.* "I'll be honest; I don't know what to do with you. I want to help you, but I don't know how."

"Can't I just stay here?"

He lay his finger to his lips. "Shh, don't say anything. Just listen. Let's say you were the sweetest girl in the world, that you didn't do anything stupid, that you didn't ride with a bunch of drug runners, that you didn't have Ice … whatever his name is, after you … what you don't get is that I'm an old White man and you're an eleven-year-old Black girl. What would people say?"

"What people? Who would care?"

A scratch sounded at the bedroom door, and Tiffany tensed.

Kappernick turned. "All right, Soldier, be cool."

"Soldier?"

"Yeah." He walked to the bedroom door and opened it. "I got a dog."

Out came Soldier.

When Tiffany saw the dog, her mouth dropped, and she shrunk back against the chair. "Oh my God, that's the Ghost! You got the ghost dog!"

Kappernick saw her fear and tried to put her at ease. "He won't hurt you, I swear. Relax." Yet Tiffany remained frozen, and Soldier glared at the girl as he slowly walked up to her. He sniffed her while she cringed and bit her upper lip. Then she extended her hand and timidly touched the dog's head. Soldier moved closer, nose touching her cheek, and after several seconds, much to Tiffany's relief, he licked her face.

Kappernick laughed. "I think he likes you."

"I sure hope so."

Soldier backed off when Kappernick told him to sit down. "Okay, Tiffany," he said, "we have a lot to talk about. I agree with you; you do need help. And once again, I'm going to let you stay here tonight. You can stay in the small room."

At this, Tiffany smiled, but Kappernick placed his forefinger to his lips. "Listen. Truth is, in the morning, I believe we have to take you to the police."

Tiffany began to cry. "Then I want to leave now. I'll find someplace. Ice Man, he owns the police. You don't know.

They come in and be with the girls—I hear them! I'll run away. I can hide in an alley."

But Kappernick knew he couldn't turn the girl out, and that night, as he lay awake in bed, he fretted. If he turned her out, where would she sleep, in a trashcan?

He'd had to talk fast and furious to keep her from running out the door, and he'd given her a fresh towel, told her to clean herself up, swearing he wouldn't call the cops while she was asleep.

He knew, though, the best thing to do, the best thing for her, was for him to call the authorities. What would Nancy have done? How would she have handled this little climbing tomboy? He knew nothing of girls, or kids, for that matter, and now he was up all night thinking about an eleven-year-old kid and a dog. Yes, this girl was a conundrum, but the guy, this asshole, Ice Man, was gonna be a real problem.

Shit! In the six days since he'd left Bruce's little stone castle, a lot had happened and he had a lot to figure out, but damn, it made his blood boil. It was like taking an elixir, a magic potion, and for the first time in a long time, Kappernick felt alive.

DAY 7

KAPPERNICK WOKE LATE, which hadn't happened in a long time. As he got dressed, he wondered if Tiffany was up, and if she was, what she was doing. He opened the bedroom door to find her sitting at the kitchen table with Soldier sitting in front of her, his head in her lap.

"He loves me," she said to Kappernick, and even though the right side of her face was still swollen, she smiled the most beautiful smile.

"Do you love him?"

"Yeah. I like him. He's like a big teddy bear. I never knew a dog before. Every once in a while, the gang would see him roaming through the park. We called him 'the Ghost' cause he'd always disappear into the woods. What do you call him again?"

"Soldier."

"Soldier." She nodded. "That's a good name. Hey, what do I call you? What's your name? I been sleeping here, and I don't even know your name."

"Just call me, Kapp." He didn't know why he'd said it. That's what they use to call him in 'nam. It just came out.

"Okie-dokie, Kapp."

"Are you hungry?"

"I could eat," she said shyly.

Kappernick fed Soldier a can of Alpo, then made scrambled eggs and watched Tiffany gobble them down. She didn't even know how to hold a fork! He considered correcting her, but thought better of it. This girl knew a lot—she had "old-girl" wisdom—but it also seemed she had a lot to learn.

"Hey," he said, "don't you have to go to school?"

The fork stopped halfway to her mouth. "I don't go to school. I haven't been to school in a long time."

"What?"

"Yeah, I don't go no more," she said, unable to look at him. Then she began to tell him why.

Yes, of course, she'd gone to school. She'd liked school, and her grandmother had taken her to school every day. But that school had been in a different neighborhood, and when her grandmother was killed and her aunt had come for her, everything had stopped. She couldn't get back to the old school—couldn't figure out how to get there, and even if she could, she couldn't afford the bus fare. Now, it was too late. She had no friends at the new school, no one to protect her back; she had no clothes, no books, and the others would gang up on her. Her aunt didn't care; she was a slave to Ice Man and the drugs he made her beg to have, the drugs that made her forget who she was, made her do ugly, despicable things. Her mother's sister looked so old, so worn. Tiffany's grandmother had tried to save her, tried to help her, but couldn't pull her away. Then, her grandmother … died.

"How'd she die?"

"She died in the hospital after she got hit."

"Hit?"

"Yeah, hit by a car right outside the house. The car never stopped; he just hit her and drove off."

Geez, it was one thing after another with this girl. My

God, what people go through! Everything sounded like a soap opera, but who would make it up? How many grown-ups would be able to handle what she'd been through and not be dragged under? This girl had survived and was still on her feet, still fighting!

The phrase "*Shoot her, Malley!*" popped into his head once more, but Kappernick ignored it.

"Okay, here's the deal," he said. "Against my better judgment, I'm going to help you, but there are conditions." Tiffany blinked, taken aback, but Kappernick ignored her. "First, you have to stop riding with the boys. There'll be no delivering drugs. And, you'll have to go to school. We'll register you this afternoon," Kappernick said. "The school's just two blocks away. We'll buy you some clothes and books, and I'll walk you to school and pick you up after, until you make friends who'll have your … back."

Tiffany got to her feet. "I can't do that," she said. "Just let me sleep here every once in a while. I won't be a bother."

"No."

"Why not?"

"Because. I don't want you here if you're not going to do the right thing. If you stay here, you've got to be all in."

Tiffany started to walk to the door. "Then let me out."

"Sure." Kappernick stood up, smiled, and walked toward her. "But if you go, don't come back, because I won't let you in."

Her chin quivered. "You're mean."

"I know." He stuck out his hand. "Good luck."

Suddenly, she hugged him. "I don't want to go!" she cried. "Please, please let me stay." And all at once, the toughness was gone, leaving a frightened little girl behind. Kappernick didn't hug her back; he stood rigid, surprised, arms out, as Tiffany sobbed real tears into his chest. Finally, he patted her back, gently talking to her. "Listen and understand: If you want to stay here, you've got to do certain things. You've got to go to school, you've got to stop delivering drugs, and you've got to promise to be real. It's gonna be hard, but that's what you've got to do if you want me to help you. I've got to be able to trust you. I've got to know my effort isn't in vain."

"Okay. I promise. I'll try."

"All right. All right, now. Dry those tears. We've got a lot to do today. First, we're going to buy you some clothes, then we're going to enroll you in school."

An hour later, they left the old Teabloom building, Soldier in tow. Tiffany, sitting tall, rode shotgun, while Soldier sat in the back, his big head sticking out the window. Too-Tall, who stood at his usual spot, hustling drugs in front of Open-Til-Four, didn't miss their departure. He kind of squinted in disbelief as Kappernick drove off.

The first part of the trip was easy. They drove to Kohl's, a small discount department store, where Tiffany bought everything from undergarments to a winter jacket (Kappernick waited patiently as she selected and tried things on), and the bill came to over three hundred dollars. He didn't care, though. Seeing her excitement and the delight on her face was worth every penny.

Afterwards, loaded down with packages, they left the store and were back on 42nd Street by quarter-to-twelve. By half-past, Tiffany, who now wore new jeans, a long-sleeved blouse, and sneakers, entered Leidy Elementary School alongside Kappernick, who led her into the office. And this was the hard part. Holding Tiffany's hand, Kappernick proceeded to concoct the wildest story of who Tiffany and he were.

"I am here," he told the school secretary, "to enroll my granddaughter in school. Her parents were killed in a car

accident in Mississippi, and I'm her only living relative."
On the walk to the school, he'd told Tiffany to just follow
along, and she now did so beautifully as if they were on stage.
Tiffany looked to be on the verge of tears, which made the
school secretary, Mrs. Ethel Patterson, lean over the counter
and say, "Oh, you poor dear."

Kappernick then made up the county where her ficti-
tious parents had lived and died, the name of an elementary
school she'd supposedly attended, and that she was an honor
student. Kappernick figured it would take them weeks to
check out his story, and by then, he'd have researched something else to have them search again. He'd just say, "Oh, did
I say that? I meant…"The lies, except for his real address and
phone number, just kept coming, and Kappernick was actually enjoying himself as he made up one story after another.

"Yes, she'll be staying permanently with her grandmother and myself. And please, don't tell any of the students
about what happened to her parents or that she's up from
Mississippi. You know how kids are. Thank God she wasn't
in the car!"

"We'll take good care of her," said the school secretary.
"We'll put her in Mrs. Lansky's class. She's an excellent
teacher." And Mrs. Patterson began to lead Tiffany away.

"I'll pick you up after school," Kappernick said in a nau-
seatingly sweet voice.

Tiffany smiled, and with just as much saccharin, replied,
"Okay, Grandpa."

Kappernick left Leidy Elementary School, shaking his head
and smiling. It'd been a lot easier than he'd thought it would
be. They believed his story! He'd have to do some research on
Mississippi schools, but geez … it was almost like they were
afraid to ask questions. Political correctness had won the day.

School let out at three thirty, and Tiffany met him at the gate, smiling. The first time he'd ever seen her smile, and it was great to see. "Hi, Grandpa." She giggled. "I got a book I need to read. A history book. Chapter five."

"Looks like you had a pretty good first day."

"I did. I like my teacher. She's nice, and really smart."

Kappernick looked at the book. "Well, this requires studying."

"Yeah, I guess if I'm supposed to be an honor student," she said, "I'd better start studying."

DAY 9

TWO DAYS LATER, when Kappernick, Tiffany, and Soldier returned from school, they found a woman waiting for them, leaning against the store window of Teabloom's, arms folded across her chest, a cigarette dangling from her mouth. As they turned the corner onto 42nd Street, Tiffany whispered to him, "It's my mom's sister, Renee."

Renee flipped her cigarette into the street, then stepped into the middle of the sidewalk as if to block their way, hands on her hips and a sneer on her face. "Girl, where you been?" she hissed.

Kappernick remained silent, studying the almost emaciated, washed-out woman in front of him. Renee's eyes were sunken, and she looked worn and much older than her years. Tiffany, who, by comparison, was ruddy and bright-eyed, didn't have to look far to see what awaited her.

"I been here."

"Here? What you doin'?"

"Tryin' to be safe. Goin' to school."

"Girl, you crazy? You comin' home, now!" She reached out to grab Tiffany's hand, but Soldier showed his teeth, growling low, and Renee drew her hand back. She chewed on her lower lip, voice softening. "You've got to come home."

But Tiffany was adamant. "No. I'm not goin' to that house, and you know why. I'm not stupid. You said you'd help me, but you can't. Ice Man's tryin' to get me. I don't want to end up like—"

"Like what? Like me?"

"Yes, like you! Look at yourself. Why you can't see it, I don't know."

"I'm your aunt! I'm the one who's supposed to take care of you!"

"But you ain't doin' it. You didn't even know I had to go to school. It took Mr. Kapp, here, to get me registered."

"Mr. Kapp? Who the hell is Mr. Kapp to you? What, he doin' you?"

"No! He's a friend. He's helpin' me, treatin' me like a person."

Renee took in Kappernick with a bitter stare and curled her lip. "Yeah, right." Then she turned back to her niece. "Girl, I'm gonna ask you one more time: You comin' home?"

"That ain't my home. I'm stayin' here, and if Mr. Kapp throws me out, I'll run like hell."

"Girl, you tryin' to get us killed?"

No one answered her.

"Ice Man gonna go crazy."

Kappernick placed a finger to his lips. "All right, that's enough for now. We're going inside. If Mr. Man wants to talk to me, this is where I'll be."

DAY 10

BRUCE KAPPERNICK'S OFFICES were on the fifteenth floor of 1800 Market Street in the Ridgeway Building. He was now a partner: Sutton, Schemski, and Kappernick, a huge place with a lot of people.

Kappernick was greeted warmly by Bruce's secretary, who led him to his son's beautifully appointed personal office with a fabulous view of the northwestern part of the city. Bruce, sitting at his desk, rose to greet his father. They embraced.

"It's good to see you. You look good, and your office is beautiful," Kappernick said approvingly.

Bruce nodded. "It is, isn't it? But it's cost me." He looked at his father and sighed. "I've paid the price, and it's cost me."

"How do you mean?

"It's cost me with you, Dad. I've been a schmuck. I'm not making excuses, but I've been snowed under with work and because of it, I've lost touch … with you. I don't want that to happen."

Kappernick gritted his teeth, all choked up. "Bruce, I love you. I'll always love you. You're my son, and right now, I'm loving you a lot."

Bruce grinned that Kappernick smile. "Hey, Dad, I got a great idea. Let's eat right here. I have a table by the window with a fantastic view, and there's a place around the corner that makes the best Italian hoagies you've ever tasted. I'll have my secretary order them for us. It'll give us more time to talk."

Kappernick thought it was a great idea.

They sat down, and instead of facing each other, they faced the window to study the view. Kappernick loved panoramic views. "This is fantastic," he said. "I could watch this all day."

"Dad, will you do me one favor?" Bruce asked.

"If I can."

"I want to be able to talk to you, man-to-man. I want to be able to talk to you like a friend. I don't want you to bullshit me, and I don't want to bullshit you. I want to be able to ask you anything, and you me. Can we do that?"

"No," Kappernick replied. "I don't think it's possible, but we can try."

"Well, it's a step in the right direction."

"Go ahead, you go first. What's on your mind?"

"Was it my family, Dad? Be honest. Was it Barbara? The kids? Did somebody say something?"

"No. Nobody said anything." Kappernick considered adding "ever," but instead he said, "Look, there has to be a purpose, a reason ..."

"Do you love my kids?"

"Of course I *love* your kids. I've watched them grow. But I just don't get it."

"Get what?"

"Get what they're all about," Kappernick explained. "When I was a kid, all I wanted to do was to get outside and play with the other kids. Playing computer games all day ... I mean, we have nothing in common. I love them, but I ... I just don't like them, if you get what I mean. It's probably my fault, but I just don't know how to communicate with them."

"Hey, I know what you mean," Bruce said, "and that worries me, because they're likable kids. Maybe we can do something that'll bring you closer together?"

Kappernick shook his head. "They don't need me. They need you."

Bruce nodded in agreement. "That's what I mean when I say I've paid. I've got to put in more time, but I hate the idea of you living alone."

"Actually, I'm not alone."

Bruce turned to his father, surprised.

"Yeah, I got a dog," Kappernick said. "A big—I mean, *enormous* dog."

"Really? You got a dog?"

The sandwiches arrived, and as they ate, Kappernick related the story of how he and Soldier became friends: how he saw the dog scrounging for food from a trash can, how he started feeding him, and how Soldier saved his life.

Bruce was fascinated. "I love it. I love the idea that you have a dog. I mean, that makes me feel a lot better. Where you are living is a bad neighborhood now, and a dog's a good idea."

Kappernick talked excitedly about Soldier. "I mean, this dog is beautiful," he said. "Smart, and at the same time, fierce. You should have seen Tiffany's face when she first saw him. I thought she was going to have a—"

"Tiffany?" Bruce put down his sandwich, wiped his lips, and blinked almost humorously. "Who's Tiffany? You got a woman?"

Kappernick stopped eating. "Okay. Remember how, every once in a while, you and I would go play golf, and we'd say before the game, 'First one who breaks a club, or goes into a rant, or freaks out, loses'? Well, that's the way it has to be now."

"Why, is something wrong with Tiffany?"

"No."

"Is Tiffany a woman?"

"No."

"Tiffany's a man?" The pitch of Bruce's voice had risen.

"No."

"Then what the hell is Tiffany?"

"Tiffany's a girl. She's eleven."

Bruce jumped to his feet. "A girl? Eleven! Dad, are you nuts?"

Kappernick held up a finger. "Remember: the first one who breaks a club …"

Bruce collapsed into his chair, shoved his face into his hands, then started to laugh. "Oh, God. This story, I can't wait to hear. I mean, Dad … you're not … you're not …"

"Absolutely not!"

"Thank God for small favors." Bruce flicked on the intercom. "Mrs. Drake, no calls for another forty-five minutes." He flicked it off, then said, "Okay, tell me. Tell me everything."

So Kappernick told him the story: how he first saw her with the gang of kid bikers and knew they were delivering drugs, how he'd heard her upstairs and had found her sleeping up there, how he'd had the tree she used to climb up onto the roof chopped down, and how she then came to him for help. When Bruce asked him why she'd needed help, Kappernick told him about what Ice Man was doing to her.

"Dad, you've got to go to the police."

"I can't. I promised her I wouldn't. I promised her, because she says the police are in on it, and this Ice Man will kill both her and her aunt."

"But this is a problem. A real problem."

"I know."

Bruce bit his lower lip and looked deep into his father's eyes as though wondering if Kappernick was still sane. "I don't get it," he said. "What are you doing? Why are you putting yourself at risk like this?"

"That's a fair question." And Kappernick seriously considered how to answer it. "You know I was in 'nam, right? 'Nam was a bitch. Some bad shit was going on there, and there was this girl about eleven years old. She needed help." He turned away to look out through the big picture window. "Well, today, this girl needs help. She's come to me, and I can't let her slip away."

"But—"

Kappernick held up a hand. "Right now, I feel as if I have a purpose, you know what I mean? This girl needs me."

"How long has she been with you?"

"A little more than five days."

"Doesn't she have to go to school?"

"I enrolled her at Leidy."

"Leidy! How the hell did you do that?"

"I told them I was … her … grandfather."

DAY 11

BEFORE ICE MAN had ever said a word, Kappernick already knew who he was.

In 1947 or '48, when Kappernick was a kid of maybe eight or nine, a horse-drawn wagon filled with huge blocks of ice would come once a week into the neighborhood. The driver would rein in his horse, walk to the back of the wagon, and use an ice pick to cut a slab of ice. Then he'd put a piece of tan leather onto his shoulder and, with tongs, lift out the just-cut slab, hoist it onto his shoulder, and carry it to the third floor of some building to put into the top of someone's icebox. To this day, Kappernick still called refrigerators "iceboxes."

Back then, Kappernick liked that iceman—a big Swedish fellow who loved to laugh. Now, the man ringing the bell at Teabloom's wasn't at all like the Swedish fellow, and it was easy to see through the safety camera that he was in no laughing mood. He rang impatiently, and was about to pound on the door, when Kappernick's voice came over the intercom.

"Yes?"

Kappernick saw Ice Man grit his teeth. "Are you Mr. Kapp?" he asked with a touch of sarcasm.

"What can I do for you?" Kappernick inquired.

"You have somethin' of mine. I think we should talk. Let me in." Ice Man had a slight Jamaican accent, and he wore white slacks with a Hawaiian flowered shirt, unbuttoned at the collar, under a light blue cashmere sport jacket, and a Panama hat. Obviously, Ice Man thought he was on some tropical island.

The man standing behind him looked like Two-Ton Tony Galento, the old-time wrestler.

"Are you alone?" Kappernick asked.

Ice Man glanced back at the wide man, and smirked. "Yes."

"Oh, great," said Kappernick. "Then, would you mind stepping aside and letting me talk to the man standing behind you? Looks like he wants something from me, too."

For a moment Ice Man seemed disconcerted and, annoyed, looked around, until he saw the camera. He smiled viciously. "Oh, him. He's my assist-tant."

"I see," said Kappernick. "Well, tell your assist-tant to go away. If you want to talk to me, you've got to be alone."

"Why? What you afraid of?"

"Him. What are you afraid of?"

"I'm not afraid of anythin'."

"Good. Then send the fat guy the fuck home. If you want to come up and talk, get rid of the bodyguard."

Ice Man told the big man behind him to go to the car. The big man nodded, disappeared off camera, and Kappernick buzzed Ice Man into the foyer.

Kappernick was waiting at the top of the steps for Ice Man, and he led him into the small living room. Ice Man glanced around cautiously. "I heard you got a dog, man."

"I put him in the bedroom to make sure he wouldn't bother you," Kappernick said, and he offered Ice Man a hard chair. "Sit down. Relax. What can I do for you ... er ... what should I call you? I don't know your real name, but I can call you Ice, or Man, or Mr. Man. What would you prefer?"

Ice Man glared.

But Kappernick smiled. "How about I call you Ice? Now, what's the story? Why did you come a-callin'?"

Ice Man returned Kappernick's smile, seeming both disconcerted and amused. "Man, I don't know whether you dumb or stupid. Maybe you crazy. You think I'm playin'?"

"Tell me what you want, and I'll see if I can help you."

Ice Man scanned the room once more. "You got something that belongs to me. Give it back, and I won't hurt you."

"What do I have?"

"The girl. Tiff. She's already cost me a lot, and she has to pay it back."

"Are you her father?"

"No. But I supported her in her time of need—I took her in, gave her a place, fed her. Now she has to pay back and be in my employ. I own her."

"Guess there's no chance in asking you to let her be, giving her a chance for a normal life; let her try to get an education, be a child for a while."

"Nope. And I hope for your sake you ain't yet taken her purity."

Kappernick curled his lip. He'd planned to show no emotion, but he couldn't help it, and he forced himself to conceal his contempt. Instead, he gritted his teeth, hid his disdain behind a grin. Now he thoroughly believed everything Tiffany had told him.

"Not to worry," he said, though he very much wanted to bash the son of a bitch sitting in front of him. "Maybe we can make a trade. What do you want for her? What's she worth to you? What will you take to leave her alone, leave her here with me?"

Now, it was Ice Man who curled his lip. Again he looked around, judging the value of Kappernick's things. "You can't afford her. She's a virgin. Do you know how much some are willing to pay to take that away?"

"I have no idea. How much?"

"If you want to be the first, you'll need twenty-five hundred, cash."

Kappernick laughed sarcastically, and Ice Man sucked in air between his teeth, hissing like a snake. He wasn't used to being laughed at.

"No. I don't want to be the first. You know what I hope? I hope the first is a boy, ten years from now; someone she loves."

Ice Man laughed sadistically and got to his feet. "I took time out of my day to find out just what you are. I've discovered, just like I thought, that you're a fool. The talk is over. Send her back or I'll kill you, old man."

Kappernick, too, got to his feet. "Kill me? I doubt that you'd do anything that stupid. You see, I believe you're a smart man. You saw the camera downstairs, and that changed your initial plan."

Kappernick shook his finger. "You know, technology is an amazing thing. Do you have a cell phone? I have one in my pocket, and I want to take it out, because I want you to see something." He removed his iPhone and pushed a button, smiling at Ice Man. "I want you to see what I just sent my attorney. It's an audio of this very conversation, and if I had your cell phone number, I'd send you a copy."

Ice Man regained his composure. "You are very, very stupid, old man." He slapped the phone out of Kappernick's hand. "Send her back immediately, or die." Then he backhanded Kappernick across the mouth.

When Kappernick sank to his knees, Ice Man spat on him. Kappernick wiped his bruised lip. "My attorney's only going to use the audio if anything happens to me or the girl."

Ice Man slowly leaned over and whispered into Kappernick's ear, "You are a dead man," then walked to the door and tried to open it. But he couldn't. "What the fuck ... ?"

"I need to let you out," said Kappernick. He rose up off the floor and retrieved his cell as he moved to let Ice Man out. He pushed a button on his cell and it started talking: *She's a virgin. Do you know how much some are willing to pay to ... Send her back or ... old man.* Kappernick clicked it off.

"Leave us alone and we will let you be. Get it?"

After the street door closed behind Ice Man, Kappernick peered out through the front window. The big man, who was waiting by a Cadillac sedan, opened the rear door and closed it sharply after Ice Man got in. Then he went around to the driver's side and drove away.

Kappernick stood at the window for some time. At least Tiffany was at school and had been saved from what would have been a horrible confrontation. He clenched his fist and hissed. In some sixty-odd years, no one had hit him and had gotten away with it. Ironically, that one time had occurred less than a hundred yards away from where he now lived, in the middle of 42nd and Thompson. He'd been beaten up by three non-neighborhood kids who pretended to be walking by, but just as they passed, one kid sucker-punched Kappernick in the mouth and he went down. Laughing, they walked away.

This, however, was different. Back then, he was fifteen. Now, he was seventy-seven and he wasn't going to physically fight Ice Man. At his age, he simply couldn't win a physical fight with an adult. He'd take the slap—for now. But, just like the three thugs, he wasn't through with Ice Man. Somehow, he'd eventually reap revenge. For the time being, he'd keep his word—he would let Ice Man be, if Ice Man let him be.

Still, he Googled The Reese Agency. Kappernick had known Roger Reese from 'nam and was glad to see he was still in business. He called the contact number, and a woman answered.

"Reese Agency."

"I'd like to talk to Reese."

"May I ask who's calling?"

"Melvin Kappernick."

He was told to hold, but it didn't take long. "Jesus Christ! Captain?"

Kappernick didn't feel like laughing, but he couldn't help himself. Reese was so flamboyant. "Yeah, it's me."

"Kapp! Man, how the hell are you?"

"Not bad, but I need your help."

"Really?"

"Yeah."

"Tell me, what's the problem?"

DAY 12

KAPPERNICK AND SOLDIER were out early, walking along the actual park side of Parkside Avenue, when out of 42nd Street came the bicycle boys. The boy who'd previously confronted Kappernick saw him and broke away, pulling up alongside Kappernick. He wore a short leather jacket and an Eagles hat with the brim on the side of his head. Old-fashioned air force sunglasses accentuated the peach fuzz on his chin, and his expression was different from the smart aleck's whose hand Kappernick had almost broken.

"Yo," he said.

"Aw," Kappernick said with some disgust, "you're not going to do anything stupid, are you?"

"Nah, nuttin' like that." He got off of his bike. "You all right?"

Kappernick stopped and stared at him. What was this all about? "What can I do for you?" he asked.

"I just want to know what's goin' on."

"What's goin' on?"

"Yeah, yeh neh. How my girl, doin'?"

"Your girl?"

"Yeah, yeh neh, Tiff. She my G."

"Really. Tiffany's your girl."

"Yeah."

"You like Tiffany."

"Yeah. She my girl."

"Does she know that?"

"Nah, I ain't told her yet."

Kappernick pointed to a park bench a short distance from where they stood. "Let's go sit down and have a talk."

"Sho." The kid strutted to the bench like he'd just scored a touchdown. "I gets how a dude your age can't be standin' on his feet too long."

"Yeah. You understand good." Kappernick laughed. "What's your name?" he asked as they sat down.

"They call me Spokes. What they call you?"

"Kapp." They touched fists. "Okay, I want to talk to you, man to man. You okay with that?" Spokes nodded. "Here's the deal: right, now, I won't lie to you … because I think you mean it when you say you like Tiffany … well, right now, Tiffany can use a friend—a real friend. Not someone who's gonna mess with her, you dig? She's having some problems—some real problems—and I think you can help. But you have to first understand that you just can't assume she's gonna be your girlfriend. You have to ask her, and if she says 'no,' you have to accept that and still be her friend. A man has to woo a girl, dig? And you've got to take it slow—real, real, real slooow."

Spokes shrugged. "How can I ask her, if I can't see her?"

"How old are you?"

"I'll be … thirteen."

"You go to school?"

"Yeah, I'm in junior high. I do pretty good, too."

"Who do you live with?"

"My moms."

"You like baseball?"

"Yeah."

"Ever been to a Phillies game?"

"A real game? Nah."

"Want to go this Sunday? I'm taking Tiffany. You can come with us if you want."

Just then, the rest of the gang showed up. "Yo, Spokes!" one kid yelled. "Let's go!"

"Get the fuck out of here, you all. Can't you see I'm talkin'?" Then to Kappernick he said, "Yeah, I want to go, to the game. Where should I meet you?"

Kappernick told him where they'd meet on Sunday, and as Spokes got onto his bike, he asked the boy why he was riding with that crew.

"Hey, I gots to work," he said. "I gots to make money. My family needs me. I'm the only one bringing anythin' in, yeh neh."

Spokes rode off, and Kappernick started walking home. He thought of the ironic current happenings in his life—on one hand, a pimp and child molester had threatened to kill him; and on the other, he was playing cupid for two preteens. He had to laugh.

For a drug runner, Spokes wasn't a bad kid, and Tiffany needed a friend. Any friend. Someone her own age. Since the confrontation with her aunt, she'd been afraid to go outside alone, afraid someone would grab her. Though she never complained, Kappernick could still see that Tiffany was bored at times. He tried to make conversation, but they had nothing in common. Sixty-six years' difference had a lot to do with it.

"Have you made any friends in school?" he'd asked. Well, she liked one girl, talked to her, but she wasn't a real friend yet. After school, Tiffany usually read and did her homework. Sometimes Kappernick would help her—go over the assigned spelling list, go over history questions.

A couple of days before, Tiffany had on a weird facial expression. She was sitting on the sofa, almost pouting.

"You okay?" Kappernick had asked on his way to the kitchen. She didn't answer. "You want to watch the game? The Phillies are winning for a change."

She scrunched up her nose as if to say, *Are you kidding?*

"Baseball?" she said.

"What, you don't like baseball?"

"It's dumb."

"Dumb?" he said. "Have you ever been to a baseball game? Huh?" When she said she hadn't and he told her they were going on Sunday, her reply was an enthusiastic, "Really?"

Then he asked her what games she liked to play, if she liked board games, and she wasn't exactly sure what he meant.

"You know, like Monopoly, card games, chess." Tiffany didn't answer. "Do you know how to play chess?" he asked. Chess was the only game he'd ever played, so when she said "no," he replied, "I can't believe it! Okay, here's what I'm gonna do: I'm gonna teach you about two things while you're here— baseball and chess." He took out his chess set and placed it onto the coffee table.

"This game is about a turf war. You're gonna have a bunch of guys, and I'm gonna have a bunch of guys. Everyone's gonna have things they can do. This is a tough game, ya know. Sure, you can climb a tree and ride a bike, but can you think? This game will determine how smart you are."

"Really. So if I beat you, I'm smart."

"I wouldn't count on you beating me for a while, and I'm not just gonna let you win because you're a girl." At that, Tiffany straightened in her seat, lips pressed together. "This game takes time to learn," he said, "but people have been playing it for hundreds of years, all over the world. All right, now listen up. This, is a pawn …"

DAY 13

THAT NIGHT, when Kappernick took Soldier for his walk, he stopped into Springer's bar for an ale. He'd told Springer several nights before about Tiffany, and the bar owner had blinked furiously, asking Kappernick if he was out of his freakin' mind. Kappernick had assured him he wasn't. Then Springer had raised one eyebrow and asked Kappernick if he was a freakin' pervert, and once again Kappernick had assured him he was not.

Just then, Perkins came through the door, took a look around, saw Kappernick, and came directly over to him.

"Perkins," Kappernick said. "Sit down and have a beer."

"I would, sir, but I think we got a problem."

Springer uncapped a beer, handed it to Perkins, and asked, "What's the problem?"

"I think two guys out there want to take the lieutenant apart. They waitin' for you, sir," he said to Kappernick.

"How do you know?"

"Heard them talkin' about waitin' and gettin' an old White man."

"Well, I'm old."

"How'd you hear all that?"

"I was in my friend's car, down the block, snoozin'—the

77

window was a-crack, you know—and some guy offered these two other guys a hundred bucks to beat the shit out of you, sir. The guy said you was White and inside Springer's Spot Lite, to wait for you to come out and do you up. I didn't get a look at the guy who hired them, but I watched as the guys walked up here." Perkins hooked his thumb and nodded his head toward the door. "They're leaning against a car right outside."

Springer took out a nightstick from under the bar and took off his apron. "Well, let us see about that."

Kappernick grabbed his arm. "Whoa, where do you think you're going?"

"I'm gonna bust me some heads—some motherfuckin' heads!"

"I'm with you, Jesse," said Perkins. "You got another one of them clubs?"

"No." Kappernick said emphatically. "I don't want you guys to get involved in this."

Springer reared back. "Hey, you think I'm gonna let you go out there, alone? You think I'm gonna let those motherfuckers fuck you up in front of my place, give it a bad reputation so white people don't wanna come in?" He glanced around and laughed. "Ruin my business?"

"Let's be smart about this."

"I'm listening."

"Well, let's say the three of us go outside together? En masse. Get a good look at who they are. Have a friendly talk. I mean, I got Soldier, here. I don't think there's gonna be any trouble."

Springer came around from behind the bar, and the three of them walked to the front door. In his right hand, Springer held his billy club at his side. "You packing?" he whispered into Kappernick's ear.

"Yeah," Kappernick replied. "I started carrying two days ago."

The two guys leaning against the car snapped to attention as Kappernick, Perkins, Springer, and Soldier marched through the door. Upon seeing the group, they looked at each other in doubt. This wasn't what they'd expected, so they shuffled and nodded.

Springer recognized one man. "Hey, Raphael. How you doin'? Come here, I want to talk to you."

Raphael was big-shouldered, with a pockmarked face and shaved head that would have made him stand out in any crowd. He sauntered over to Springer. Both men were well over six feet tall and stood eye-to-eye.

Springer smiled. "I want you to meet a special friend of mine. This here's Mel. I don't want anything to happen to him, you dig? What you doin' around here, anyway, dude? You drinkin'?"

"Nah." Raphael forced a nervous grin. "We just passin', Jesse. Ain't nothin' to it." Then he nodded a "let's go" to his friend, and they ambled off.

"They're from Thirty-Ninth Street," Perkins said. "They were up here with a purpose, that's for sure."

Kappernick considered the comment. "That's only four blocks away."

"Yeah, but around here"—Springer looked around—"that's a lot of dead territory.

DAY 14

SUNDAY WAS A PERFECT DAY FOR BASEBALL.

The doorbell rang, and Tiffany wondered who it was as Kappernick answered the intercom.

"It's Spokes," he said.

"Spokes?" She blinked. "I ain't ridin' no more. I promised you I wouldn't."

"Yeah, it's not that. I invited him to the game."

Tiffany was dumbfounded. "You did? How come?"

Kappernick shrugged as he let in Spokes.

"Yo," Spokes said as he came through the apartment door, wearing a Ryan Howard Jersey and a Phillies cap. As usual, the brim was tilted off to the side, and the too-big jersey came down to just above his knees. He immediately strutted over to a befuddled Tiffany, holding something behind his back.

"Hey, I got this for you," he said, holding out another Phillies cap. "Yeh neh, it's like a gift. You can have it—free."

Tiffany took the cap with an expression of disbelief.

"Put it on. Let's see how it looks," said Spokes, and she did. Spokes nodded. "Yeah, that looks good," he said. "Real good."

Tiffany gave him a look of pure disdain, one that sort

of said, "Boy, you crazy!" and while Kappernick locked up, Tiffany walked down the stairs with Spokes right on her heels. At the car, she insisted on sitting in the front seat and told Spokes to get in the back. On the way to the game, they didn't talk at first, both staring out through the window as Kappernick drove, humming to himself, until Tiffany burst out, "You know I ain't ridin' no more."

"Yeah, I know." Spokes said. "What you doing?"

"Goin' to school. Learnin'."

"That's good."

"So why you here?"

"To see ya. I miss ya."

"What? Really? You crazy?"

"Nah, I'm serious."

Kappernick turned on the radio and listened to soft rock.

Suddenly, the two kids were talking as if they'd never met before. Spokes had gone to Leidy and had had the teacher who now taught Tiffany, and they soon discovered they had a lot of things to talk about, none of it about drugs or bikes or gangs. As they jabbered away, Kappernick hummed to Jim Croce's, *Don't You Know I had A Dream Last Night*.

Kappernick had gotten third-level seats. The game was great, and the kids loved all of it—the huge scoreboard, the Philly Phanatic, the game itself. They ate cheese steaks from Tony Deluca's and a Schmitter from McNally's; they laughed a lot at Kappernick, who yelled at the umpire on every ball and every strike. In the end, the Phillies lost big time, but it didn't matter. The experience was fantastic.

On the way home, Kappernick heard Tiffany ask Spokes, "Do you play chess? … No? Oh, that's a shame. I could teach you, if you want. You got to be smart to play it. People been playin' it for a hundred years. It's a game of war, like two gangs fightin' for turf …"

DAY 15

MONDAY MORNING, Kappernick's cell phone rang around eleven o'clock. It was Bruce.

"My boy! How you doin', kid?"

"I'm good, Dad. How you doin'?"

"I'm hanging in there. What's up?"

"How about coming up for dinner tonight?"

"I'd like that. Can I bring my house guest?"

There was a moment of silence, and then: "Sure, why not? I want to meet her."

"Did you tell Barbara?"

"No. You told me not to say anything, and I didn't. Let's surprise her. I'll just tell her you're bringing a guest."

"Geez. I can't wait."

Kappernick didn't tell Tiffany where they were going; he just said they were going out to eat. Tiffany assumed it was a fast food place on City Line Avenue, like Colonel Sanders or Ruby Tuesday. She loved going to those places. It was a rare treat; seldom did she eat in restaurants. Her grandmother, who always cooked, didn't "cotton" to eat-out places, and if her mother liked them, she couldn't remember. But, because she was going out, Tiffany put on her clean jeans and a flowered blouse she'd picked out when Kappernick had taken her shopping, then she put on a colorful pair of socks and white sneakers. Her curly hair stuck out of her new Phillies cap. As they walked out the door, Kappernick told her she looked nice.

They drove across City Line Avenue at 54th Street, and Tiffany noticed they didn't turn right as they usually did. They were in Merion where the homes were bigger and brighter than any she'd ever seen before. Soon, they turned down a tree-lined drive where the houses were huge, the lawns long, and the trees old. They pulled into a driveway and parked behind a Mercedes.

Tiffany peered quizzically at Kappernick.

"My son's house," he said. "We've been invited for dinner."

Kappernick rang the bell, then opened the door, which he knew was never locked, and walked in. Tiffany followed, though with a mild look of concern … until her mouth dropped open.

She'd never been in a place so beautiful and so clean! Barbara, wearing a white apron over her skirt and blouse, exited the kitchen, wiping her hands as if she'd been interrupted washing dishes.

"Dad—!" she started, but when she saw Tiffany, her previous thoughts vanished and she did something that surprised Kappernick. She smiled, cocked her head, and beamed. "Hello," she said and, without taking her eyes off of the girl, walked over to Kappernick, kissed him briskly on the cheek, then stuck her hand out to Tiffany. "I'm Barbara. Who are you?"

"I'm Tiffany."

"Tiffany's my house guest," said Kappernick. "She's been staying with me."

"Really," Barbara said, maintaining the lilt in her voice. "That's … wonderful. How old are you, dear?"

"I'm eleven, almost twelve."

Just then, Bruce walked in from the study. "Hi, Dad."

"Tiffany, this is my son Bruce, and Barbara is Bruce's wife."

"I didn't know you had a son, Mister Kapp."

"Yep. I got a son, and he has two sons. Where are Daniel and Jacob?"

Barbara kept drying her hands, still without taking her eyes off of Tiffany, who was more than a little interested in looking around. "They're upstairs," she said. "I'll call them. Is your mother also staying with Dad, Mel … Kapp?"

"Nope. My mom's been in jail for five years."

"Oh … that's a shame. Let me call the kids. No, on second thought, I'd better go get them. They're probably deeply involved with their homework." Barbara left to round up the boys, while Bruce led them into the office.

"Boy, this place is really somethin'," said Tiffany. "You must be a billionaire."

Bruce laughed. "No, not by a long, long, long shot. Sit down. How you doing? Is my dad treating you okay?"

"Yeah. He's the best." Tiffany blushed. "Your dad's been great. I never knew my dad. Mr. Kapp's house is the best place I ever lived. He took me and Spokes to a Phillies game yesterday." And she touched her new cap.

Bruce smiled broadly. "He used to take me, too, back in the day."

Barbara entered the room with Jacob, who was a few months younger than Tiffany. "Daniel's studying his Haftorah. He'll be down for dinner. Tiffany, this is Jacob."

"Jake," he said, correcting his mother. He waved to Kappernick. "Hi, Gramps." Kappernick nodded. Then Jake did something that surprised him: he extended his hand to

Tiffany, who took it, almost ladylike, and smiled.

"Call me Tiff," she said.

"Hey, you like to play computer games?"

Tiffany shrugged. "I never have."

"Really? Come on, I'll teach you."

Tiffany looked at Kappernick, who smiled. "Go ahead," he said. "Jake's a computer wizard."

Barbara waited until they left the room, a whimsical smile on her face. "Okay ... will somebody please tell me what's going on?"

At first Kappernick was reluctant to talk about Tiffany, worried that Barbara might get on the phone afterwards and within minutes tell everybody she knew. And Barbara knew a lot of people. Within hours, Kappernick imagined, everyone in Merion would be discussing his business. But Barbara was adamant, wanting to know everything, her eyes glistening with the excitement of a story she knew *had* to be electrifying. She swore absolute secrecy, and even held her hand to God. Finally, Kappernick consented, and he started from the beginning—the young bikers, hearing noises upstairs, and the climbing tree Tiffany used to get in; he alluded to the fact she was in some danger, but didn't discuss Ice Man; and he ended with her living in the small room off of the kitchen, how she studied every day, and was doing well in school.

"She's a very bright girl. I'm very proud of her."

"What do you plan to do with her?"

"I don't know."

"You certainly can't keep her."

"Why not?"

"Because, it's just not done. Old men just can't take in young girls."

"Why not?"

"It's just not done."

Kappernick was about to say "Why not?" one more time, but the return of Jacob and Tiffany, along with Daniel, interrupted them. Daniel was a good six months from being bar mitzvahed, but he was acting superior, showing off, strutting around as if he were twenty.

"Hi, Mel," he said casually. Kappernick didn't like the show. He called Daniel over and offered up his hand, and when the boy took it, Kappernick grasped it firmly, applying pressure. Daniel winced and tried to pull his hand away, but couldn't. Pain began to show on his face, his whole body cringing.

"Gramps!" he said.

"That's better. I'm your grandfather and I expect to be treated with respect. You will call me Gramps until I give you permission to call me something else. Do you understand?" Daniel nodded, and Kappernick eased up on the pressure but didn't completely let go. "Now," he said, "you owe me a hug." And Daniel gave that gladly.

Over dinner there was plenty of talk, and Kappernick couldn't remember a more convivial family time. Tiffany wasn't the least bit shy and contributed to the conversations, unabashed, while Kappernick marveled at how she forthrightly asked and answered questions, seeming totally at ease in a setting that would have intimidated others. She exhibited a precociousness that made the adults smile and wonder from where it emanated—how did a child who had so little, have so much strength and wisdom? At the table, she mentioned her grandmother several times, and Barbara asked her about the woman.

"She died," Tiffany explained. "She got hit by a car in front of the house and died." And later, someone asked her about her father. "Never met him," she said. "But Granny said he was a pure man."

Kappernick watched Barbara's face when Tiffany said

these things, and he could almost see what she was thinking. Against all odds, this young girl had forged ahead, managed to survive. Now, Kappernick saw a light in Barbara's eyes, an admiration he'd never seen before.

After dinner, as they made to leave, Barbara hugged Tiffany, then kissed Kappernick on the cheek. "You are an amazing man, Melvin Kappernick," she whispered into his ear. "I want to help. Let me know if there is anything I can do."

On the drive back to 42nd Street, Kappernick asked Tiffany how she was doing.

"Really good, Mr. Kapp," she replied. "I'll never forget tonight in my whole life. They must be really rich. It was like a castle."

"No. They're not *really* rich. It just seems that way, given where we live. The dichotomy is so dramatic. But remember this: they had the opportunity and they took advantage of it. Bruce had the opportunity, and I'm proud of him for working so hard. Sometimes too hard."

"But he had something just as important."

"What's that?"

She smiled at Kappernick. "He had you."

Tiffany couldn't see it, but Kappernick's eyes misted up. "I was there when he needed me," he said. "I think he knew he could count on me." Then, to change the subject, he asked, "So you had a good time?"

"Oh, yes."

"What did you like the best?"

"Well, I was up in Jake's room, which is bigger than your whole house, and he was showing me computer games. I wasn't doin' too well, but then I saw he had a chess set, so I challenged him to a game."

"How'd you do?"

"I beat him!"

Kappernick laughed. "Good girl."

DAY 16

AS WAS THEIR DAILY ROUTINE, Kappernick and Soldier walked Tiffany to school, then stood at the gate as she entered the yard, where she was always met by another girl whom Kappernick assumed was Tiffany's *almost* friend. Now, as he turned to walk away, he heard footsteps behind him and a woman's voice yelling, "Sir! Oh, sir!"

A white-haired, rosy-cheeked woman stopped abruptly before him, and Kappernick had to draw back to avoid their lips touching. She appeared out of breath from running.

"Are you Mr. Kappernick?" she asked, and when he acknowledged he was, she stuck out her hand. "Hi, I'm Mrs. Lansky, Tiffany's teacher."

Kappernick smiled. "Hello."

"I need to talk to you."

"I'm all ears."

"No, not now. My class is waiting. Can we meet after school?"

"Are you asking me out on a date?" he said, then immediately added, "Just kidding. Sure. When?"

"Can you do it today?"

"I can meet you after I take Tiffany home. What do you take in your coffee? I'll bring a thermos and two cups?"

"It's not necessary."

"I want to."

"Black with a Sweet and Low. I'll be in Room 215."

"See you then."

Mrs. Lansky smiled an acknowledgement and pivoted away. Kappernick watched her as she strode off. She wasn't a bad looking woman. Slim, with a very nice rear end.

That afternoon, with a thermos of hot coffee and two Styrofoam cups, Kappernick found Room 215, where Mrs. Lansky sat at her desk, working on some papers. Except for the student desks and chairs—which in Kappernick's day were screwed into the floor—the room, he thought, hadn't changed. Pictures the kids had drawn and papers they'd written hung all over place. Kappernick pulled up a chair to sit across from the teacher, smiling to himself. As a kid, he'd been in this very position several times. He poured Mrs. Lansky a cup of hot coffee, and as he filled his own, he watched her open the Sweet and Low. Then she looked up, and Kappernick smiled at her, waiting for her to begin. She sipped the coffee, then sat back and folded her arms.

"Okay, Mr. Kappernick, what's going on?"

"You tell me. You said you wanted to talk to me. Obviously, it's about Tiffany. How's she doing? Is she adjusting?"

Mrs. Lansky was momentarily taken back. "Yes, she's adjusting amazingly well. And she's extremely smart."

"Oh, I'm so happy to hear that. What's the problem, then?"

"Well, as of today, we—Mrs. Patterson and the school—haven't received her records from Moosesalaga, Mississippi. And to be very honest, there is no Moosesalaga, Mississippi."

Kappernick laughed. He'd totally forgotten what name he'd made up, though he knew it had started with an "M." "Well, and for good reason," he said. "Who'd want to live in a town named Moosesalaga?"

"I'm not laughing."

"I can see that. I don't have the slightest idea where Mrs. Patterson got Moosesaaa-whatever its name is, but the name of the town is Mantachie, in Itawamba County. I think the school she attended was Chickasaw Elementary, I'm not sure, but it was right off of Jacinto Road. Why?" he said, dumbfounded. "What's going on?"

Mrs. Lansky pursed her lips. "I … I'm not sure."

Kappernick quickly changed the subject. "You know I went to Leidy as a kid, right? In the old school, across the street. Things were different then."

"Yes, they were. And that's what concerns me. In my almost forty years of teaching, I've seen some strange things. I'm retiring next year, and I don't want—"

"Retiring? You don't look old enough. I bet Mr. Lansky is looking forward to that."

"My husband died two years ago."

"My wife died two years ago."

"I'm sorry. But could we get back to—"

"Will you have dinner with me?"

"What? I…"

"Please. Wednesday night. We can talk then. What can it hurt? Where should I pick you up?"

"Rules and regulations" was the title of the note Kappernick had put on Tiffany's door, and under the heading he'd written: "We'll talk after dinner."

Dinner consisted of Campbell's Tomato Soup and hot dogs. After they finished, Kappernick got a yellow-lined legal pad and rewrote: "Rules and regulations" at the top. Just below, he wrote: 1. Cleaning: a. room, b. clothes.

Tiffany made a face and rolled her eyes, but Kappernick tapped the paper with his pencil. "Listen," he said, "when you came here, this place was clean. I put things away. You've got to, too. You're not going to come here and just freeload. You've got to earn your keep, so I expect you to keep your room clean, and wash and dry your own clothes."

"I don't know how."

"I'll teach you. It's easy."

"If I wash all of my clothes, I'll be naked."

Kappernick got up and brought her one if his long dress shirts. "Use this until we get you something that will cover your naked body." Then he went back to the list.

"Suppose I won't do it," she said. "What will you do then, huh?" Tiffany crossed her arms over her chest.

A dark cloud rolled across Kappernick's face—where the hell was her appreciation?—and he leaned across the table. "Then I'll throw you out on your ass. I'm not kidding. I didn't ask you to come here; you asked me. I'm not your father, and I'm not your mother! I'm not gonna be picking up after you. You want to stay here, then you've got to toe the line. And it's just not this." He tapped the yellow pad. "There's more. So let me know now—right now—if you're in or out."

Tiffany's eyes teared up, and her lower lip began to quiver. "I'm sorry. I don't know why I get this way. I do appreciate everything you've done."

Kappernick softened. "Awright, awright, we'll just chalk this little temper flare-up to … I don't know … which sometimes goes awry."

She wiped away a tear. "What else?"

"It's not like I'm sending you into the coal mines. This is easy stuff," he said, and she nodded that she understood.

"All right, once a week, you've got to make dinner, and when you're not making it, you've got to help clean up." He bit the end of his pencil and thought if there was something he missed. "You've got to keep up with your studies, of course, and … I think … that's it."

"You missed something."

"I did? What?"

"Chess."

"Chess? Chess isn't a chore."

"Write it down. One game before bed."

"Okay, I'm writing it down. But only if I'm around. I have an appointment tomorrow night and I may not be home until late. You'll be in charge. Don't let anyone in."

DAY 18

"HIS NAME WAS NORMAN MALLEY. In 1968, he was twenty-five. He was in my squad in Vietnam. How the hell he got in my squad, I'll never know. Fact is, he should never have been in 'nam. He wasn't prepared; like a lot of them, he didn't know anything, and he was psychologically messed up. According to some reports, he lost it in basic, became unstable and should have been given a medical discharge. Actually, he was a pacifist—a pacifist! In 'nam! But—and this I found out later—his father was running for governor or some high office and needed, for political reasons, to say his son was a marine, a fighting man who was fighting the good fight. Can you imagine?

"So the old man got him transferred to some reserve unit in 1962. The reserve unit met once a month, and he lasted there for five meetings before the top sergeant, who ran the entire outfit, saw what he was and got rid of him. Supposedly the top said, 'I can't stand looking at you. You're a coward. I want you out of here. I think you ought to move to New York or someplace where you can never find a unit, and write me a letter each month saying you looked and looked but were unable to find one, and I'll keep you off the books.' Back then, things like that happened all the time, so for five years, he never went to meetings, to summer camp—nothing. And in that time, his father died. Exactly three months before his enlistment would have been up, he got a letter from the government who, at the time, needed men in 'nam, saying he had thirty days to find a unit or they were sending him to Vietnam. And that's how he ended up in 'nam, in my squad. I mean, Malley didn't even know how to fire his weapon! Didn't want to know."

Kappernick had been looking down at his plate, having not touched the T-bone steak the waiter had put down in front of him. He just kept on talking until a small hand landed on his, and he suddenly looked up into the eyes of Linda Lansky, who wore a concerned look.

She forced out a choked chuckle. "What is all this? Who's Malley?"

Kappernick swallowed hard. "Huh?"

"I mean, we were talking about Tiffany, and suddenly you went into this space and were talking about Vietnam."

"Oh, I'm sorry." He wiped his forehead with his napkin. "I just got lost for a minute."

"Are you all right? It was scary, like you went into some kind of trance."

"Yeah, I'm all right. Let's just forget it."

"Well, if you want to talk about it …"

Kappernick needed someone to talk to—someone his own age who'd also lost a loved one; someone he thought might understand. Linda Lansky, he thought, for some unknown reason, was that person—a sympathetic ear. The waiter had taken their orders, then Linda started to ask questions about his made-up daughter who'd died in Mississippi and the family she left behind: Tiffany. He was unable to make up any more stories, and out of the clear, blue sky, he said, looking down at his plate: "Let me tell you about Malley."

And that's how he'd begun. As if hypnotized, Kappernick had gotten lost in the past.

Now, when Linda said, "Well, if you want to talk about it…" he promptly replied, "No. Not right now."

DAY 19

THAT NIGHT, while Kappernick lay in bed, wondering what he was *indeed* doing. He'd almost told Linda Lansky the whole story. He'd wanted to; that's why he'd taken her to dinner. But now, he realized he was lucky he hadn't. What good would it have done to get her involved? He liked Linda. She was a woman—a real woman—but she'd have never gone along with the mess he'd created for himself. What had he been thinking?

It'd only been a little over two weeks, but he felt very close to this tough little girl. Yes, she was tough—very tough. Tough enough to climb a tree, figure out how to get into what she thought was an abandoned house, and brave enough to do it. And, more importantly, smart enough to see what her future would be if she'd stayed with her aunt. But what could he do? He couldn't keep her; she wasn't his kid. Yet, in some ways, even in this short period of time, he felt closer to Tiffany than he had to Bruce when Bruce was that age. Where was he when Bruce was eleven? On the road, selling shoes, schlepping samples from New York to small stores in the midwest, riding a horse through the woods of Fairmount park, trying to forget.

But Bruce hadn't needed him like this girl needed him.

Still, he worried. People would think the worst, because that's what people do. Everyone—his son, his daughter-in-law, Springer. Surely, Linda Lansky would be no different. If only he hadn't promised Tiffany not to tell the authorities. That was his downfall; once he gave his word, it was etched in stone. If only he could see where this was going.

The other little girl flashed through his mind, the one whose image he couldn't forget—the tattered dress; the dirty, outstretched hands; the tears running down her face. And Malley, the men shouting.

Maybe he should have gone to Florida and bought a condo in some gated community, married again. He thought of the Cat Stevens song "Father & Son" and started to hum, "…find a girl settle down; if you want, you can marry …" Then he laughed out loud. So many things to consider … until he thought how, when he left Teabloom's earlier that night to pick up Linda, he'd found a note taped to the front door. It'd been printed in black magic marker and it read: "I haven't forgotten you, motherfucker. Don't forget me. I want what's mine." No signature, but Kappernick didn't have to look on the surveillance video to know who'd sent it.

He curled his lip. He'd have to do something about Ice Man, who obviously wasn't going to leave them alone. On his nightstand lay his holstered short-muzzle .38. During the day, he'd been wearing it on his belt at the hip, slightly behind his back. Now, he reached over, picked up the weapon and examined it. He didn't have to see it; he could feel it as he ran his hand down the cold barrel. Maybe, he thought, almost absentmindedly, it would be best to eliminate Ice Man.

DAY 20

THE NEXT MORNING, after walking Soldier and Tiffany to school, Kappernick spotted Too-Tall coming out of Open-Til-Four. The big man saw him coming, and he raised a disparaging eyebrow.

"You tryin' to get yourself killed, Mr. Melvin?"

"No, not really."

"Then, you just plain crazy. You fucking with the wrong guy, 'cause Ice Man is crazy."

"You work for him, Too-Tall?"

"Nah, I'm in business for myself. But Ice Man is nobody to fuck with."

"You know where he lives?" Kappernick asked, but Too-Tall couldn't say. "How about where he hangs out?"

"There's an old, broken-down deli on the corner of Thirty-Ninth and Girard. He gets there around noon. Sits in the back. Be careful. I'm beginning to like you."

Now Kappernick raised a questioning eyebrow.

"Yeah, that's right, that's what I said." Too-Tall nodded. "You make me feel like I live in an integrated neighborhood." And they both laughed.

That noon, Kappernick parked along the park side of the street with a perfect view of the deli bearing a sign that read:

"Benny's." He sat in his car, sipping coffee from a paper cup. Didn't take long before Ice Man came strutting down the street, wearing his Panama hat, sunglasses, dark slacks, and a reddish sport jacket. One of the guys who'd been waiting outside of Springer's Spot Lite was with him.

Kappernick watched them talking and laughing as they strode past the old Girard movie theater that had, years ago, been converted into the "Say Your Prayers" tabernacle. They passed by a seedy men's clothing store, a beauty shop, and went into Benny's Deli. Ten minutes later, they emerged with coffee and a bag of donuts, and headed up 39th Street. Kappernick moved his car up Girard far enough to see them enter a dirty, poorly stuccoed building on the corner of the next block, then he drove back to where he'd first parked, left the car, and entered the store.

He remembered it as a kid—the place was where the Faust gang used to hang out. A pool table still sat in the back room, but now the place was dirty and dilapidated, with booths sporting torn, black leather seats lining the right hand wall and a door beyond them that led out to 39th Street.

That night, Kappernick asked Tiffany exactly where her aunt Renee lived.

The next day at noon, Kappernick waited on 40th Street, the block he'd seen Ice Man first appear. Once again, Ice Man was on time. The pimp seemed a punctual man, and he saw the door through which Ice Man emerged. Just like the day before, he was with a second man—the huge guy who'd driven him over to Teabloom's. They'd come out of the place Tiffany had told Kappernick about, obviously the place Tiffany's aunt did business.

This time, Ice Man wore a suit, looking like a business-man. Well, now Kappernick knew where he could find the businessman if he needed him in a hurry.

Kappernick drove into the park to let Soldier run, and as he watched the dog traverse the grassy field, he considered killing Ice Man. Who the hell would miss the son of a bitch? Maybe that's what this was all about. Maybe he was meant to be back on 42nd Street. He was an old man, with not much time left. If he took out a bum like Ice Man that had years left to hurt people, kill people, enslave little girls, wouldn't it be worth it? What would he be giving up? A couple of years? That might be the perfect solution; a good way to take out the bastards, the assholes, and the scum of the world. He'd be doing the community a favor. If he got caught, he'd go to jail, but that wasn't his main problem. His main problem was the girl. What would he do with the girl? If he killed Ice Man and then got caught, Tiffany would be all alone. What would happen to her?

Soldier finished his sniffing and running and came back to Kappernick to stand at his side.

"What would you do, boy?" he asked the dog. "What would you do?"

On his way back to the car, Kappernick saw Spokes sitting on his bike, waiting for him. The young drug delivery boy greeted him in his usual sing-song way, "Hey m'man what's happenin'?"

"You tell me. We haven't seen you in a while."

"Yeh neh, chillin'."

"Don't you ever go to school?"

"Hell, yeah, I do. I gets so many A's, they think I'm Albert Einstein. Yeh neh, A-bomb here, A-bomb there."

"Yeah, I get it. Why don't you come over and beat Tiffany at chess?" Kappernick smirked. "Yeh neh, get back at her for the way she obliterated you."

"Hey, man, that won't happen again, believe me. I read me a book, and I'm gonna teach her good, this time. When you want me, Mr. Mel?"

"We eat at seven."

"I'll be there." He turned his baseball cap to the side. "Catch yeh," he said, and peddled away.

Kappernick drove home and parked his car in his usual spot. As he got out, he saw Perkins dressed smartly and carrying a suitcase.

"Hey, Perkins, what's up?"

"Not a thing. How you been?"

"I'm okay. Going on a trip?"

"Nah, just working, is all."

"Yeah, what do you do?"

Perkins held up the valise. "I'm in the suitcase business."

"You sell suitcases?"

He smiled. "No. Well, not exactly, but if you need a suitcase, let me know."

That afternoon, when Kappernick met Tiffany outside of school, he saw Linda. He waved to her, and she waved back.

Tiffany noticed the exchange and smiled. "Do you come here to pick me up or to make eyes at my teacher?" Then she playfully skipped ahead and sang out, "You got a crush on teacher! You got a crush on teacher!"

Kappernick chuckled. "Hey, she's a very pretty woman, but she's way too young for me."

"Oh, you're not so old."

"Yes, unfortunately I am. Oh yeah, I almost forgot," said Kappernick, "we're having a guest for dinner. It's your night to cook, so add a plate."

"Who's comin'?"

"One of your favorite people."

"Who that?"

"Spokes."

"Spokes? Who invited him?"

"I did. He wants a chess rematch. Says he's gonna slaughter you."

"Yeah, right. He must be out of his mind."

"What are you making for dinner?"

"The only thing you taught me: hot dogs, baked beans, and openin' a can of vegetable soup."

"Maybe you should take out a cookbook at the school library."

"Ha, ha."

That night at 6:45, Kappernick buzzed in Spokes, and in his usual way, the young hoodlum sauntered into the apartment, tipped his cap to Kappernick, then looked around for Tiffany. She marched out of the kitchen, acting like boiling water and throwing a bunch of hot dogs into the pot was a real ordeal.

Spokes immediately made a mistake with the first enthusiastic words out of his mouth: "Hey, m'woman!" to which Tiffany rolled her eyes and walked back into the kitchen. Spokes, noticing the disdainful reaction, wondered aloud, "What I say?"

Tiffany came back out, hands on her hips. "First of all, I'm not 'your woman.' I'm nobody's woman. I'm not even a woman yet, though I'm slavin' in the kitchen like one. I'm only eleven. I won't be a woman until next year."

"Okay … then … I say … hey … m'girl!

"No. Don't say that, either."

"Why not?"

She rolled her eyes again. "'Cause I'm not your girl."

"Hey, you mad at me?"

"No."

"You want me to leave?"

"Nooo."

Spokes scratched his head. "I don't get it. What we supposed to be?"

"Friends. Can't we just be friends?"

"That's what I thought we were. Look, I walk down the street, I see one of my homies and I say, 'Hey m'man.' I see you, I say, 'Hey, m'woman.' Yeh neh, man ... woman. Yeh tell me you ain't no woman, so I say, 'Hey, m'girl.' Yeh don't like that—ain't no big thing—so I'll call you whatever yeh want. I'm your man—ooops, I mean ... I'm your *friend*."

Spokes was fast on his feet for sure, and Tiffany appreciated the way he maneuvered around her rebuke. She smiled, and he smiled back. "What should I call you?" he asked.

"Tiffany. Tiff. Now go in the living room and talk to Mr. Kapp until I call you for dinner."

"Yes, ma'am." He removed his cap and bowed. "Saw that move on old time TV," he said. "But, speaking of moves, I'll be honest with you. I came here tonight for one reason only: to teach you a lesson in chess, yeh dig? It ain't about you being my friend; it's about the game." With that, Spokes walked into the living room, announcing loud enough for Tiffany to hear, "I was sent in here by Tiff to be with you, m'man." He stressed "m'man."

After dinner, they played chess. There hadn't been much talking during dinner, and there was even less during the games. For the most part, Kappernick sat in his lounge chair and read, while a particular game went on. Occasionally, he'd get up to look at the board, but refrained from commenting. Tiffany took the first game easily—in less than twenty moves. This defeat did not deter Spokes, however, who went on the attack in game two, but lost in the end. In the third game, it looked as if Spokes was winning, when Kappernick announced it was 9:30 and that would be all for the night. Both combatants groaned.

"We can save the board and you can finish it next time," he said. "From what I saw, you both played well."

Kappernick put Soldier on a leash and walked Spokes out. "Listen, Mr. Mel," said the young biker as they reached the front door, "you gots to be careful. I overheard someone's out to get you."

"Was it Ice Man?"

Spokes looked down at his feet. "Yeah."

"Did he send you?"

"No." The kid shook his head. "Not exactly. Not to get you. He said he needed to talk to Tiff, but you wouldn't let him. Said you was getting in the way of family. But I know that ain't true. I'm sorry, Mr. Mel. I don't want anything to happen to her, and I don't want anything to happen you. You believe me?"

"Yeah, kid, I do. Thanks." Kappernick opened the door. "You be careful."

The street was empty. Kappernick watched Spokes stride away, then he walked up to Springer's Spot Lite and sat at his usual place at the bar. Springer set him up with his favorite ale and asked him how he was doing, to which Kappernick grimly told him he was okay. Instinctively, Springer toweled the bar. "Darnell was in here looking for you," he said. "You just missed him."

"I saw him earlier today. I didn't know he was in the suit-case business."

"Yeah, he's been in it for years."

"Really? What company does he work for?"

Springer raised an eyebrow, confused for a minute. "What company ... does he work ... ?" Then he started to laugh.

"What's so funny?"

"You. You're funny. The suitcase business isn't exactly what you think."

"Tell me."

"Okay. Here's how it works: Perkins dresses real nice, takes a suitcase filled with old crap, and goes down to the Greyhound Bus Terminal, where he sits until he sees someone who looks like a good target carrying a suitcase. When that person isn't looking, he switches his with theirs, then walks out. He brings the case to his place and goes through it. It's like a treasure hunt—you never know what a newly acquired suitcase may hold. Sometimes nothing, sometimes something."

"Jesus!"

"Yeah, it's almost foolproof. If they ask him what he's doing there, he says he's waiting for a friend. If they see him switch bags, he says he made a mistake and apologizes. So far, neither scenario has ever happened. He has it down to a science."

Hearing this, Kappernick was physically shaken. "What the hell happened? Perkins was a good soldier."

"He probably was. I don't know. Shit happens. He probably mustered out, couldn't get a job, didn't want to become a real criminal and so figured out a way. A bag here, a bag there ..."

As Springer walked up the bar to help another customer, Kappernick thought: *Other people run away from this kind of shit. They go to Florida and hide in gated communities. Me? Schmuck that I am ... I'm right in the middle of it.*

DAY 21

PERKINS LIVED on the third floor in an efficiency apartment at the rear of one of the brownstones that lined Parkside Ave. He'd been there for nearly sixteen years. Bernard Segal, the old Jewish man who owned the building, kept the foyers clean, rarely raised the rent and, unlike other owners Perkins had rented from, was responsive to problems. Although it was cold in the winter and hot in the summer, Perkins loved the place. He liked its location, and he enjoyed sitting in the worn wicker chairs that Segal kept on the front porch, rocking and looking out into the park.

Under the one window in his room sat an old porcelain sink next to a small gas range and an apartment-sized refrigerator. The very tiny bathroom had only a stall shower, and not four feet from the bathroom door stood Perkins' easy chair, reading lamp, and TV. On the other side of the room was a single bed and a nightstand. The walls were lined with bookcases that were filled with books and one small rug covered the floor in front of the reading chair. Except for one wooden stool and a suitcase propped up by the door, that was the contents of the apartment, and still the place looked crowded. But Perkins didn't mind. The rent was low, and it included all utilities.

From the sink, Perkins filled a teapot with water, put it on the stove, and turned on the fire. He'd just gotten up and was dressed in his boxer shorts. As he waited for the water to boil, he whistled and extracted a Tetley tea bag from a near-empty box, and was about to insert a slice of bread into the toaster when a knock sounded on his door.

Perkins raised his eyebrows at this odd occurrence and stared at the entryway. No one had knocked on his door in a long time.

"Just a minute," he called out, putting on a pair of pants held up by suspenders, then muttered, "Just a damn minute." He limped over to the door and swung it open. "Now, who—" There stood Kappernick, smiling, with his big dog, Soldier. Perkins was pleasantly surprised. "Captain—er, I mean, sir?"

"Hey Perkins. How you doin'?"

"Fine. Fine. Just fine, sir." He resisted the temptation to salute.

"I wanted to talk to you. I was out walking my dog and … can I come in? I can leave the dog out here. He won't bother anybody."

"Sure, sure. Come on in. I got some tea on the stove, and I got an extra cup."

"Good. I'll have some. Should I leave the dog outside?"

"Nah, he won't be no bother. You sit in that comfortable chair there, while I brew the tea."

Kappernick looked around, immediately seeing the only other place to sit was a stool. "No, I'll take the stool," he said. The room was small, but clean, and what impressed Kappernick the most were the books that filled the shelves.

Within minutes, Perkins had handed his old lieutenant a cup of hot brew, then sat on the edge of his TV chair, unwilling to sit all the way back since it wouldn't be respectful. He looked quizzically at his old frontline officer, then shrugged as if to say: What's going on?

"Perkins." Kappernick looked him straight in the eye. "I've been thinking about you. I want to make sure you're okay. Frankly, I found out about your suitcase business just the other day, and while it's really none of my business, I'm worried. You were a damn good soldier, Perkins—damn good! What the hell happened?"

Kappernick remembered that group of brothers with great affection; those ethnically diverse men had come together as one cohesive unit—all of the moving parts worked, and each man knew what was expected of him, knew what his job was, and they all understood they needed to work as a team. In those days, Perkins was small, lean and, as they said in the corps, strak, meaning everything was always in order, clean and precise—his weapon was always immaculate, his fatigues creased, his boots polished. Now, the only major difference, Kappernick thought as he looked around, was the absence of hair. Perkins was almost completely bald. Back then, Perkins had loved the marines; the corps was his place in the world—his life, his home. And the corps loved him because Perkins had a talent: he was a sharpshooter, a sniper, a long-distance dead-eye. He could shoot the whiskers off of a squirrel at a hundred yards, and more than once he'd taken someone out a football field away.

"Well, I ain't complainin'," Perkins said. "I can't complain. I … well, things just went bad."

"How so? What went bad?"

"I got out in '70," he explained. "Honorable, and all. As you know, I'd taken a bullet in the leg and I couldn't go anymore. But in all honesty—and it wasn't the corps' fault—I just wasn't ready. The only skill I had was shooting that sighted M1. I could fire that sonofabitch," he said fondly, remembering it almost wistfully. "Things … they changed back home. I'd gone in as a kid, and when I got out, there was nothing I could do. No one would hire me, no one respected me. I was lost, you know? My head was fucked up, my leg was busted up, and my heart was broken because the corps was behind me, you know what I mean? Hell, you should. You're the one who put me on his back and pulled me out of there, remember?"

Kappernick nodded.

"Did a lot of menial jobs to survive. Lot of latrine work. Still do. Cleaning toilets, that's me. Anyway—and I'm not complainin'—things got tough. I could go on welfare, but that ain't me. I just never tried. Anyway, about twenty-five years ago, my sister, who lives in Baltimore, sent me some money to visit her. I packed a bag and went down to the bus station, and while I was sittin' there waitin' for my bus, don't you know it, somebody took my bag! He got me, but he left me his bag. Left it right where mine was! Mostly it was a bunch of crap, but it did have a book."

He pointed to the top of a bookcase. "It's right up there. See these books, they all came from bags and suitcases, and I've read them all." Perkins blinked, then hung his head, seeming momentarily choked up. He bit his lip. "You know," he said in almost a whisper, "we risked our lives for them, but they don't give a damn for us. They treat us bad. We became invisible. I see the suitcase business as a way of them paying me back for what I gave them. Sometimes the bag I leave them is worth more than the one they had."

"Do you need anything?" Kappernick asked. "Could you use some money?"

"No, sir. I'm fine. I'm all right."

"If you need anything, or need me, don't hesitate. I'm right around the corner. And, if you don't mind, I'm gonna call the VA to see if we can get you off of latrine duty."

DAY 22

KAPPERNICK WAITED until Saturday morning to call Linda Lansky.

"Hey," he said, "I've been thinking about you. You busy tonight? You want to have dinner?"

There was a long pause.

"Are you busy tonight?" he asked again.

"No. Just a little surprised."

"Why? You think just because you get old, you don't want to be with people?"

Linda was talking about absenteeism. How the rehabbing mania, the gentrification of the city caused kids to play, what she called, "long-term hooky."

"You see, if a block has sixty houses, and each house has four apartments, and each apartment has an average of two kids, then we're talking sixty times four times two. That's four hundred and eighty kids. And, in Philadelphia, this gentrification is taking place all over the city. The rehabbers are working on twenty streets. That's ..." Kappernick watched her calculate in her head. "… close to eight thousand kids. Now, these families can't afford to move into more affluent neighborhoods, so they move deeper into the ghettoes like displaced persons. They don't know anyone, their kids don't know anyone and have no one to protect their backs; they're picked on, taken advantage of, beaten up, made to pay their lunch money to bullies. Is it any wonder they don't want to go to school?"

Kappernick loved her passion. "Wow. You are totally all in."

Resolve filled her gaze. "I've been working on this problem for four years. Yes, we're making Philadelphia more beautiful, but we're also destroying neighborhoods and displacing hundreds of kids. I can see what these kids are going through, how they're hurting." She studied Kappernick with a deep light in her eyes. "That's why I'm trusting you. Tiffany's lucky to have someone like you to look after her. I'd hate to see her fall into that hole I just described to you."

Kappernick took a deep breath. "Let me tell you a story."

"Uh-oh. I hope it's not about … what's his name … Malley."

"In a way it is. Look, I've only known you for a short time, but I think you're a good person and I believe I can trust you. Can I trust you?"

"Is this about Tiffany?"

"Yep."

"Tell me. What is it?"

"I'm not her grandfather. In fact, I'm not related to her at all. I've only known her for a little more than a month."

"But she's living with you."

"Yep."

Linda considered running the hell out of the restaurant yelling, "Police!" but she didn't. Instead, she listened, and at first, like everyone else, her mouth dropped open. But as

Kappernick told her what had happened—about the tree, about hearing her up on the third floor, the pallet of rags, Tiffany's aunt, and Ice Man—Linda's lips closed and she listened in rapt silence.

"So, she has her own room and cleans it, washes her own clothes, makes her bed and cooks once a week," Kappernick said. "I also taught her how to play chess. Last week she had a friend over—twelve years old and totally in love with her. She taught him how to play the game and, believe it or not, they sat in the living room and played for two straight hours. Only problem is: she's afraid to go out alone, afraid Ice Man will get her. It's just like you said—there's no one there to protect her back. Spokes told me that—"

"Spokes! You mean, Dezi McClendon?"

"I don't know this kid's real name."

"There's only one Spokes. You got him to sit still for two hours?"

"No, she did. She bosses him around, and he listens. Honestly, though, I think he's a pretty good kid."

"Very smart," Linda muttered absentmindedly. "But I'm concerned. Very concerned. Why? Why are you so reluctant to go to the proper authorities?"

Kappernick sighed in frustration. "Okay, it's not just that I gave her my word. This girl is terrified of Ice Man. She won't go out on the street alone, afraid one of Ice Man's cronies will grab her. She used to climb up a tree, enter an abandoned building, and sleep on a dirty floor to avoid being near this guy. But"—he held up his hands— "let's forget all of that for a moment. Let's say I go to the authorities. Let's say I convince Tiffany to tell all. Let's say the cops believe her. What are they going to do, run right out and arrest him? Give me a break. Or if they do, he'll be out in two minutes. But if I know the bureaucracy, reality is, they probably won't believe her and give her back to her aunt, or worse—they'll arrest the aunt and put Tiffany in an institution, where she'll remain for the next seven years of her life. No, I can't do that."

"You seem so sure."

"Heh. Let me tell you a little story. About ten years ago, my wife and I were friendly with a psychiatrist and his wife. One night, the four of us were out to dinner, and this guy, the psychiatrist, is depressed. Why? Because that afternoon he was on a committee that hears domestic violence cases, and they, the committee, heard of a case where a three-year-old girl has syphilis. She's three! Syphilis can only be transferred through intercourse. My friend's depressed because they didn't arrest the sonofabitch who did it! Three years old. No, I can't put Tiffany through that."

"You like this girl."

"I do. But mostly, I admire her. She has guts and brains, and I want her to have a chance. I mean, she was able to see what her life would be and, unlike most kids, she's not willing to just go along. Blows my mind how bright this kid is. Must have been the grandmother who had the brains."

"And you're not … touching … her …"

Kappernick couldn't hide his annoyance. "I have not laid a glove on the kid," he said, stressing the word "kid." "Hand to God. I mean, would I be here telling you, if I had? Give me a break."

"Why did you tell me, Melvin? I mean it's not like you and I … You know, you could get arrested."

"Yeah," he laughed. "Ironically, I could get cuffed for endangering the morals of a minor." Then he got serious. "Linda, I told you for a lot of reasons. First of all, I like you. Ah, I can see by your annoyed look that you think that's irrelevant. Yes, I know, I'm way too old for you, but I like being with lovely women. What can I do? More importantly, though, you know Tiffany. You see her potential and I was hoping you might have some answers. You're her teacher."

At that moment, Kappernick's cell phone rang. "Hey," he announced to Linda, "it's my kid—my real kid, Bruce. I'm gonna answer it, okay?" And Linda nodded as he took the call. "Hey, boy, how you doin'?"

"I'm good, Dad, how about you? How's the kid?"

"I'm good and she's good. What's up?"

"Listen, it's supposed to be a beautiful day tomorrow, and we're planning a trip to the zoo. Do you and Tiffany want to join us?"

"The zoo? Yeah, that sounds great. What time?"

"Eleven."

"Cool. We'll meet you there. Thanks."

Kappernick hung up, then smiled at Linda. "My son, the lawyer. The zoo. Want to come?"

"I … we … no … What will people think? What will Tiffany think?"

"Who cares? You're worried what people will assume? That's the trouble! Sure, better you should sit inside all alone on a beautiful day."

"How do you know I don't have plans?"

"Do you?"

Linda was about to protest, but the objection died on her lips. "I'll meet you there."

Kappernick smiled. "Really?"

"Yes. Now I want to meet the whole family."

Kappernick sat back, still smiling, clasping his hands behind his head to study Linda. He felt good, better than he had in years. He'd just finished a marvelous tournedos (the most delicious cut of the fillet of beef) dinner, was sitting across from an extremely interesting woman, and his son had just asked him to join him for a Sunday at the zoo, when a jazz quartet started to play. He started snapping his fingers, then said, "Hey, do you dance?"

"I've been known to, every once in a while. Why?"

"Why? Well, we're here, we've finished dinner, there's a band playing, and there's a dance floor, that's why. And the song they're playing is one of my favorites, and so appropriate."

Kappernick got up, held out his hand. Linda took it, and as they walked to the dance floor, she asked the name of the song. "It's an old Sinatra tune," he said, taking her in his arms and moving to the music. "It's called, 'I've Got You Under My Skin.'"

DAY 23

WHEN KAPPERNICK TOLD TIFFANY they were going to the zoo, and his son, daughter-in-law, and kids would meet them there, she was excited. She'd never been to the zoo. She almost squealed with delight, then spent about an hour selecting a Go-Phillies T-shirt, tight-fitting jeans, and a pale gray hoodie sweatshirt. The zoo was only about ten blocks from 42nd Street, but Kappernick chose to drive. If they walked, they'd have to pass by the 39th Street and Benny's Deli, and he didn't want to do that; there was too great a chance of seeing one of Ice Man's gang. The zoo's main parking lot was a half-block away from the entrance.

It was a beautiful morning. Bruce, Barbara, and the kids waited for them at the main gate when they arrived. Bruce and Kappernick hugged. Barbara kissed her father-in-law's cheek, then hugged Tiffany. Kappernick hugged the boys, and as he did, he saw Linda approaching.

"Well, look who it is!" said Kappernick. "Hello, Mrs. Lansky. Isn't this a coincidence? Mrs. Lansky, I want you to meet my family. Mrs. Lansky is Tiffany's fifth grade teacher."

Despite everyone's cordiality, the meeting was somewhat awkward; Tiffany didn't quite know how to act or what to say, and she looked at Kappernick with an "I knew it" grin.

"Actually it wasn't a surprise or a coincidence," he said. "I've come to know Mrs. … Linda, and I invited her to join us."

Tiffany let loose an enormous smile, which Barbara understood immediately. With a smirk as if the two of them shared a secret, she took Tiffany's hand and together they walked to the zoo's entrance gate. The boys followed, shortly joined by their grandfather and Linda. Momentarily dumbfounded, Bruce stood there with his own smirk, until Barbara yelled back to him, "Honey, you've got the tickets!" After that, things went quite smoothly.

Kappernick strolled with Linda, behind Bruce's family, who'd already adopted Tiffany. He felt very pleased and satisfied, and in the case of his son, Barbara, and their kids, absence may have indeed made the heart grow fonder. Both Daniel and Jacob seemed pretty nice when they didn't have their faces in their computer games.

Bruce told him Barbara and the boys had actually insisted on inviting him and Tiffany. Seemed Mah Jong and silly telephone conversations took a backseat to motherly instincts. Bruce had taken a day off to be with his family, and walking next to him was a lovely younger lady, a mere child of sixty-something, who watched him with admiration in her eyes. He couldn't help smiling.

Everybody had stopped in front of a fence that corralled the giraffes. The park was crowded on this first real day of Spring. "Listen, everybody!" said Bruce. "It's time for a picture." And everyone thought this was a grand idea. The kids joyfully fought for positioning, which almost brought tears to Kappernick's eyes, because they fought to be next to him. In the end, Tiffany stood to his right, Jacob to his left, Daniel to his younger brother's left, Linda to Tiffany's right, with

Bruce and Barbara on the ends. They'd asked someone passing by to take the shot.

As the newly appointed photographer, an older man, tried to line up the photo, Kappernick spotted another guy emerge from the crowd. He'd seen him before, outside of Springer's Spot Lite. He was one of the guys who'd been sent to beat him up.

This guy wore a long raincoat.

This guy was taking a weapon out of his pocket.

This guy had murder in his eyes.

PART TWO

BARTON BERK

BARTON BERK sat back in a soft leather chair and smoked a filter-tipped Marlboro from a long cigarette holder. He kicked off his shoes, put his feet up onto the matching ottoman, and gazed out through the picture window of his luxurious apartment. Though he maintained many residences, this was his true place; here, he was himself. Checking his watch, he knew he didn't have much time to enjoy the view; he had to get to work.

After finishing the cigarette, he sighed heavily, left the easy chair, and went into the bedroom, where he removed his rings, his watch, and his shirt and tie. He thought about changing his trousers, but he didn't have time. No one would know or care about the trousers anyway.

Dressing hurriedly, he put on a white button-down shirt, bow tie, wedding band, and wire-frame glasses. Then he donned a short, white lab jacket where, on the left hand side, sat his name tag: B. Berk. Under the tag was the store logo, CVS, where he was the head pharmacist. Then he took the elevator down to the parking lot and passed by the BMW (although he couldn't resist touching it) and took the old Chevy.

Driving northeast, Berk thought about his day. He'd had some tension, had to slap around Monique, who'd had given him lip. Another time, he might have let it slide, since she was a good producer. Still, he had to slap her face, careful not to mar her looks, and just to be sure she understood, he punched her in the kidneys a couple of times. Lately, he'd lost some prestige and he had to draw a line somewhere. She'd cried loud enough for everyone to hear, "Please, Ice! I didn't mean it, Ice!" He couldn't remember exactly what had set him off. It didn't matter, though. He'd been looking to hit someone, and she'd stepped into his line of fire. He thought that kind of shit was over. He didn't enjoy hurting people, he just wanted them to obey. Motherfuckers!

All right, he had to get it out of his head, had to calm down, to be Barton Berk. He had drugs to dispense.

He smiled grimly. What a life!

Yes, that white motherfucker had surprised him with that audio tape, and he'd taken the slap in the face as though it hadn't fazed him. Ice Man wanted to kill him. Luckily, Barton Berk had had the sense to walk away, thinking he'd get him later. Stupid white sonofabitch could expose Ice Man, reveal his real identity. He had to figure something out. He'd tried—he'd spent hours working on a solution—but no answer had come. Then the two bunglers, outside of the Spot Lite—what a fiasco! Walking away! That's losing face. Those sons of bitches were more afraid of what those punks outside that bar might have done than what he, Ice Man, would do for their not doing anything!

The girl—this guy had fucked with his business. Actually, it was Richie Wright—aka Spade Coolie—who'd put the idea in his head. Personally, Ice Man had never fucked with pedophiles, but Coolie had said there was big money in it. They'd accidentally met one morning at the 39th Street Deli. Coolie always dressed like a pimp, and that day he'd worn a black cowboy hat, a black shirt, a snake-skin sports jacket, and matching cowboy boots. Talk about wanting to stand out. "Hey, m'man, wassup? I been thinkin' 'bout you."

"Tryin' to decide, is dat bad or good?" They slapped hands.

"Could be profitable. How's that little girl of yourn? How old's she?"

"Who you talkin' about?"

"You know, the young one, the kid."

"Who?"

"Don't bullshit me. Don't you got some real young pussy livin' at Thirty-Ninth ?"

"Tiffany? Josie's kid?"

"I don't know her name. She pale, got bushy hair."

"Yeah"—he snorted—"you talkin' about Tiffany. She ten or eleven, mon. Couple years, I'll break her in. Why? What's it to you?"

"Yeah, right." Coolie scoffed. "Couple years." But then he saw Ice Man was serious. "You crazy, motherfucker, the big money's now."

Coolie lowered his voice to a whisper. "Listen, I got me a pettyfile who's willin' to spend big money."

"Yeah, what we talkin'?"

Ice Man had been planning to slowly break Tiffany in, to get her used to her surroundings, so to speak. But Coolie was talking big, big money, which put everything in a new light. Initially, Coolie told him twenty-five thousand a pop was the appropriate fee, and if she continued to have that "baby" look, she could make big money like that for a long time. Not twenty-five, thirty dollars a pop, but twenty-five thousand! Handled correctly, she could become an industry— porn movies, pictures.

Ever since that conversation with Coolie, Ice Man had thought about how to break her in once she was living under his roof, but he hadn't wanted to beat her into submission;

he'd wanted to finesse her, make her fall in love with him so she'd do, out of love, what he asked. Under the circumstances, however, that was hard to do since things seemed to continually get in his way. First, the grandmother, and then the aunt, Renee. It was like they were both watching him. He didn't want to lose Renee; she was a good whore who earned good money, two to three hundred a night, if he kept her drugged. She loved him, obeyed him, did what he told her to. The only thing she loved more than himself were the drugs he fed her. Sometimes, if she was real good, earned good, he'd let her service him in bed.

One night, after making him feel especially good, Renee started talking about her sister, Josie, and her baby girl, Tiffany. Renee had seen the girl on the street and mentioned how she was growing up and how good she was looking. Josie would have been proud of her.

It started Ice Man thinking, and Renee saw how this interested him. To please him, she began talking about what if, for Josie's sake, they took her in.

Renee instinctively knew what his designs were for Tiffany, but he didn't want to blatantly expose his plans, especially so soon after the grandmother's … accident. But because of Renee's jealousy, the timing with Tiffany was never right. By the time he'd gotten free from other things, it was always so late. He'd go into Tiffany's room when she was already asleep. He'd get in bed with her, try to finesse her, press his hard one against her, try to kiss her, force her hand down to touch him. But she always fought him, kept saying, "No!" Two, three times this happened until her protests finally irritated him so much, he slapped her across the mouth and grabbed her by the neck. "Next time I come in here and you say 'no,' I'll fuckin' beat the shit out of you. Next time, you'll do everything I tell you to do."

But there was no next time. It was like she'd disappeared—he came to the house one night and her bed was empty. Where the fuck was she? Took him almost three weeks to find out. She was with some fuckin' old white-eye motherfucker! Dat motherfucker was costing Ice Man, and Ice Man did not like it! It was costing him face, and more importantly, some serious money!

He banged his fist against the steering wheel, cursing aloud, and as he pulled into the rear parking lot of CVS, the veins in his forehead began to pulsate, having momentarily lost all rationale. *Fuck dat motherfucker! I should have killed him in the apartment! Fuck the tape!*

And just as his anger was about to peak, a cell phone rang. Not Berk's phone, but Ice Man's. Berk took a deep breath. He had to calm down, even though the phone was jumping around on the passenger seat next to him. He picked it up and answered it. "Yeah?"

"Hey, brother, this is Raphael. I know I'm on your shit list since me and Omar fucked up outside of the Spot Lite, but I mean to make up for it. I just seen your main fuckin' man."

Berk switched to his Jamaican accent. He'd only been to Jamaica once, on a five-day trip. He was no more Jamaican than he was Caucasian. "Yeah, mon, who dat be?"

"Da old white guy you want done. And he got the girl with him. Look like they goin' to the zoo."

"Can you put a bullet in dat motherfucker's head for me?"

"Yeah, I can do it."

"Without fucking it up?"

"Don't you worry. What'll it be worth?"

"Ten grand, mon."

"It's as good as done."

Ice Man looked up at the bright, sunny day and thought, *It's a good time to die.* Then he looked at himself in the rear-

view mirror and, forcing a smile, he put on his non-magni-
fying, horn-rimmed glasses and left the car. Dr. Jekyll and
Mister Hyde; Superman and Clark Kent; Barton Berk and
Ice Man.

TOWANDA HALL

WHEN TIFFANY'S GRANDMOTHER was angry, her eyes would widen, her huge breasts would heave, and the tips of her teeth would appear under pressed lips.

Tiffany remembered how, when she was five, she'd heard her granny banging on her mother's apartment door. "Josie, you in there? Josie, I'm talking to you!" had been the shouts that came through. Back then, Tiffany stood transfixed, terrified, in the middle of the living room, sucking her thumb, staring at the door. She saw the doorknob turn and the door being pushed open. With a grunt, her grandmother shoved aside the debris and entered the room, then the old woman stopped short, lower jaw dropping open then snapping shut as she looked around the room in horror.

The place was in chaotic disarray—the few pictures on the walls were lopsided, glass broken; the floors were littered with papers, bills, dirty dishes, filthy clothes; and roaches and silverfish were everywhere.

"My Lord!" she hissed. She momentarily ignored Tiffany and shouted out, "Josie!" to no reply, only the sobs of the little girl standing on top of a pile of debris. The old woman looked down at her. "Girl, what's your name?"

"Tiffany."

"You're Tiffany?"

"Yes."

"Where's your mom, girl?"

"I don't know."

"How long she been gone?"

"I don't know."

"You been here all alone?"

"Yes."

"When's the last time you ate?"

"I don't know."

The old woman teared up. "Girl, you come here. I'm your grandmother, Towanda, and I'm gonna take you home with me. Your days of going hungry and living like this are over."

Tiffany walked tentatively, almost staggering, over to her grandmother and fell into her arms. The old woman clutched her to her breast, tears running down her face. Without closing the door, she wrapped Tiffany into her own coat, carried her out of the building, and hailed a cab.

The taxi ride took them to East Oak Lane, only twenty minutes away, yet it was a different world. Before entering the house, the old woman shook out the coat in which she'd wrapped her granddaughter and examined Tiffany. "There will be no roaches in my house, little darling."

Tiffany's grandmother was like a ray of sunshine on a dismal day. Her house sparkled—the furniture was polished; the shelves were filled with delightful objects, books, and magazines; and best of all, the aroma from the kitchen was tantalizing. "We gonna feed you first"—her grandmother used the universal "we"—"and then we gonna bath you, and get you some decent clothes. Yes, that's what we gonna do."

That night, Towanda put Tiffany to bed in what once had been Tiffany's mother's room. She kissed Tiffany on her forehead and told her not to worry, that she was now in her granny's hands.

"I'll leave the door ajar in case you need to use the bathroom," she told Tiffany. But Tiffany lay in bed, unable to sleep for a long while. When she was just about to doze off, she heard her grandmother praying in the adjoining room. "Dear Lord," she said, "as you know, I'm not a religious woman, but I ask you now to help me. This little girl needs me. She's been deeply hurt, and I should have come to her rescue long ago. I let my own foolish pride stand in the way. I'd turned away from my daughter—both of my daughters—when they needed me. Never thought my Josie would do the things she did, and now the police are looking for her. I tried, Lord; You knows I tried. Tried to raise her and her sister right. But I failed. I'm not making excuses, Lord, but I was alone. I had no help, and I honestly don't know what I did wrong. I promise you now, Lord, I won't let this girl down. This little girl needs me. Please help me to help her. I pray to you. Thank you. Sincerely, Towanda Hall."

Towanda lay in bed, thinking about the day she'd abandoned Josie, when she found out what she was, what she'd become, and why she'd stayed away. Things had gone to hell so quickly. She'd been a good girl—both of them had—but the devil himself had been standin' outside the church, catching them as they fell down the steps. *Good Lord! Why? Was it the neighborhood? Was it that I was working all the time? That they had no father? That the schools were rotten?*

Soon, light crawled in through a faded lace curtain. Towanda's chest heaved, and tears rolled down her cheeks. Yes, Josie had had a baby out of wedlock—a girl, the child in the next room. She and the baby had lived with her for about six months and everything seemed fine. Then, without notice, she disappeared, taking all of her things and leaving only a note: *"I need a place of my own, a place closer to work. Renee's going to move in with me and help take care of Tiffany."*

With that note, Towanda was alone. The house was empty, and she was stunned. Not until days later had she realized she'd been robbed of her blood. She read the note several times—Josie hadn't said where they'd moved. Towanda figured they'd call to let her know, but days drifted into weeks and still no call. Soon, she became frantic. What was going on? What should she do? What had she said, or done, to drive them away?

Then she received a letter addressed to Josie. She opened it. Josie's job was letting her go for chronic absenteeism! How was she even supporting herself?

When people asked Towanda about her girls, she just smiled and made up stories, and as the weeks and months fell away, she became more reclusive, slipping into a depression that immobilized her, sapped her of her strength. Until one day, coming from the market with a couple of bags in her hands, she passed by her haughty neighbor from down the block, Lonnie Jones. "Oh, Towanda," Lonnie said, "I just saw your girls going into that house on Mole Street. You know, that old, boarded-up place—the old Victorian?"

Boarded-up, old Victorian!

Towanda hurriedly stowed the groceries and rushed over to Mole Street. She wanted to see her girls! She thought she knew which house Lonnie had referred to—the one made of cut stone, with old-fashioned turrets. She thought it was being restored, but despite its historic beauty, it had become an eyesore over the years.

She turned the corner onto Mole Street and saw Renee coming out of the old place on the arm of some man. No one walked like Renee. Towanda shouted out to her, but a car screeching by drowned out her words. By the time she'd recovered her composure, Renee and the man were already in a car, driving away.

Instead, she strode up to the old house.

A black, rusty, ornate iron fence guarded the Victorian, wrapping around the entire building like a worn-out belt. Towanda opened the creaky gate and headed up the broken, slate path lined with neglected grass. The paint on the porch was chipped, boards broken. Windows were covered with plywood, and the front door was slightly ajar.

Towanda pushed it open to an empty, cold, dark interior that reeked of nauseating foulness. The older woman gagged, put her hand over her mouth, and was about to turn away, when she heard noises from the upper floor. A voice that echoed through the building, reverberating off the walls, followed by weird laughter.

As she cautiously climbed the stairs, the overwhelming stench of urine and feces again made her gag. She reached the landing, then passed a room where a man was huddled on the floor in the corner, back to the wall, legs pulled up to his chest, head between his knees. Suddenly, he lifted his head, turned to the side, and vomited next to where he sat. He didn't move.

The next room had a table and some chairs, and a decrepit sofa, where the people there acted like they were dead. Zombies. In the next room, she found her Josie, who was on her knees before a man whose pants were down around his ankles. She clutched his naked buttocks with his penis in her mouth. Towanda stood there shaking while the man grabbed Josie's hair, pulled her mouth away from him. "You gonna do what your Ice Man, say?"

"Yes, Ice. Yes, Ice."

"When I tell you to suck a man's dick, you suck that dick! You don't say the word 'no' to your Ice Man. Now get back on there and do me up!"

Josie obeyed, and Ice Man groaned. Towanda breathed

in deeply—an audible gasp. The man grasping Josie's head heard it and turned.

"Who there?" he said, momentarily letting go of Josie, who turned as well.

She swayed as if in a drunken haze, face gaunt, eyes deep in her skull. "Momma?"

"Momma?" the man said incredulously. "Dat your momma?" And he began to laugh, turning to face Towanda, swinging his fading erection. "Come here, Momma, and get you some of dis." He turned back to Josie, grabbed her hair. "Get back on. That's it. Do it good. Hey, Momma, can you do it this good? You taught her good."

Towanda heard his laughter all the way home.

Back then, Tiffany had been less than a year old. The four years following were difficult for Towanda—she was terrified, repulsed, appalled, and disheartened. Just the thought of what she'd witnessed had sickened her, not because Josie was on her knees, but because she, Towanda, hadn't done anything about it. She'd run away. In her heart of hearts, she prayed Josie would come back to her, that she was being held against her will, that she'd break away. But she knew it was only a pipe dream. It hadn't looked like Renee was being held against her will, not when she drove off with that dandy in that fancy car. And neither was Josie chained. And that man—he'd had a fire in his eyes like Satan himself!

No, Josie hadn't tried to run to her momma when she saw her. After the initial shock, there was almost a smile on Josie's face, as if she didn't care.

Disgust filled Towanda's heart, overwhelmed her. And because it had overwhelmed her, it had also immobilized her. She was haunted by the laughter of the maniac Josie obviously worshipped, and she blamed herself, kept reliving the past. They'd been such good children. If only she hadn't done some things, or had maybe done some other things, the situation might have been different.

A year passed.

Towanda woke up one morning, put on her robe, and went downstairs. Despite the violent rainstorm the night before, the sun shone brightly. She made herself some coffee and looked around her house, unable to remember the last time she'd dusted or vacuumed. At that moment, she didn't care.

Carrying her coffee cup to the front door, she made to retrieve her newspaper, but when she opened the door and bent down for the paper, she gasped. Standing on the top step and holding a small suitcase was her younger daughter, Renee. Towanda's heart pounded and her chin quivered, eyes tearing up.

"Baby!" she cried, holding out her arms. She couldn't help herself. Renee had deserted her, hadn't called in over a year, yet she was still her baby girl.

"Hi, Momma. How've you been?"

Renee did not rush into her mother's arms. Instead, she coolly kissed her cheek. Kissed it like some foreign dignitary who'd come to inspect.

"I need to stay for a few days."

Stunned, Towanda did not move. "Just a few days? It's been more than a year, and this is how you greet your mother? Just a few days? Why? What's going on?"

"I got in a little trouble. Nothing to worry about, but I gave the police this address."

A sudden, enormous tension tightened between the two women, lasting several moments. Renee broke the silence first.

"Are you not going to invite me in?"

Towanda never thought she'd say it. Had her disappearance happened a few days before, had Renee not stayed away for so long or had taken her so totally for granted, her answer might have been different. But this day she said, "No. Absolutely not!" and the smugness vanished from Renee's face. "I don't know you. I have no idea who you are. You're not the daughter I raised; you're some pimp's whore. You think you can just walk in here and bullshit me, but that ain't the way it gonna be."

"Momma, I never asked you for anything before. I need you now. Please."

"Never asked me for anything? That's because I gave you everything, worked my fingers to the bone for you. You want to come in here? Then you got to tell me everything, and it got to be the truth, you hear me? 'Cause if I see you're lying, I'll know, and I'll throw you right the hell out."

While they sat in the kitchen, Renee grudgingly tolerated a grilling from her mother:

"Who you living with?"

"Josie."

"Where's that?—look at me when I talking!"

"You think you're a policeman?"

"Maybe that's what I should have been. Now what's the address?"

"Why do you want to know?"

"No, this isn't I ask you, you ask me. This is: I ask you, and you answer me. Now what's the address? Is Josie working? How's the baby? Who's taking care of her? What she doin'? Is she working? Now what is the trouble you got in?"

"I got caught with some, marijuana is all."

"Oh, is that all? Did you get arrested? How much marijuana was it?"

"Not much, just a small bag. It wasn't even mine."

"Did they put you in jail? Oh, Lord, two nights. Oh, Lord, my baby girl got a record."

"They say if I stay clean, since I haven't got a record, it'll be expunged. That's why I have to stay here."

A knock came at the door, and Towanda went to see who it was. A police officer stood on the porch, pad in hand.

"Is there a Renee Hall living here?"

Towanda told him there was. "I'm her mother, Towanda Hall."

"Is she living here now, ma'am?"

"Yes. She's lived here all her life. She's a good girl."

"I'm sure she is, but I'm not here to determine that. Is she here now, ma'am?"

"Yes. She sittin' there."

The officer looked over at Renee. "Could you come here, miss, and bring your identification with you." He checked the cards against the picture. "While you are out on bail," he said, "you may not change address without notification."

Towanda shook her head and *tsk*ed. "All this, for a little bit of mother nature?" she said.

The officer raised an eyebrow. "We don't consider a pound of marijuana a little bit, ma'am."

After the officer left, Renee smirked. "Those cops, they lie like crazy."

At that moment, Towanda Hall hated her younger child, something she thought had been impossible. But she couldn't turn out her baby girl.

One morning, three days later, Towanda went to the address Renee had given her, to find Josie. But the landlord said Josie had moved out the day before, and when she told Renee what had happened, a smirk appeared on her younger daughter's face.

"What made you this way?" Towanda asked. "Was it me? Was it something I did?"

"It was what you didn't do; what we didn't do. We never did anything, never had any fun, never went anyplace or saw anyone."

"It wasn't enough that I worked hard for you," said Towanda, "kept a roof over your head and fed you?"

"You're from another time, Momma. You remind me of that old lady in *A Raisin in the Sun*. You think like that, and you act like her. That time's long past; a hundred years ago! We—Josie and me—we want to live, have fun."

Towanda wanted to say: *I was alone! I read to you, I held you when you cried, I rocked you in my arms!* But she didn't. Somewhere along the line she'd lost her girls, and after seeing the look on Renee's face, she was sure words wouldn't matter. She now resigned herself to the fact that nothing would save her younger girl.

"Yeah, well, I'm sure prison will be a lot of fun."

In three months, Renee was sentenced to eighteen months at Graterford Prison, and the next time Towanda would see her younger daughter was nine years later, when Tiffany turned eleven.

TIFFANY

BECAUSE HER GRANDMOTHER read her sophisticated books—and didn't just read them, but discussed them—her reading and comprehension skills were off the charts for elementary school levels. More importantly, Tiffany seemed to understand how fortunate she'd been to have been found by her grandmother and taken in. Before long, Tiffany could see what her grandmother was thinking. When they were on the street to take care of some business or to purchase something, if they saw boys hanging out in front of a store, Tiffany would think: *Grammy's gonna say something about those boys*, and sure enough, she would.

"You see those boys, Tiffany? They don't care about nothing. Why? 'Cause they ain't got nothing to care about. They don't care about nobody, and nobody cares about them. Even if you loved them, they would use you, beat you, and throw your heart away."

Or: "Girl, I want you to know real love. I want you to love someone who cares about you, someone who enjoys just holding your hand while you study the stars. Someone who will lie in the grass with you on a summer's day. Don't you do something you don't want to do. Don't let nobody use you, or force you to do something you don't want to do."

Or: "You see them fools? They is high on drugs. Drugs is bad for you. Why? 'Cause it takes away your spirit, robs you of your soul, and makes you weak. You can be great if you can be strong."

Or: "Life ain't no bowl of cherries; it's hard work. But livin' a good life is worth it."

Or: "You're smart, and you're good. You're gonna go to college, make somethin' of yourself, make your grammy proud."

Or, when Tiffany would ask about her mother, Towanda would say, "Your momma got in trouble. She's in prison and will be there for a long time. A man, like one of those boys on the corner, took her on a ride that ruined her life."

"Why?" Tiffany would ask, and her grandmother would reply, "I don't know. People do dumb things. That's why you have to be careful. You have to choose the right thing. You can't let people use you or abuse you."

For nearly five years, these conversations became a part of the general discussions between grandmother and grand-daughter. Towanda loved to talk, and Tiffany loved to listen, because she knew her grammy was honest and sincere and could neither afford to play kids games nor dilute their dialogue or talk down to her. And because her grandmother treated her almost like an adult, Tiffany began to understand and see things few her age did.

Then one early Spring afternoon, a knock came at the door. Towanda was in the kitchen cutting vegetables for their dinner stew, while Tiffany was reading her fourth Harry Potter book. The girl put down her book and opened the door to a man and woman standing on the porch, peering through the glass storm door. At first Tiffany didn't recognize the almost-anorexic woman, but when the woman spoke, she knew exactly who it was.

"Well," said the woman, forcing a smile, "you must be Tiffany. Do you know who I am?"

"Yes. You're Aunt Renee."

"Yes, that's right. My, my, my, how you've grown! You must be ten by now."

"Almost eleven." Tiffany flipped the latch on the storm door into the "lock" position. Renee saw it, and for a moment, her eyes went dark, when Towanda came out of the kitchen, wiping her hands on her apron.

"Who is it, Tiff—" The words froze on her lips.

"It's your daughter, Momma."

"Oh."

Lip curled, Towanda went to the door. She hadn't seen her younger daughter since Renee had been sentenced to eighteen months at Graterford, more than five years ago.

"This is Mr. Mann, Momma. We need to talk to you. Will you invite us in?"

Towanda glared at Mr. Mann, jaw trembling with anger. She knew exactly who he was.

"Tiff," she said, "you go into the kitchen and shut the door." When her granddaughter was out of earshot, Towanda turned on Renee. "No," she hissed, "I am not going to invite you in. What do you want?"

Renee's eyes darkened again as she stared at her mother. "Well, I just spoke to Josie and she said she wanted Tiffany to come live with me, so..."

"Are you out of your mind?" Towanda blurted out. "Let Tiffany come live with you? Over my dead body. You dare to come here"—she pointed at Mr. Mann—"with that no-good bastard? You crazy! Get out of here, or I'll call the police, and you take that no-good piece of crap with you." And she slammed the door in her daughter's face.

She went into the kitchen, out of breath, clutching her

chest. Tiffany had never seen her grandmother so irate, her anger like a strong wind that couldn't be contained.

"Grammy," Tiffany said, worried, "what's wrong?"

"Nothin', darlin'. Nothin' for you to worry about. Just need to catch my breath, is all." After a long time, Towanda finally caught her breath, and when she did, she straightened her apron and whispered barely inaudibly, "Over my dead body."

One month later, her dead body lay in the middle of the street, killed by a hit-and-run. Police determined the car must have been going pretty fast, since a nearby neighbor sitting on his porch saw the whole incident and had said, when the car hit the old lady, it sent the body "sky high."

Not-so-ironically, Tiffany's aunt Renee had been in the vicinity, and she met the girl outside of school, just the way her grandmother did, and told her sympathetically what had happened. Tiffany had to come home with her now.

After hearing the news, Tiffany was so distraught, she couldn't think straight. The eleven-year-old cried and sobbed as Renee put her in the back of a sedan, drove her to Towanda's house, helped her pack her things, and then whisked her away.

The transition was startling, going from her grandmother's cozy, immaculate home to where Renee lived and did business. Other girls lived there and did their business, as well, but they mostly stayed to themselves. Some were sympathetic to Tiffany, though they otherwise ignored her.

Renee made up a cock-and-bull story, telling Tiffany that because Towanda had been hit by a car—a hit-and-run— she'd be buried by the state, with no funeral. In her grief, Tiffany didn't quite believe it, but what could she do? She had no idea where she was, no place to turn, no one to protect her back. Renee said she was there to help, but as the months passed, Tiffany saw her aunt had other concerns, one of them—the most important one—was pleasing someone they all called "Ice Man."

Tiffany held an almost-instant dislike for Ice Man. She remembered seeing him with Renee at her grammy's door and had a vague sense she'd seen him before that, although she wasn't quite sure where. She also remembered her grammy's anger, the overpowering rage she'd tried so desperately to control but could not hide. Aunt Renee and the other women fawned over him, almost bowed to him when he came into the house, and his callous smugness annoyed Tiffany almost as much as his intense cologne or aftershave. When he was angry, tension filled the air, and everyone was careful of what they said, how they acted. Everyone was always on guard, walking on eggshells, so as not to awaken the tyrant, the madman.

Ice Man had paid little attention to Tiffany for the first month after she'd come to live at the house on 40th Street, and for the most part, she was left to her own devices. Renee rarely spent time with her because, every time she did, Tiffany would ask about Towanda—Where was she buried? Who could have run her down? Were the police looking for that person? … and Renee would constantly put her off, telling her they'd talk later and for Tiffany to go to her room, to not get in the way. Somebody was always coming over that Renee had to see.

So, Tiffany suffered from the boredom, the loneliness, and a lack of communication, staying in the tiny room Renee had given her, often brooding. Until one day she wandered into the backyard, a place full of trash bags and junk. One thing stood out, however, partially hidden behind some empty cardboard boxes: a beautiful Schwinn mountain bike. Though the yard was enclosed by a six-foot-high fence, it still had a door that led out to a littered alleyway that wound its

way down to Girard Avenue. Within fifteen minutes of finding the Schwinn, Tiffany was riding it in close-by Fairmount
Park, and every morning from then on, she took it out for
long rides. She didn't know who the bike belonged to, and
neither did she care, and it seemed no one else did, either.
And no one, not even Renee, cared that Tiffany was gone
or missing. Riding cleared her head, allowed her to think
about how abruptly things had changed, and had it not been
for the bike, Tiffany wouldn't have been able to tolerate her
current situation.

As she rode and explored the park, she often thought
about her grammy, sensing something was wrong, though
couldn't quite figure it out. And then, several days after she
started riding regularly, she saw them coming—five of them,
all boys, all around her age, pedaling on all sorts of bikes.
They swarmed around her like bees that she'd found and had
accidentally disturbed their nest. One boy, wearing a light
leather jacket, a faded black derby, and a silk scarf, grinned
at her with a playful light in his eye. The others followed,
grinning stupidly. No one stopped riding, and as they all sped
down the street, he spoke to her.

"Who you?" he said.

"Tiff," she replied. "Who you?"

"Spokes. What you doin'?"

"Duh. Ridin'. Just ridin', is all."

"Want to ride with us?"

"Where you goin'?"

"Around."

"Sure."

"Think you can keep up?"

Tiffany glanced derisively at him as if to say *that won't be
a problem*, and he laughed.

"Okay," he said, "then let's go." And the pack took off,

almost leaving her in the dust. Tiffany had to pedal hard to keep up.

They rode for about two hours, and at first, Tiffany didn't realize what was happening until she understood they were delivering packets from place to place, though it didn't dawn on her what those little packages were and she didn't ask any questions. By the end of the day, Spokes gave her ten dollars and told her if she wanted to ride with them again, it would be okay, and if she did, where they'd meet up the following day.

Riding with the pack kept Tiffany smiling, gave her a purpose and a respite from the gloom of Renee's house. She always looked forward to riding with the Cadre (a name they called themselves), almost as if she'd been accepted into the group, free of requirements. And the pack seemed oblivious as to who she was; they didn't even know she was a girl at first until, on the third day, her hat had blown off and her hair had fluttered out.

"You a girl!" Spokes said in astonishment.

"Duh."

"Okay. I don't care, as long as you keep up."

"Huh. You got nothin' to worry about on that score."

Spokes rode away, smiling. Normally, the pack tolerated no shenanigans; their major, and usually only, concern was doing their job, which spanned an area from 42nd Street where Too-Tall was, to as far north as 52nd Street, as far south as the north end of the zoo, and as far west as the Drexel and Penn campuses. They had little time for fun and games, but on several occasions, after finding out Tiffany was a girl, Spokes started doing things that, under normal circumstances, would be anathema to their purpose—pranks and monkeyshines that brought unwanted attention and might foil a delivery. All of that showing off had ended when Melvin Kappernick had almost broken his hand and Too-

Tall had told him that if he did anything stupid like that again, he'd break every bone in his body.

Tiffany had just finally started to adjust and accept where she was, when one night, Ice Man entered her room, took off his clothes, lifted her covers, and lay down next to her. She'd been lying on her side when she heard him come in, and she froze. He pressed right up against her, putting his arm around her so her back was to his chest, his penis against her buttocks. She shivered. His body cologne stifled her. He whispered into her ear, "You feel me? Yeah, you feel me." His voice was soft, yet hard, the accent Jamaican. "No, I'm not gonna take you tonight. Tonight, I'm gonna let you dream about what's up against your pretty little ass. Tonight you gonna dream about touchin' it, and holdin' it, and kissin' it, and makin' it happy. Soon, you gonna be my number one little girl."

Then, without another word, he got up, got dressed, and left the room.

When the door closed, Tiffany was breathing hard, but it wasn't from sexual arousal, it was from fear. That night, she didn't sleep much, and when she did, she woke in a cold sweat. She worried about what to do. Unfortunately, she couldn't confide in Renee; her aunt was totally under Ice Man's thumb.

The next morning, Tiffany thought about how to escape and where she could go, and different ideas ran through her mind, though nothing seemed rational. That night, she locked her bedroom door and heard the knob rattle around midnight. The following day, after she'd returned from riding, she discovered the lock had been removed.

Previously, she hadn't thought about Ice Man, until, hiding in her room, Tiffany realized Ice Man only appeared at night, usually from ten into the wee morning hours. If she wasn't there at night, he couldn't get her. But where could she go?

Three nights later, Ice Man entered her room after midnight, easily pushing aside the chair she'd propped up against the door. Tiffany turned over onto her side, away from the door, and pretended to be asleep. He undressed and, as he'd done three nights before, moved in close to her, spooning her, pulling her to him. This time his erection found the separation of her buttocks, and he pressed against her, moving rhythmically into her. "Please…" she whispered—a frightened sob, a plea, but he ignored it by taking her hand and making her stroke his erection. It took some time, but after he'd achieved an orgasm, he wiped himself off on her cover sheet, dressed, and abruptly left. When Tiffany heard the door close, she wept silently. This wasn't the way it was supposed to be.

The next day, quite by accident—while the pack went into Open-Til-Four and Tiffany went into the empty lot across the street to find a place to relive herself—she found a tree leaning against one of the four nearby deserted buildings. Later that afternoon, after the pack had dispersed, she climbed the tree and found one of the roof hatches with no latch on it. It opened easily, and with just a little ingenuity, Tiffany descended into the third floor of Teabloom's.

The cracked window shade allowed in enough light to illuminate the decrepit room's torn wallpaper and littered floor. She walked over to the window and lifted the shade. Suddenly, the place lit up with a Dickens-like mauve effervescence; even through the caked pane of glass, the area brightened with a cozy warmth. It wasn't scary. No, not at all.

Tiffany stood in the center of the room and, like a decorator, considered how she could make it work. She tried the light switch by the door, but there was no electricity. She'd need a way to light the place at night. And she'd need a bed. What if she had to use the bathroom? Suppose she needed water or got hungry? No, it wouldn't work … she'd have to find somewhere else. But where?

Three nights later, Ice Man again came into her room, and this time, Tiffany fought him, repeatedly saying "no," struggling as he forced her head down into his groin. She only stopped fighting when he slapped her hard across the face, and his anger at her refusal to listen and obey resonated through the air.

Cruelly, he made her take his erection into her mouth, holding and moving her head up and down until he ejaculated, the volume of his sperm almost choking her. Then, grabbing her by the hair, he whispered, "Don't you ever fight me again, you hear? Next time I come in, you spread your legs, you hear? You do what you suppose to. You listen to your Ice Man, and obey."

That was the last night she slept in that bed.

The next morning, Tiffany made a decision. Throwing all caution to the wind, she climbed the tree up to the third floor of Teabloom's and, having lugged up some old towels, newspapers, and a pillow she figured Renee wouldn't miss, all in a heavy-duty trash bag, made a pallet in the abandoned room. With the money Spokes had given her since she started riding with them, Tiffany purchased several dozen candles, a heavy-duty chain, and a lock. She appropriated a broom she'd found on the porch next to Renee's house, and she spent the whole day carting things into the empty lot and carrying them up the tree into the deserted building. She chained the bike to the fence post, camouflaging it with broken branches, and for the next six nights, slept there in the empty room … until Melvin Kappernick caught her.

Her mouth had dropped open when she heard the person behind her tell her to stop and raise her hands, and for the briefest of moments, Tiffany considered running, but there was nowhere else to go, no escape. Never in her wildest dreams did she ever think anyone else was in the building, and more so that it would be the old white man who'd almost broken Spokes' hand.

When Tiffany finally faced him, she discovered they shared the same expression of disbelief: he, that she was a girl; and she, that he was the man the pack had previously picked on. In a way, she was relieved. Something sat in his stare that was less sinister, more concerned. Once he'd recovered from his initial surprise, he actually seemed calm, almost annoyed that she'd invaded his privacy. He talked to her, listened to her, and allowed her to stay. Then, after he'd taken her in, he'd made no demands, except for doing the dishes, keeping her room neat, and doing her homework. No lust sat in his gaze, and he went out of his way to protect her.

Except for her grammy, Mr. Kapp was the best thing that had ever happened to her. He walked her to and from school. They ate out three to four times a week. He bought her school clothes, solved her school problems when she asked, and except for the occasional expressions of annoyance, he never yelled at her or threatened her in any way. His face was so expressive, Tiffany often knew what he was thinking—sometimes, he was so proud of her, like when she beat his nephew and Spokes at chess, or when she spelled every word correctly on her take-home list, or when she told Renee why she'd run away. Often, she'd come out of her room and see him sitting in his easy chair, reading the newspaper or watching some political show on TV, and it made her feel safe. Very early on Tiffany felt, had she known her father or her grandfather, she would have wanted them to be exactly like Mr. Kapp.

And that day at the zoo, after she'd rushed over to be next to him for the picture the stranger was taking, as she was gazing up at him in admiration, she saw his face drain cold.

DAY 23

KAPPERNICK WORE A SMILE. This was worth everything. Not only was it a beautiful day, but he was also *at the zoo* with people he really cared about.

Now, he stood in the middle of the group, waiting to have his picture taken by a stranger, arms around the two kids each by his side, trusty cane in his right hand and dangling down behind Jacob's back. He smiled at Jacob, then at Tiffany, then looked up … and that's when he saw the guy coming out of the crowd.

The man wore a topcoat, a brown fedora, and sunglasses. He stood out, because the only reason the zoo was so crowded was because of the warm, sunny day. Kappernick immediately recognized him as one of the men from outside of Springer's Spot Lite. As the man reached into his pocket, Kappernick went into action. He could see a pistol coming out and, shoving the kids aside, he rushed toward the stranger taking the picture. This startled the would-be photographer so much, his arm instinctively went up to protect himself, bumping into the arm of the shooter as he fired. The shot went high, and Kappernick whacked his attacker's shoulder with his cane. Unfortunately, the force of the blow was partially deflected by the stranger who, not knowing what was going on, blocked Kappernick from grabbing the shooter, who in turn fled deep into the crowd, shedding his topcoat and hat.

For the briefest moment, everything stopped, even the giraffes stopped chewing. And then … utter confusion.

People started yelling and running, and lost in the chaos was the man who'd had every reason to run. Kappernick spun around, breathing a sigh of relief that no one had been injured. Bruce started to say something, when his father stopped him.

"Come on," he said, "let's get out of here."

With haste, they moved toward the exit gate, and once outside, Kappernick grabbed Barbara's arm to get her attention. "Listen, I need a favor." Tiffany clutched at his own arm, shaking. "Would you take Tiffany home with you for a few days?"

"No!" Tiffany gripped his arm tighter. "I want to stay with you."

Kappernick ignored her and stared at Barbara, in whom there wasn't the slightest hesitation. "Of course, she'll come with us." And in that moment, Kappernick couldn't have been more proud of the woman his son had married.

Tiffany, though, wouldn't hear of it. She threw her arms around him, crying into his chest. "No, Mr. Kapp, please. I want to stay with you."

He patted her shoulder, then pushed her firmly away. "Hey, what's this? This isn't like you. You're the bravest kid I know. It's not like you're going to purgatory, and it'll only be for a few days. You'll have a lot of fun beating the guys at chess, and you know it's for the best. Now, go with Barbara."

"But—"

"No buts. Do as I tell you. I'll call in to let you know what's going on."

Reluctantly, Tiffany allowed Barbara to pull her away.

Bruce came over, followed by Linda Lansky. "Dad, I want to get the kids home, but I need to talk to you. Follow us—"

"I can't. I need to take care of some things. I'll call you tonight."

"Don't do anything stupid. Promise me."

Kappernick smiled. "I love you. I'll call you tonight. Don't worry."

"I do worry."

"You never did listen to me."

Bruce grabbed his father and hugged him. "Call me tonight." Kappernick watched Bruce march his grandsons to the parking lot, then he felt a hand on his arm. He looked down at Linda and forced a smile. "Tiffany won't be in school for the next couple of days."

Linda was shaking nervously. "You are such a lousy date."

"Gee, and I thought you were having a good time," he said, trying, unsuccessfully, to be lighthearted.

"I was, right up until somebody tried to kill you." What was it about this man that kept her there talking instead of running like hell? Maybe he simply had the ability to calm her. Linda took a deep breath.

"Come on, I'll walk you to the parking lot." Kappernick took her arm and they started to walk. Nothing was said between them until they reached her car.

"I'll call you tonight," he said.

She looked up at him and whispered, "Be careful," then she kissed his cheek. Smiling, he touched the spot her lips had been. "Thanks," he said, and he opened the car door for her.

Forty-second Street lay empty. Even Too-Tall and his two side-kicks appeared to have had taken the day off. Obviously, word of what had happened at the zoo hadn't yet reached the street.

Kappernick checked his car and locked it. Inside the apartment, Soldier greeted him warmly.

"We've got to get the hell out of here, boy," Kappernick told him. "Can't take any chances."

He went into the bedroom, grabbed his .38 and an extra round of ammo. From above the closet he pulled down his suitcase and packed a couple of pairs of pants, along with some shirts, undershorts, and socks. Then he went into the kitchen, threw dog food into a bag, and when he was sure he had everything he needed, he set the door alarm, picked up Soldier's leash, and whistled for the dog. Soldier scrambled down the stairs, and together, they left the building.

Kappernick considered himself a good man. A man who, all his life, tried to do the right thing, the honorable thing—as a little kid growing up on 42nd Street; in high school, in college, in the army; Vietnam, his job, his marriage. He stubbornly lived by a code of ethics that ruled his life, one in which he had no idea where it had come from. He'd never pondered upon it, nor wrote it down, nor stayed up nights outlining how he should act or what he would do in certain situations. This ethical set of laws was innate; it'd always been there. And it was what his grandfather, Morris Teabloom, had taught him: "Things have to be so," meaning things had to be right, loose ends tied up. And when things were "just so," he'd say, "Nah," and hold up his hands as if to say, "Now, it's right."

Once, Kappernick remembered, his grandfather was making change for a sale, and he couldn't find a nickel in the till (an old cigar box) to make the exchange complete. So he told the customer to wait, that he'd go to the third floor to recover the exact money he needed. The customer, in return, told him not to worry, that he'd get it next time. But Morris wouldn't hear of it, and he walked the stairs to retrieve a nickel he'd left there. He returned, out of breath, and placed the coin into the man's palm. "Nah," he'd said, "now it's right."

Kappernick wondered if having thought momentarily of his grandfather had given a star an extra twinkle somewhere in the cosmos. The memory of Morris Teabloom had almost been entirely obliterated, and would certainly be gone forever once Kappernick passed. No one, he was sure, had thought of the old man in fifty years, so what had "making it right" done for him? That's the way it was, the way it is, and the way it always will be. No one will remember, no one will care. He regretted doing a few things in his life, and he regretted not doing some things. The one thing he probably regretted most was not protecting Malley, and he didn't want to regret not killing Ice Man. Maybe that's why he'd survived this long; maybe that's what old men were supposed to do—when you come to the end of the trail, or at least close to the end, you do something for the good of the world? Nah—you take out a piece of crap. Maybe that was his predestined mission, why the gods had kept him alive.

In this case, he'd be the judge and the jury. No doubt Ice Man deserved to die. Sure, he could go to the police, but really, what good would that do? They might arrest the sono-fabitch, but could they hold him? And what would happen if they couldn't? What would he plot? Who would he hurt? Hell, he might even come after Tiffany, or Bruce and his family—no telling what he'd do. No, the best thing to do, for all concerned, was to take him out. If everyone thought the way he did at that moment, though, there'd be utter chaos. Anti-abortionists would kill doctors who performed abortions; terrorist groups like ISIS, who slaughtered thousands, would be justified.

Kappernick shook his head. Those people he'd leave to

the government. This was different. This was personal. Ice Man had to go.

All of these thoughts tumbled through Kappernick's mind as Soldier crisscrossed the open field of Belmont Plateau looking for a place to relieve himself. In the distance, outlined against the night sky, glimmered and glowed the city of Philadelphia, which was a sight to behold and gave Kappernick hope. Sitting on the hillside, with crickets chirping, the night alive with stars, and the shimmering cityscape outline, all seemed right with the world.

Soldier, having done his business, came back and sat next to him as Kappernick stared out into the night. Kappernick, almost without thinking, scratched the dog's ear, talking to him as if he might have some answers. "So, what do you think, fella? Are you with me on this?"

ROGER REESE

ROGER "WOBBO" REESE had put on some pounds since his tour in Vietnam. Like, eighty. After he mustered out of the marines, he joined the Philadelphia Police Force and spent ten years as a detective sergeant in the homicide unit, chasing killers. But his inability to control his weight had been the deciding factor in his leaving the department.

Though he was a big man at nearly six-foot-three, his enormous weight made him a liability—to himself and to his partners. His problem? He just couldn't stop eating. While others had a BLT on two pieces of white toast, Reese would cut a loaf of rye bread long ways and stuff it with all sorts of deli meats, tomatoes, onions, and mayonnaise, then down it before the guy with the puny bacon sandwich took his first bite, after which he'd stare at the guy nibbling on the BLT, hoping he'd offer him half. People had all sorts of nicknames for him, which he good-naturedly absorbed. They'd come in to the station and ask to see, "the fat man." "You mean, Detective Reese?" the desk sergeant would say. "Yeah," the person would reply, "the fat man."

Reese could take a joke, but he wouldn't be fucked with. If he wrapped his big arm around your neck and squeezed, you were in trouble. If he hit you anywhere—chest, arm, gut, kidneys—you knew you were being hit. Like being hit with a battering ram or a sledgehammer. He'd killed a couple of men in 'nam, mostly Cong, and three others, while on the force. When he left the force, Reese went into business for himself: Reese & Associates, Investigations.

First time they met after the phone call was at a Kentucky Fried Chicken on City Line Avenue. While Reese downed a twelve-piece pack of barbecued poultry, Kappernick filled him in, and with every new detail, Reese asked his one-time lieutenant the same question, "You out of your freakin' mind?" Like Springer, Reese couldn't fathom why Kappernick had moved back to 42nd and Viola! Just like Bruce's and Linda Lansky's, his face took on a strange look when he found out about Tiffany, but he dropped his stare and nodded in understanding when Kappernick said, "She reminded me of that little girl. You know the one in 'nam, the one … Malley … I couldn't let that happen to this one."

"Jesus, you still carrying that around?"

"I guess I am. Some things you just can't get rid of. I thought it was gone, but this kid, Tiffany, brought it back."

"It wasn't your fault. Malley fucked up. He shoulda dropped her."

"It wasn't his fault and it wasn't her fault. He was a pacifist. Sure, he was a victim, but so was she."

"You gotta let it go."

"Can't. It was on my watch."

Reese shook his head at the absurdity, then whispered, "Yeah, I get it. What about the kid? Is she okay?"

"Amazingly, I think she is. I'm continually astounded by her guts and brains. We thought those kids in the war zone went through something. I can't imagine what this kid went through. I remember when my kid was almost three we let him watch a Disney movie on TV. I think it was Snow White.

I mean, it was a Disney movie! Well, something scared him so much, he couldn't sleep. He kept saying, 'I'm afraid, Daddy.' He couldn't sleep. Took hours of talking to him, holding him, to finally get him to shut his eyes. I'm thinking Tiffany never had anyone to talk to her or to hold her when she was afraid, and that kills me, you know what I mean?"

"You know," said Reese, "it's been a while, but I still know some people on the force."

"No." Kappernick was emphatic. "That won't work. The girl says cops are there every day, banging the hookers."

Reese shook his head. "Yeah, cops have dicks, too. What about this tape you got?"

"I fucked up. It was on my phone, but"—Kappernick dropped his gaze—"I ... somehow erased it. It was an accident. I'm not a computer guy. I took it to the Apple store, but they said it was gone."

Reese pushed aside the box of chicken bones and used a toothpick to pry some meat out of his teeth. "What do you want me to do, Kapp? How can I help?"

Kappernick leaned in. "I want to know everything about this guy."

Soldier had heard him first before Reese had even said a word, and the big dog let out a threatening growl. Kappernick saw him coming and stood as he approached.

"Jesus," Reese said, "couldn't you pick a restaurant? Belmont Plateau, are you kidding me? If I sit down, I'll ruin my suit, and it'd probably take me an hour to get on my feet again."

They shook hands. "Look at the city, Reese. Appreciate the beauty."

"Yeah, right," came the sarcastic reply. "Real nice."

"Okay, let's go to my car, then. We can talk there."

"Thank you."

"You got anything?"

"Yes, I do. But let's get into the car before we start talking."

Because of Soldier, they sat in Kappernick's car, and Reese opened a manila folder, letting out a heavy sigh. "This is real interesting stuff. And this Ice Man, it turns out, is a real character. Smart, shifty, and dangerous. I had to talk to some of my old friends to get started, but here it is: He first appeared on the Philly scene about fifteen years ago. He doesn't have a record, never spent a night in jail, though he was pulled in several times. He was always questioned and then let go. As I said, smart and cagey. He likes real estate—owns three houses, has six or seven girls working for him…"

"And he's never spent a night in jail? How can that be?"

"He's smart. And he deals. Mostly cocaine. Tiffany's mother was one of his whores. Word has it she took the rap for him. Got fifteen years."

"Jesus, what the hell did she do?"

"Stabbed a guy. Killed him. Pled guilty."

"Holy hell!"

"Only she didn't do it."

"How do you know?"

"The guy was six-three. She's five-four. The trajectory of the wound was downward. She would have had to be stand-ing on a chair."

"Then…"

"I don't know. She kept saying she did it. What were they going to do?"

"She was protecting the bastard."

"Most likely."

"This motherfucker is something else." Kappernick shook

his head in disbelief. "Anything else?"

"Yeah. Lots. I haven't even gotten to the interesting stuff."

"I'm listening."

"This guy isn't your ordinary pimp. Believe it or not, he's got a degree from NYU. He was born in the Bronx, and his father was a sales manager for Encyclopedia Britannica, his mother a school teacher. As I said, he's never been arrested, or at least booked or brought to trial, but as a kid, he had a couple of depraved incidents. When he was ten, he took to killing dogs and cats; when he was twelve, he beat up a schoolmate with an iron pipe—nearly killed him. Somehow, it never even went to trial, though, and the guy never even got a reprimand. When he moved to Philadelphia—and no one knows why he moved—he changed his name. Oh yeah, I forgot, his real name is, get this … Barton Berk. Now, here's the real killer—this guy has a job. A real fucking job!"

"What's he do?"

"He's a fucking druggist."

"I know he sells drugs—"

"No. He's a real druggist. He works in a drugstore, filling prescriptions. He's a pharmacist."

"Now that's interesting. Where's the store?"

"In the Northeast. The address is in the file. He has the two-to-nine shift. Drives there every day. He lives downtown, alone, in a swank building."

Kappernick turned to Reese and smiled. "This is excellent work, Reese. I appreciate it. What do I owe you, my friend?"

"Nada. This one's on the house. But before we split, I just want to reiterate: I think you should go to the cops." Reese saw that weird Kappernick smile and immediately knew that wasn't an option. "Okay, I won't ask again but … what are you planning to do?"

"I'm not sure. At this point I haven't decided. But I have

a favor to ask, and this can't be a freebie."

"I can't guarantee that. Go ahead. Ask."

"Can you put a watch on my son's house?"

DAY 34

ON CITY LINE AVENUE, not four miles from 42nd and Parkside, sat the Sunnyside Motel, where Kappernick and Soldier eventually found themselves. A party was going on down the hall, the ruckus causing a baby to cry in the room next to theirs. The mother must have been at the party; she wasn't responding.

Pick the kid up, for cryin' out loud! Kappernick thought.

When Bruce was very young, he'd sometimes wake up and start crying—*Waaaaa! Waaaa!*—and Nancy's eyes would jolt open. She'd wait a minute or two, listening intently, to see if it persisted, and if it did, she'd hop out of bed to hold him and rock him back to sleep.

Had anyone done that for Tiffany, Kappernick wondered, or did they just let her cry and work out her own fears? Kids were so vulnerable, so impressionable. But they knew, even as they were manipulated, what fear was.

Fear's innate. Worry, concern, relief—the endless cycle. How had Tiffany turned out to be such a good kid? Who'd been there to help quell her fear, her crying, put her back to bed? According to Reese, it certainly hadn't been her mother.

Kappernick thought about the little girl in Vietnam, his ruminations always the same: the girl would emerge from the

166 \ TED FINK

hut with tears running down her face, skinny arms stretched out, in her tattered dress, pleading inaudibly. You wanted to take her into your arms and wipe her tears away. That's what Malley had wanted to do. Why was she crying? Because she knew … she knew the pack of explosives strapped to her back would kill her. She didn't want to die. She didn't want to hurt anyone. But what could she do?

The girl had been maybe ten or eleven. Malley had shouldered his weapon and started to go to her, when she'd shook her head, telling him not to, to stay away, while at the same time continuing to stagger toward him. "Don't be afraid," he'd said, smiling. And those were the last words he'd ever utter. The explosive device strapped to her back had killed him instantly, and had blown her apart. A piece of the girl's arm had landed gruesomely at Kappernick's feet.

Immediately, the squad had taken cover.

And the whole area had exploded in a firefight.

Later, after it was over, a decrepit old man would tell them a Cong—a Charlie—had gone crazy, taken over the village, killing people for no reason and raping the young girls who couldn't run. He was killed in the firefight.

For the rest of Kappernick's life, the girl's face would haunt him. Not because the explosive had killed Malley (although that was bad enough), but because of the fear in the girl's eyes before the detonation. She'd only been a peasant girl—in the scheme of things, few would miss her. Kappernick, however, would be one. He just couldn't let it go.

Fear. Oh, yes—fear!

BARTON BERK

BERK WANTED TO CALL IN SICK, but he couldn't do that. He hadn't missed a day in years. Still, that fuckin' idiot, Raphael, was so dumb—so fuckin' dumb! At the zoo! Who did he think he was? Paul fuckin' Simon? He had to put it out of his mind, had to focus. He had to fill prescriptions. He couldn't afford to *kill* anybody with the wrong ingredients!

Taking a deep breath, Berk studied the next prescription, about to put it together, when an associate interrupted him. "A customer needs to talk to you, sir. He's at the will-call station."

Berk told the girl to fill the order he'd been working on and walked, with some annoyance and almost absentmindedly, to the counter, where a man stood with his back to him.

"Excuse me," said Berk, "can I help you?"

The man turned, smiled, and before Berk realized who it was, the old man grabbed him by the white lab jacket, yanked him forward him, and slapped him hard across the face. With some effort, Berk pulled back to see a sinister smile on Kappernick's face.

"I owed you that one, motherfucker!"

"You … you…" the pharmacist whispered, eyes ablaze, jaw quivering in anger.

"Go ahead, bitch, call the police."

Berk looked around before hissing, "I'll kill you ... do you hear me?"

"No, I'll kill you," Kappernick mouthed, almost mockingly. "Do you hear me?"

A guard approached from the front of the store, having been at the register when he'd heard the slap and wondered what it was. "You okay, Mr. Berk?"

Kappernick smiled nastily, while Berk forced his own smile.

"Yes, yes I'm fine," he said.

Kappernick turned to go. "I'll be back to pick it up. Have it ready." Then, in a fake "old man's voice," he said to the guard, "These young whippersnappers think a man's got time to kill. They don't know you could die at any minute."

The guard walked Kappernick back to the front door, laughing despite himself. Then the old man turned to stare back at Berk, who was still leaning on the counter, watching them.

Kappernick waved. "See you soon, sonny."

DAY 26

TWO DAYS LATER, a police car pulled up alongside Kappernick as he walked Soldier. Inside, sat two cops. The one riding shotgun had his window open.

"Hey, old man," he said, "you live around here?"

"Why?" Kappernick asked, turning on the camera of his cell phone in his pocket. "Did I do anything wrong?"

"Don't get smart. We want to talk to you."

Taking out his smartphone, Kappernick said, "Well, I want to talk to you, too," and he squatted down to get a picture of the cop who was driving. "Do you know Ice Man? Did he send you?"

The officers looked at one another, then at Kappernick, unhappy. The driver stepped on the gas, and the car pulled away.

MORRIS MORTON

MARINE CAPTAIN MORRIS MORTON was a psychiatrist who'd heard a lot of horrifying stories in his tour in Vietnam, but this one took the cake. Morton helped mitigate soldiers' guilt, helped to ease the pain, and, most importantly, helped get them back into combat. In a lot of ways, he resembled a priest listening to confession. In fact, many times he wished he was a priest. "Say three Hail Mary's and repent. Never do it again…" but that was impossible in 'nam. In 'nam, they would, in all likelihood, have to do it again.

Guilt came in all forms and all degrees—getting out of a detail where someone got hurt, losing a friend, killing an enemy. Everyone saw things, horrible things, and everyone hurt in different ways. Kappernick, was no exception. All men in combat had to develop a hard bark, and for officers who sent men into combat, it had to be especially tough. Unfortunately, a thick skin wasn't nearly enough sometimes.

Morton studied Kappernick, trying to understand. "Look, Lieutenant, it wasn't your fault…"

"Malley shouldn't have been on point. I did it as a punishment, tried to teach him a lesson. I wanted him to understand that every man counted, that every man was there for a reason, that every man depended on the guy next to him."

"Did the men not trust him?"

"Doc, for Christ's sake, he was a pacifist. You don't go around talking non-violence in a war zone—not with guys counting on you. I wanted him to know fear."

"You don't think he was afraid?"

"I think his father knocked all of that out of him."

"The senator."

"Yeah. I once asked him why the hell he was there, and he said his father wanted him to see action, to be a man."

"Why didn't he put in a request for a transfer?"

"He did. And I signed it and sent it off—twice."

"I see." There was a long silence. "But you can't blame yourself," he said. "The girl was carrying—"

"Oh, I don't blame the girl. I can't blame her. She didn't strap that shit on her back. I blame the motherfucker who did it, the one who made her do it, the one who threatened her and abused her. She knew she was gonna die. In that split second before she blew, I saw she didn't want to die. The fear, the terror—it won't go away. I wish that sonofabitch, the one who made her do it, the one who'd used her, had lived long enough so I could have have killed him myself."

"Because he killed Malley?"

"No, because he killed the girl. He robbed her of her chance to live."

"You don't feel bad about Malley?"

"Of course I feel bad about him. Actually, I'm grateful to him. You see, he saved my life."

"How so?"

"Had he not gone to her with open arms, I probably would have. I couldn't have killed her. I mean, how do you kill a ten-year-old girl?"

DAY 28

KAPPERNICK STUDIED his cell phone, then put it back into his pocket. He wanted to call Linda, just to hear her voice, but he knew what she would say: *What are you doing? Where are you? Are you crazy? Let the police handle this—please!* So, as much as he wanted to hear her voice, he *didn't* want to hear it.

Nancy would have asked the same questions, but in a different way. She would have used every tactic—pleading, debating, anger, reason—yet in her heart, she would have known why. She would have understood. When you meet a new woman, though, your past is dead; she'd never know what you were, or why you are what you are, and never be able to imagine the body you once had, the strength you once possessed, the way you used to run, dance, sing. And neither would she know the little pieces of information, the accumulated data, that made you think the way you did. Long-time wives understood all of those things; newcomers, no matter how wise, never could.

Kappernick's cell phone vibrated in his pocket, and though he didn't recognize the number, he answered it anyway. He didn't say anything, just listened.

"Captain?" Still, he didn't respond. "Captain, it's me, Darnell. Darnell Perkins."

"How'd you get this number?"

"Jesse gave it to me. Told me to call."

"Why?"

"He said it was important that you meet him. He wants to talk to you."

"Why doesn't *he* call me?"

"I don't know."

"Can I trust him?"

"I think so, sir."

"Can I trust you? Are you with me?"

"Yes, sir. Semper Fidelis. Semper Fi—always faithful. I've always been with you, sir—always. You once saved my life, and I'll never forget that. Jesse closes the place at two. Can you meet after that?"

"Yeah, I'll call him at two, just after he closes. I'll tell him where we'll meet. And, Darnell … I want you to be there."

A fine rain punctuated a grizzly night. Kappernick had chosen an all-night diner that sat alone in the Roxborough section of the city. The building was long and narrow, fifties-built and retro-hip, with worn, red leather seats on chrome stools that lined a Formica counter.

From a window booth at the back, Kappernick had a full view of the parking lot, and his car was one of few. He'd called Springer shortly after he'd arrived. Though he wasn't sure what the barkeep wanted, he was interested in what he had to say. The old waitress, who could barely stay awake, took his order for coffee, and after she delivered it, Kappernick took out his .38, placing it on the seat next to him. He liked Springer, but he was taking no chances.

At ten after two, Springer and Perkins walked in, saw him sitting at the back, and waved. Kappernick nodded and, with his eyes, told them to sit across from him.

Springer and Kappernick studied each other.

"Everybody's talking about you," Springer started.

"I figured they would be. I'm glad they're just talking."

"I got a visit today."

"I'm sorry, I didn't want to get you … either of you, involved."

Springer's eyes narrowed. "Well, we're goddamned involved. What you doin', trying to get yourself killed?"

"Not really."

The barkeep shook his head in disbelief. "Not really? Not really? This Ice Man's goin' nuts, and they say he's gonna kill you. He don't play. He even got the cops lookin' for you."

"Yeah, I met them yesterday."

"You…" Springer moaned in frustration. "Look, normally, I wouldn't give a shit if a White man gets his head blown off. But I like you. You and me go back, all the way back. But this ain't like throwin' fists in the street. These people shoot to kill. They'll kill you. He gonna get you."

Kappernick's gaze grew as cold as ice. *Not if I get him first.*

Springer seemed to read his thoughts. "Why?" he said. "Just tell me why? Why would you, a White man, come down here and get involved?"

"I told him. I said, 'Just let the girl be. Let her grow up, have a childhood.' But he wouldn't."

"The girl? Is this about the girl? For Christ's sake, you know how many kids in that neighborhood are fucked up? Screwed up? What's one stupid Black girl mean to you?"

"Suppose it was your girl?"

"But it isn't. I took care of my kid. Jesus Christ Almighty!"

Until that moment, Perkins hadn't said a word, having sat there silently, taking it all in. But now, unable to contain himself, he tentatively raised his hand, as if in school, wanting to speak.

Springer stared at him in bewilderment. "What?"

"Let me tell you a story, Jesse…"

"Darnell, we don't need a story right at this minute. You just listen—"

"No, you listen! I got somethin' to say, and I aims to say it. All right with you, captain? Now, first off, the captain ain't no captain. He's actually a lieutenant, but to us, he was like a captain, because he was cool. He cared about us. But that's neither here nor there. You see, we got called into this village—a stinkin', smelly, shitty bunch of crappy hovels—and out of this hut comes a kid, couldn't have been more than ten, and she's got dynamite strapped to her back. Blows herself up. Kills a guy named Malley. It was bad, a terrible horror. It threw us, all of us, for a loss. I mean, the whole squad was fucked up because of it. Morale couldn't have been lower. We hated everyone who had slant eyes, and we questioned everything."

Springer raised his eyebrows, exasperated, tired of war stories. "Darnell, what the hell does this have to do with what's happenin' now?"

"Don't you see? It wasn't the girl. It was the son of a bitch who strapped the shit to her back. The captain here made us see it. Ain't that right, captain? Ain't that the way it was?"

Kappernick looked at Perkins with a new respect. He was so spot on. He remembered that meeting, when they'd all talked about it. Yeah, that meeting had had impact. Now, Kappernick smiled and nodded.

"Is that what it is, Kapp?"

"This Ice Man is the same kind of motherfucker who used that girl in 'nam like she was a landmine. Darnell hit the nail on the fucking head."

"Call the cops."

"The cops!" Kappernick scoffed. "The fucking cops are

being paid off. No, this has to be handled outside the law. He's got to pay."

"Pay? How? What do you plan to do?"

"What's he tryin' to do to me? What do you think his plans are?"

There was a long silence.

Springer chewed on his lower lip. "You know, Kapp, I don't owe you anything. I mean … I got a family … I …"

"Did they threaten you, Jesse?"

Springer shrugged. "Yeah. Both the cops and one of those two assholes who were gonna beat the shit out of you that night. They wanted me to bring you in, tell them where to find you."

"I wish you weren't involved, but this is something I have to see through."

"I'm with you, captain," said Perkins.

"Thanks, Darnell, but I don't want you to get hurt. Stay out of it."

"No, sir, I ain't stayin' out. I'm all in."

Springer smiled, shook his head. "You're both fuckin' crazy. You know, Kapp, you haven't changed. I remember back in the day, when three guys punched you in the mouth while you were walking down the street. Punched you for no reason." Springer turned to Perkins. "Punched him for no reason! Don't you know, this son of a bitch found those bas- tards, found out who they were, where they lived, and broke their legs with a baseball bat. He waited outside their houses, hid in the bushes until they got home, and got 'em."

"Got two of them. The third guy joined the army before I could get him."

Springer shrugged again. "Awright, fuck it, I'm in."

BARBARA KAPPERNICK

BARBARA MYERS KAPPERNICK sat on the bed in the room Melvin, her father-in-law, had slept in for two years after his wife, Nancy, had passed. Now, it was the room Tiffany Hall would sleep in.

Barbara had her arm wrapped around the young girl, trying to console her. Tiffany wasn't doing well; she'd fallen into a depression after the incident at the zoo, and no matter what Barbara tried, she couldn't shake the despair from the young girl's eyes. Her motherly instincts couldn't bear that Tiffany was suffering. Barbara loved her sons deeply, yes, but she'd always wanted a girl. She and Bruce had talked about adopting, taking in a needy child, a girl from Chili or Panama or some other poor country. Now, Barbara couldn't imagine a child more in need than Tiffany.

"Why is all this happening?" Tiffany asked. "Is it me? Is it my fault?" She hadn't cried, though her chin quivered as she fought back tears.

"No. Don't even think that," Barbara told her. "Believe me, trust me, it's going to be all right. Don't worry."

"I'm afraid," she whimpered. The first time she'd ever said those words aloud.

"Don't worry. You're safe here. We'll protect you."

"You don't know. The Ice Man's bad—real, bad."

Barbara drew the girl closer. *It isn't fair. It just isn't fair,* she thought, and despite herself, only half-believing it, she replied, "It's going to be all right."

Tiffany pulled away slightly, looking earnestly into Barbara's eyes. "I'm mostly worried about, Kappy. He's too old to fight Ice Man."

For a moment, Barbara stared at her, confused, and then, because of its absurdity, she laughed. "Kappy?" No one had ever called her father-in-law "Kappy" before. She couldn't help herself. "Kappy?"

And through the fear, Tiffany started to laugh, too. "Yeah, that's what I call him. Not to his face, but in my head."

A knock came at the bedroom door, and Jacob peeked in. "A lady on the phone wants to talk to you," he said to his mother. "Hey, Tiff, you want to do something?"

Tiffany looked up at Barbara, and Barbara nodded, adding, "Let's not talk about the zoo thing."

Linda Lansky was on the phone, and she wanted to know if anyone had heard from Melvin. Barbara told her they hadn't, and for about an hour they talked about Tiffany, considering, very seriously, calling the police, with a whole myriad of reasons why they should, but just as many why they shouldn't. Mainly, Barbara was afraid it'd throw Tiffany into an even deeper depression. The girl had already lost everything, everyone, and Barbara wasn't sure Tiffany could tolerate another separation. Linda agreed.

"Listen, Barbara, would you mind if I stopped over tomorrow after school?" she asked.

"Not at all. I'd welcome it."

The front doorbell rang, and Barbara yelled for Bruce to get it.

Bruce was in the den, working on a report due the following day, although because the event at the zoo, his concentration wasn't where it needed to be. With more than a little agitation, he swung open the door to two men standing on his step. One was a huge African American who had to weigh well over 350 pounds, and stared at Bruce, who was a little taken back.

"Are you Bruce Kappernick?"

"Yes," Bruce answered, hesitant.

"My name's Reese. I'm a friend of your father's. Here's my card. I'm going to have a man watching your house for the next couple of days. This here is Harry Frye." Frye, almost hidden by Reese, nodded. "Harry will be parked on the street. If you have an alarm system, use it. Keep the back door and windows locked. Now, who takes the kids to school?"

"Wait a minute. Are we in danger?"

"I don't know, but we're not going to take any chances, are we?"

Bruce shoved his hands onto hips and walked around in an angry circle. "Did my dad send you?" He didn't wait for an answer. "Where is he? Where is he?"

Reese raised an eyebrow, shook his head. "I don't know."

"When's the last time you saw him?"

"Last night."

"Where?"

"In the park."

"In the park? In Fairmount fuckin' Park?"

"Yeah. Listen, I know you're worried, but the captain … he can take care of himself."

"Take care of himself? Jesus Christ, he's seventy-seven years old!"

"Yeah, but seventy-seven ain't what it used to be."

DAY 30

KAPPERNICK WAS SEVENTY-SEVEN, and since seventy-seven wasn't what it used to be, he thought: *If it ain't what it used to be, I'd sure hate to be feeling like what it was.*

His body was tired.

He needed a nap.

He hoped he could sleep.

The last couple of days had been hectic, to say the least. He'd just arrived back at his motel room from slapping that sonofabitch across the mouth, which felt good—really good. But he knew after he'd done it, there would be no turning back.

As he drove to the CVS where Berk worked, he'd actually considered negotiating a truce, but the idea was short-lived. He knew it was impossible. Ice Man had tried to kill him, in broad daylight, in front of his family.

He almost didn't recognize the guy behind the counter; the druggist seemed different somehow. It wasn't just the glasses on the tip of his nose, or the way he parted his hair; it was his whole demeanor—softer, more civil. But with the slap, Ice Man quickly returned, eyes glaring, hate burning, anger radiating. Kappernick saw him in that split second, and Ice Man in return saw Kappernick, who'd been hoping that the sonofabitch would jump across the counter so he could kill him right then and there. But Ice Man had maintained self-control. Motherfucker. He'd wanted to provoke the bastard, wanted Ice Man to come to him, to make a mistake. Mostly, though, he wanted him to worry, to suffer, to know fear.

Kappernick wasn't sure how long he lay there before he fell asleep. A sharp knock on the door woke him. His eyes snapped open. Soldier was there, growling with lip curled. Kappernick reached for his weapon on the night table next to the bed and yelled, "Who's there?"

"It's Benny Bittle. You called me."

"Are you alone?"

"Yep."

"Step back from the door."

Kappernick looked at Bittle through the peep hole. He was indeed alone. He told Soldier to cool it, then opened the door. Bittle was short, stocky, and sported a full, black beard and a full head of black hair, with large, intense eyes behind black-framed glasses. The suit he wore was dark gray, ten years old, pant legs cuffed. He hauled a large suitcase that he now rolled into the room, and after he stood the case on its end, he looked around.

"Mind if I check out the bathroom and the closet?" He studied Kappernick, then added as he walked to the closet, "No credit, no checks, no credit cards."

"And no questions."

Bittle slung the suitcase onto the bed and opened it. "I brought a sampling of what you said you might need. I have more that I can bring later, if this doesn't suffice."

"No, I think you have enough here to choose from. Does the twenty-two have a silencer?"

"Absolutely. Look, the silencer is nothing more than a suppressor. It suppresses sound. Because this is a low caliber, you don't hear nothing. And that Colt is a hell of a piece, if you get close. It's what the pros use. Twenty-twos ain't what they used to be. It's a semi-automatic with an enormous capacity. Sixteen rounds, and it can wreak havoc. Once that shell gets inside, it wanders. And it's light." He studied the weapon as he handed it to Kappernick. "I can let you have it with the silencer for two grand."

"Wow. That's huge."

"Hey, the pistol's two hundred ninety-five. You can go into any store and get one, and that's what you'd pay. It's the suppressor that costs, and it costs because you can't go into a store and get it. To get a suppressor, you gotta fill out a form like you were trying to get a machine gun. Might take maybe nine months. You need something tomorrow, you pay for it. I'm not trying to take advantage of you, but that's what I can get for it."

Kappernick bit the bullet. "Okay, I'll take it. I also need a rifle. Something I can break down. It has to have a sight, with an accuracy of a hundred yards."

Bittle smiled, and he held up a finger to emphasize his delight. "I got just the thing. Here, check this out."

From the large suitcase he took out a small briefcase, the kind and size a lawyer might use, and emptied the contents onto the bed. Within minutes, he assembled the most beautiful rifle Kappernick had ever seen.

"This is an Accuracy International sniper rifle. It collapses into nothing. If you don't want to look like a Wall Street broker, it can fit snugly into a backpack or a gym bag. Here, hold it."

Kappernick was immediately impressed by how light the weapon was.

Bittle went on. "This is a killing machine. This is what connoisseurs of the trade use to take out a man. Now, there are fifty or sixty sights that can be used, but personally"—he pulled out a particular sight—"I recommend a Schmidt & Bender optic. One-inch barrel, 308-caliber. This weapon is considered the best tool in the trade."

LINDA LANSKY

LINDA COULDN'T BELIEVE HOW, all of a sudden, she was involved in what her mother would have called "pure *mishegas*." Absolute craziness! Until this madness, her life had been normal.

When she was twenty-five, she'd married Harry Lansky, and she and her husband were both teachers. She taught fifth grade and had received a master's degree in elementary school studies, and he taught high school English. Even though they had no children, which they'd wanted badly, they were still happy because they cared deeply for each other and had rationalized that teaching gave them many, many children they could call their own. Teaching also gave them time, especially in the summer, to travel to exotic, far-off places around the world.

So for many years, life was sweet. She and Harry were both avid readers and they never lacked for conversation; they both loved movies and the theater. In fact, life couldn't have been any sweeter … until Harry had developed a debilitating dementia, and then life became hard.

At first, it'd started with mild memory loss, little things like not being able to find his keys or forgetting why he'd gone into a room, until it eventually developed into forgetting how to get to his classroom or the route that led to the school. Within a year, he could no longer teach, and two years after the initial signs, he merely sat at home in his easy chair. He'd gained considerable weight and watched TV endlessly. The disease had lasted seven years, little by little robbing Harry of not only his memory but also his mind until all he did, day after day and year after year, was sit in front of the TV, watching soaps, not remembering what he'd just seen. He'd only gone to the bathroom when he was told to, and after several mishaps, he'd worn a diaper at all times. Linda, however, continued to work, leaving him daily with a caregiver.

Dementia not only debilitates the victim, but it also tears apart the loved ones. Each time they see what he or she has become, they also see what that person once was, and no matter how hard they try, those images can't be hidden.

So when Harry finally passed, as much as Linda had hated to admit it, it'd been a relief. The body that had been left behind in the overstuffed easy chair hadn't been Harry for many years.

After the funeral, Linda settled into being alone. She'd already been alone, really alone, for several years before Harry had passed, though in a different way. She still had to take care of him, make sure he was fed, take him to the toilet, tell him to wipe himself, pay the caregiver who came in from nine to five, six days a week. During those last years, her classes, the schoolkids, and the book she was trying to write all kept her mind active, kept her going, and had helped her from brooding over her loneliness.

She'd worried what it would be like after she retired. What would she do? Take some courses? Finish her book? Play bridge once a week? Jesus! She'd accepted that the excitement of life was now behind her and, for all intents and purposes, so were men—once she'd met Harry, other men had no longer been in her thoughts, and they'd been married for almost forty years, so she wouldn't even know what to say to a man, how to act, where to find one.

Linda was about to say *c'est la vie* to that whole idea, when out of the clear blue sky appeared Melvin Kappernick. He was the kind of guy you'd find at a dude ranch—tall, slim, leaning against a fence, chewing on a long piece of straw, a cowboy hat pulled down over his craggy face, and a big smile that spread from ear to ear. Yet he wasn't a "howdie-pardner" kind of guy. No, Melvin was bright, well-read, and sensitive. Linda liked him, and she felt that Melvin liked her. She hadn't felt this way in many years.

Despite all of the misgivings about Tiffany, Linda found herself constantly thinking about Melvin. Sure, he had some problems, but who hadn't? She'd had such a good time at the zoo—she liked his son and daughter-in-law, and their kids; she'd liked walking with Melvin. The day had been so beautiful, and then … then the craziness, the *mishegas*. Someone had actually tried to kill him! Shoot him right there in front of everybody! It'd been insane, totally insane.

For the past couple of days, that was all Linda could think about. She hadn't heard from Melvin, and she wasn't sure she really wanted to. Still, she couldn't get him out of her mind. When she'd left school just twenty minutes before, her thoughts were so clouded by the incident at the zoo, she couldn't remember where she'd parked her car. She'd driven home in a sort of daze, and had pulled up to her house in a state of worried consternation. She was halfway up the steps leading to her front door when she heard the pull of a chain. Linda looked up to see a huge dog staring at her.

She froze.

She wasn't a dog person, and the size alone of this beast almost scared her to tears. But the dog wagged his tail as he stuck out his big tongue and licked her face. Linda wiped her wet cheek with the back of her hand, then let out a "Get back!" and to her amazement, the brute retreated and sat down. Even sitting, he was still imposing.

She took a deep, shaky breath. She'd seen this dog before. It was Melvin's. He'd been walking the dog the day they'd first met. She looked around, then back at the dog.

"Where is he?" she asked. "Where is your stupid master?"

The dog hung his head sadly, and that's when Linda saw the note wrapped in his collar. It might as well have been in its mouth. With a thumb and a pointer finger, she cautiously removed the note, then sat down in a porch chair. The envelope, with her full name printed on its face, contained a single, folded sheet of typewriter paper with a letter that had been meticulously handwritten.

> *Hi, Linda. I know you're probably saying, "Is he out of his gourd? How dare he leave this beast on my porch! What the hell am I going to do with it?" Well, I'm sorry, but I knew no one else who'd love him as much as I do. His name's Soldier. I hope you like dogs.*

At that point, Soldier got up and put his huge head on her lap.

> *If you give him two cans of Alpo a day, (the bag is behind the storm door) water, and a few pats on the head, he will protect you with his life. He's the smartest dog I ever met. His being with you will put my mind at ease. I need to know that you'll be safe until I get back. You've kinda gotten under my skin. Take care and thanks.*

> *Sincerely, Melvin*

Linda lowered the letter, then looked at the monster whose head rested in her lap. She timidly patted his brow.

"What am I going to do with you?" she said. "I've never had a dog. You know … that buddy of yours is totally crazy."

RAPHAEL DIEGO

RAPHAEL DIEGO hadn't left his room in more than three days. He knew he was in trouble; the debacle at the zoo was gonna cost him. Now, all he wanted was to get out of his ten-by-ten cubbyhole. It was worse than a prison. At least inside a prison they fed you.

Here, in his "home sweet home," he was starving. The electricity to the fridge had gone off a while back, and whatever he'd had in there (which wasn't much in the first place), now stunk to high heaven. Right now, he could go for a cheesesteak—shit, he could go for ten of them! But he couldn't go anywhere, or show his face. Ice Man was waiting for him to do just that.

Maybe he should have gone to the 39th Street pad right after he'd run out of the zoo. Taken his beating like a man. But he hadn't. His first instinct had been to head to his own hole-in-the-wall, then bite his lip at his own stupidity. But no one just says: "Here I am, boys! Beat the shit out of me!" And because he hadn't faced the rap-song, he was worse off. He'd seen Ice Man beat up someone before. It wasn't pretty. Ice had made five guys watch it as a lesson. The guy strapped to the chair kept passing out from the pain, but Ice Man kept waking him up with smelling salts so he could inflict more.

No, Diego wasn't going to volunteer for that.

One window in Diego's flat looked out onto the street. He lifted the shade and peeked out. It was quiet. Jesus. It was like Christmas-fucking-Eve. He was trapped—fucking trapped! He couldn't even make a call. The Cricket cell phone in his pocket had run out of minutes. He was fucked—totally fucked!

Thoughts of running filled his head, but where would he go? That nobody came looking for him, that Ice Man hadn't sent any motherfucker to knock on his door, was a bad sign. Real bad. Maybe Ice wanted him to run? Get him outside the territory? Yeah, if he could make it out of the hood and into the railroad yard, he could jump a car and ride, hop a freight and disappear. All he had left in cash, though, was a hundred and thirty-five bucks. Shit, he'd have to get to another state, stick up a store, and just lie low. Yeah, that's what he had to do.

His tiny closet had a small gym bag, and in it, Diego crammed a few things. Then he threw on a khaki jacket hanging on a hook at the back of the door, and put up the collar. Into the coat pocket he shoved his .44, and into his pants he stashed a switchblade and his money.

That's all there was. That's all he had. He checked the street once more. Dead as a doornail; nothin' was happening.

He opened up the front door and peered out into the dimly lit hall, where a single bulb dangling from a wire cast a strange light against the walls. Diego took a deep breath and walked out into the hallway, gym bag in his left hand, fingering the weapon in his pocket with his right.

Every house on that hundred block of Poplar Street had porches. Diego stepped out onto his porch and breathed heavily, walked down the three steps to the sidewalk and hurried down the street. On the next corner stood a dinosaur—an old pay phone. He'd call Ice Man and tell him he was leaving.

He strode over to the phone, set down his gym bag, then fumbled for some change in his pants pocket … and that's when the bullet went into his leg. He cried out and sank to the ground, and before he could get his hand out of his pocket, the shooter was on him.

Jesus Christ, motherfucker—it was the old White guy! Diego groaned, and the old guy whacked him on the side of the head with the gun's long muzzle. Not twenty feet from the pay phone lay an alleyway, dark, dirty, and reeking of tomcat urine. The old guy, having seen what Diego was trying to do, wrenched the gun out of Diego's coat.

"Got anything else, shitface?"

"No."

"No?" The old man stared into his eyes. Then his face went crazy, and he hissed, "You lying fuck, I'll kill you right now."

"Okay, okay, please! I got a switch in my pants pocket." Diego moaned again. The old man stepped back and made him take out the knife, toss it into the street.

"Now, listen carefully. There's an alley back there, about twenty feet from where we now stand. I want you to get up and hop to it."

"No. No."

"You want to live? Then, you do as I say, or I'll kill you right here."

Bleeding and crying, Diego struggled to his feet and, hopping, made it over to the alleyway. Just as he entered the trash-filled passageway, the old man pushed him to the ground.

"Now tell me everything!" the old man demanded, shining his cell phone's light into Diego's face. When Diego refused, the old man smacked him in the teeth with the barrel of the gun.

"Okay, okay! Ice Man made me do it, man. He was gonna pay me ten grand. That's how much he wanted you out of the way. He hates you, man. He gonna kill you, man. He gonna get you good!" Radiating pain made his voice whine.

"Really? Let's give him a call and see what he says. What's his number?"

"What? His number?"

"Yeah. Let's give him a buzz."

"I don't know his number. Are you crazy—?" But the old man raised his pistol to hit him again, and he blurted out the number.

The old man dialed and put the call on speaker. The phone was answered with a "Yeah?"

"Hello, Icy." The old man sneered at the phone. "How you doin'? You fill my order, sonny?" No response. "Hey, your buddy wants to talk to you."

Silence.

Kappernick held the phone out to Diego.

"Ice? Ice! He got me, Ice. Hurt me bad! Blew my knee off! Are you there, Ice?"

There was silence for several moments before the cell clicked off. Diego stared at the phone, then looked up at the old man with a whimper. He began to weep. "What are you gonna do with me?"

"You want to live?" the old man asked.

"You're not gonna kill me—you wouldn't kill me! You can't kill me!"

"I said, do you want to live?"

BARTON BERK

MOTHERFUCKER, COCKSUCKER, SONOFABITCH!

Ice Man stared furiously at his cell, then threw it against the wall, jaw quivering, hands shaking. This was the second time in three days he was so pissed off he couldn't think clearly. Had anybody walked by, he would have punched him in the mouth; he needed to hit someone, to hurt someone. He peered around the room. Those who hadn't left sat silently, not looking at him, while Marissa, one of the whores, walked in, took one look at the group, and immediately left.

The group consisted of three of Ice Man's flunkies: Timmy Savage, the other dummy he'd sent with Diego to beat up the old man outside of the Spot Lite; Ruby Brown, his personal bodyguard and driver who looked like a sumo wrestler, though with a brain as thick as his body; and Martin Mobley, a young shooter whom Ice Man liked, because Mobley enjoyed hurting people as much as he did. Mobley was deep chocolate in color with semi-bulgy eyes. Ice Man snarled within as he studied his … *men*. None of them were worth a shit. But that's what you get for hiring crap. You get what you pay for.

That old man, that Kapp, had to go, had to be killed. This was the third time he, Ice Man, had misjudged him, underestimated him, not taken him seriously. That sonofabitch was smart, too fucking smart, and he'd done things that infuriated Ice Man, things no one had ever dared to do. If he could find him, he'd kill him, slowly. And now, Diego! He'd personally wanted to hurt Diego, make an example of him, take him apart for being so stupid—so fucking stupid! Too late for that. Originally, he'd considered letting Diego keep a low profile until the heat cooled; let him lie low, stew in his own idiocy. But he'd waited too long. That old man had gotten to him first. Motherfucker! He had to fucking pay … but how? He couldn't even find the son of a bitch! He'd put someone on the old man's place, but the whole building was dark. That old piece of shit wasn't there; both he and the girl were gone. Maybe he should just burn the fucking place down!

For a while he'd thought the old man had run, until he showed up at the store. And now, *Diego*. It was too much—too fucking much! He had to do something, had to hurt him! He stood there as if immobilized … and then he smiled, sure of what he had to do. An eye for an eye.

"Mobley!" he yelled. The Black man looked up, and Ice Man gritted his teeth. "Come here."

JESSE SPRINGER

"THIS HAS NOTHING to do with race," was what Kappernick had told him. "This has to do with what's right, with defending oneself, with respecting yourself."

Springer had nodded. He'd understood what Kappernick was saying: If you let someone put his hand into your pocket, it'd be hard to keep others from doing the same; if you let someone punch you in the mouth, everybody would try to knock your teeth out; if you let someone try to kill you, if he didn't get you, someone else would. In order to live in peace, you had to defend yourself.

The bar business had taught him. Growing up in West Philly had taught him. He'd learned very early, if you were weak, people would pick on you. Springer was not weak. Few dared to pick on him. People knew Springer made sure his bar was a safe place to drink; funny business, monkey business, and stupidity wouldn't be tolerated. He'd worked too hard to have some asshole undo what was his, and thereby do him harm. His business had been good to him. The Spot Lite had put his three sons through college, and had given his daughter a wedding she'd always remember; it allowed him to be ready to help out any of his family, or to have a special present for any of his eight grandchildren when it was birthday time. It had even allowed him to take his wife to Italy, and Paris, and Berlin. He worked hard, had fared well, despite working in a dismal neighborhood. Springer had no regrets.

Rarely did he get involved in neighborhood affairs. On 42nd Street, there was no business association, no community association. Who would it consist of? What would he do, have a meeting with Chang who owned Open-Til-Four, or with Too-Tall? The thought was preposterous. No, he was alone on the edge of the desert's tattered fringes, observing the wasteland of West Philadelphia.

Initially, he couldn't understand Kappernick, didn't get why he'd come back and was living alone above the old store in a neighborhood that was no longer his. Given all that, though, he liked him, always had. Most people run from their past, run from the poverty. What he really couldn't understand was why Kappernick had taken in the girl. What did he owe her? Why did he care? What could he do for her? What would he do for her? He, Springer, wouldn't have done it. And maybe, just maybe, knowing he wouldn't have gotten involved, is why he'd said he'd help. And he did help.

Earlier that day, when Kappernick had called, Springer, without hesitation, had gotten him Diego's address, which took all of three calls and ten minutes. If helping was gonna be that easy, he'd have no complaints. Those simple calls had eased the guilt he was feeling. Guilt, for not doing anything.

After all these years, Springer felt he owed Kappernick, or at least owed the family something. Loyalty. Old Mrs. Teabloom, Kappernick's grandmother, with her big stomach, sagging cheeks, and heavy hand, had helped him out, gave him his first job carrying boxes of fruit and delivering orders, had showed an interest. She'd taught him how to ring up sales, make change, gave him some hard-earned money in his pocket. Even as he tended bar, these thoughts were constantly with him.

Springer washed a couple of glasses under the counter, then looked at the wall clock. Almost closing time, with only two people left in the bar. One of his regulars, Oscar Tweedson, was falling asleep on his stool, and the other guy, who sat at the end of the bar, was calling for his tab.

On his way to collect, Springer shook Tweedson. "It's time to get going," he said, and Tweedson woke up, staggered over to the door, and left with the stranger.

As the two sots walked out into the night air, Springer locked the door behind them, then counted his cash, turned off the outside lights, did one last check of the place, and turned on the alarm. Finally satisfied, he left by the back door.

Thankfully, his car was only fifteen feet away and, with a sigh, Springer opened the Chevy's door, sat down, and started the engine. He was about to turn on some music for the drive home, when he felt the muzzle of a .45 press against the back of his head.

BARTON BERK

ON THE SECOND FLOOR of the house on 39th Street where Tiffany's aunt worked and lived, Ice Man used a back room when he was on location, and Ice Man was definitely on location when Mobley and Brown brought Springer in.

He smiled when his boys carried—actually, dragged—the unconscious owner of the Spot Lite into the sparse chamber and deposited him on a wooden chair in front of an old oak table. Springer's nose bled; blood had splattered over his white shirt.

"It looks worse than it really is," said Mobley. "I had to whack him a couple of times. He didn't want to come inside."

"No problem. Where'd you get him? Anyone see you?"

"Nah. Got him in his car after he closed. Nobody was around."

"Good. Tie him to that chair, and tape his hands to the table. Ruby, get rid of the car; take it back to where you found it. We'll wait for you to get back before we begin. I'll get things ready."

Against one wall stood a locked metal file cabinet, which Ice Man unlocked and from which he extracted a huge roll of duct tape and a substantial hank of rope. He handed them to Mobley, who hog-tied Springer to the chair. Then Ice Man meticulously removed a pair of plastic surgical gloves from a black medical bag and, sitting down in an easy chair, the only other piece of furniture, he donned the gloves, then made sure the bag contained everything he needed. An old-fashioned floor lamp stood behind the chair, and on the chair's arm hung a glamour magazine, which Ice Man thumbed through while he waited for Brown to return.

Once the big bodyguard had reappeared, Ice Man told him to wipe the keys clean and put them into Springer's pocket.

Then he got to work.

He carried the bag over to the table and from it took out a small vial of smelling salts to restore the barkeep's consciousness. Springer's eyes snapped open. Immediately, he noticed he was crudely tied down and taped to a chair, and he looked up into Ice Man's eyes.

Ice Man smiled. "Well, look who it be. If it isn't the owner of the Spot Lite. How you doin' man? Good to see you. Glad you could make it."

"What the hell is this? What do you want?"

"Just a little talk."

"Why am I strapped to a chair?"

"Well, I want to make sure you be tellin' me the truth, man."

"The truth? The truth about what?"

"About your friend, de White man. I want to know everything you know. Now, what do you know?"

"Not much."

"Do you know where he is right now? Where that coward be hidin'?"

"No. If I did, I'd tell you." The night they'd met at the diner, Springer had asked Kappernick where he was staying, but Kappernick wouldn't say. He'd said he wanted Springer to stay out of it, that he'd handle it, that Springer had a family and a business to worry about.

"But you his friend. You must know where I can find him."

"Look, I knew him as a kid. I worked in his grandmother's vegetable store. He came into the bar. That's all there is."

"Really," Ice Man said and, reaching into the black medical bag, extracted a hammer and four-inch spike. "You remember Mr. Mobley, here? Mr. Mobley say you were willin' to fight for the man. That sound like a friend to me."

Springer's eyes widened at the sight of the hammer and spike. "Look, I just didn't want no trouble outside my place. I would have done the same for anybody."

"I think you lyin'. Please, for your own sake, do not lie to Ice Man." And with that, he slammed the hammer down onto the little finger of Springer's right hand. The barkeep howled at the excruciating pain.

"You scream like that again, I'm gonna pull every tooth out of your lyin' mouth," said Ice Man. "Now what can you tell me?"

"I swear, I don't know anything, I swear! Please!"

Ice Man smiled briefly, then he slowly, tortuously, searched through the black bag. Springer gritted his teeth, eyes blinking wildly, until Ice Man shook his head.

"Can't find the scalpel. You a lucky man. Well, I think this will do." And he picked up the spike in his left hand, placed its tip on the back of Springer's right hand, then raised the hammer …

"Wait, wait! I do know something! I do know something!"

"What you know?"

"I don't know where he is, but I know he has a son. He told me he has a son."

"A son? What's his name?"

"I don't know."

"Where he live? What he do?"

Springer's jaw quivered. "I don't know where he lives—I swear! But I think Mel said he was a lawyer. I may be able to find out. Give me some time."

Ice Man shrugged. "I'll think about it, man." And with that, he smashed the spike through the back of Springer's hand, pinning it to the wooden table. "But I don't want you to go anywhere while I'm considering the possibilities."

DAY 35

KAPPERNICK ANSWERED his cell phone and listened while Perkins gave him some bad news.

"I think they got Jesse."

"How do you know?"

"I went by the Spot Lite today and his wife was there. She was worried. Jesse didn't come home last night. In all the years they were married, he's never done that. She called his cell, but he didn't answer. The money from the night before was in the safe, so he wasn't robbed, and his car was still parked behind the club. Do you think they killed him?"

"I hope not. That's why I didn't want him involved. He has a family; it makes him vulnerable. You see what can happen? Are you still in?"

"Yes, sir. I'm all in."

"Okay. I want to meet with you soon. I'll call you back and let you know where and when."

Almost immediately, Kappernick's phone started singing again. This time, it was Reese.

"Kapp?"

"I'm here."

"I just wanted to check in with you. This morning, around four o'clock, the guy I have watching your son's house saw a

208 \ TED FINK

car slowing down in front of it. What made him nervous was that it'd come back for a second look. Normally, he'd have followed them, but he thought better of it. Maybe whoever it was wanted to see if anyone was watching. Since he was alone, he didn't want to be drawn away, you know what I mean?"

"Your guy did the right thing. Did he get a look at them?"

"They were two Black guys, which made it even more suspicious, since there aren't too many brothers in that neighborhood. He got the plate number, which I checked out, and just as I suspected, the plate was reported stolen two months ago."

"I'm worried."

"Look, it may be nothing, but to be on the safe side, I'm going to put two more guys on. It'll be a little expensive."

"Don't worry about the costs. Do it."

"I will. But, Kapp … I'm thinking the smart thing to do would be to go to the cops."

"I'm thinking you may be right. If things don't work out, I may do that tomorrow."

"Tomorrow? What do you mean?"

"Nothing. Just babbling. I'm counting on you, Reese. Keep my kid and his family safe."

"I'm on it," the big detective replied, then clicked off.

Kappernick stared at the phone in his hand. He was worried—real worried. He lay down in bed and closed his eyes. He was tired—very tired. His whole body throbbed with apprehension. He'd never felt this way, even when bullets were flying in 'nam. Yes, that had been dangerous, terrifying, but so different. He'd been young and dumb back then. This time, he'd just been plain stupid, having endangered his whole family.

Even though it was early in the day, he considered taking a sleeping pill, though he resisted that temptation. Yes, he was tired, but he still needed to be alert, needed a clear head. If only he could get one good hour of sleep. If only …

He'd been busy. Posing as an electrical repairman, Kappernick had thoroughly cased the 40th Street house. He'd checked the back alley, and had even gone to a realtor that had posted the availability of a third-floor apartment almost directly across from Ice Man's 40th Street whorehouse. The real estate agent said he didn't have time to show it.

"Look," he'd said, "it's a dump. You won't like it. But if you really need to see it today, here's the keys."

Kappernick had gone to see the place and it was perfect for what he was planning, so he made a duplicate set of keys before he'd returned the originals—he'd only need the apartment for one night. Then he'd driven into Center City, into the garage where Ice Man parked his car, took the freight elevator, and got off on Berk's floor to slide a note under his door. It read: *Hope you're not working too hard, Dearie. See you soon, Icy.*

Then he'd gone back to the garage and flattened both rear tires on the pharmacist's car.

Up to that point, Kappernick thought things had gone, as the English say, "brilliantly." But the two recent phone calls that had immediately heightened his anxiety meant he had to speed up his plans.

DAY 36

PERKINS LAUGHED—a high-pitched cackle. "How'd you find this place?" he asked, and laughed again, unable to contain his excitement.

Kappernick stared. Had he made a mistake, asking Perkins to be a part of his plan? "You okay?" he said. "You gonna be able to do this?"

"Yes, sir. I'm fine. Just a little nervous."

They'd entered the building through the back yard. When Kappernick had been there earlier, he'd unlocked the gate to the alley—homes constructed in the early part of the nineteenth century had alleyways between the rows—and the set of keys he'd duplicated had included one that opened into the dismal, single-bulb hallway that he and Perkins had taken to the third-floor apartment.

Once inside, Kappernick had removed a backpack he'd been carrying and placed it onto the floor in the middle of the room. From it, he'd taken out a miner's headlamp and a twenty-amp electrical fuse. He'd strapped the lamp onto his head and turned on the light, which allowed him to find the fuse box, where the realtor had removed all of the fuses to keep, he assumed, anyone from running up an electric bill. He opened the box and screwed in the fuse, hoping it would produce light. And it did. A small, overhead fixture flickered on, dimly illuminating the room.

Hands on his hips, Perkins giggled with delight.

"Be quiet. Control yourself, and listen up. If anybody hears us, we're fucked."

Perkins saluted. "Okay, it won't happen again, I swear."

Kappernick opened the case containing the rifle he'd bought from Bittle, and Perkins slapped his hands over his mouth to keep from shouting with joy.

"Oh, my God!" he whispered. "It's beautiful."

"Can you put it together?"

"May I?"

"Absolutely."

Suddenly, all of the childishness and silliness was gone as Perkins, with masterful skill, assembled the weapon. Once he had it together, he studied it in awe, and Kappernick again saw the soldier he once knew. He handed Perkins the Schmidt & Bender optic sight. Perkins snapped it on, then held out his hand.

"Ammo," he said.

"In a minute." Kappernick walked over to the window and lifted the shade. "Come here. I want you to see the target. You see the building across the street, with the gray porch?" Perkins nodded. "That's the house."

"I know the house, I know the place," Perkins said. "You can't live in this neighborhood and not know the place."

"Good. Give me twenty minutes. You have your watch and cell phone?"

"Yes, sir.

"Okay. We'll synchronize our watches when I leave. Here, put on these gloves. Don't leave any prints. Think you can still shoot?"

"With this piece, I can shoot their eyes out."

"No, not the eyes. I don't want you to kill them. I want you to disable them, take off their kneecaps. Think you can get their knees? After twenty minutes, the first guy who comes out of that house, cripple him. Next guy out, do the same. I want two guys lying on that porch, yellin' and screamin'. Can you do that?"

"Yes, I can."

"Then, I want you to pack up and get the hell out of here, using the alley. Understand?"

"Yes, sir. Twenty minutes. After that, I shoot the fuckin' kneecap off the first guy out, do the same with the next. Then I pack up and leave the way we came."

"Right. Make sure you leave after that—go home and stay there. Don't try to get in touch with me; I'll contact you. Okay, here's the ammo. Let's check our watches. Remember, don't kill anybody. Just disable them, and then get the hell out. You got it?"

"Yes, sir."

"Okay, soldier, I'm counting on you."

"*Semper fedelis*, captain."

Kappernick handed him the box of bullets, and they shook hands. "Good luck. And ... thanks."

"You, too, sir."

BARTON BERK

BERK BREATHED HEAVILY. The old fuck was trying to be cute. Well, he, Ice Man, would do what Donald Trump had suggested: kill every member of the sonofabitch's family.

He'd sent Mobley and a kid named Zits Marshall to check out his son's home. Luckily, Kappernick wasn't a common name. He'd send the old fuck a message: You don't fuck with Ice Man.

That's when he saw the folded paper that had been slipped under his door. He got his .45 from the bedroom, marched back out into the living room, and threw open the door. No one was there. He retreated into the apartment and, slamming the door, reread the note.

Hope you're not working too hard, Dearie. See you soon, Icy.

A rage boiled. Ice Man. Icy! Just who the fuck did this sonofabitch think he was! He dared come to his home! The old man had to be taken care of today. It was getting late. He had to be at work, but he'd found, in the garage, the car he used for commuting had been sabotaged. He glanced at the Mercedes; he couldn't arrive to work in that car. That car belonged to Ice Man.

Reluctantly, Berk called the CVS and told the manager he wouldn't be in—the first time in all the years he'd worked there he'd ever missed a day.

He marched upstairs, stormed into the apartment, and changed into a white-flecked sport jacket over a new black shirt. Then he donned a new panama hat and sunglasses, and drove the Mercedes to 40th Street.

By seven thirty, everyone was assembled in the upstairs room. Springer still sat with the spike pinning his hand to the table. He'd lost considerable blood, and he was moaning, drifting in and out of consciousness. Ice Man looked at him with disdain.

"When it gets dark, Mobley, I want you to take Springer to his car and drop him off." He winked, and Mobley smiled, knowing without being told what Ice Man wanted.

Later on, just before the bug-eyed man was ready to leave, the boss whispered, "Once you get rid of him, come back here. We got plenty more work to do." And with that, he jerked the spike out of Springer's hand, careful not to get any blood on his clothes. The barkeep shrieked and collapsed. "You'd better pull the car up front. This here pussy can't take the pain."

Mobley went downstairs and opened the front door, lit a cigarette and walked to the end of the porch, where he took a long drag … when he felt his kneecap explode. He let out a horrendous scream, then tumbled down the stairs. Everyone heard, though what they didn't hear was Perkins' delighted giggle from the third-floor window of the building across the street.

"What the hell was that?" Ice Man snapped.

Savage, who was about to put handcuffs on Springer, shrugged.

"Go find out what the trouble is," said Ice Man. "And be careful."

Savage peered out to the sidewalk below. "Looks like Mobley fell down the stairs."

"Go help him."

With a nod, Savage bounced down the stairs, opened the front door, and took three steps, before he, too, was hit in the leg, the bullet shattering his thigh. He tumbled down the steps.

Perkins watched the two men writhe on the ground, and almost immediately, the door opened again. This time, it was Ice Man. Perkins could have finished it right then and there, but his job was to follow orders. Instead, he broke down the weapon, shut the window, drew the decrepit shades, and left the building the way Kappernick had taken him.

Across the street, Ice Man was like a whirling dervish, mind spinning, momentarily immobilizing him ... until he heard the girls screaming.

"Stay in your fuckin' rooms!" he shouted, but one paying customer didn't listen and was pulling up his pants as he came down the stairs, wanting out. Brown black-jacked the customer cold and dragged him back into his room. Outside, both Mobley and Savage squirmed in pain, yelling for help.

"Ruby," Ice Man shouted above the din, "come here, man!" The big man waddled down the stairs. "I want you to go back up and bring down that sonofabitch, Springer. We gotta get out of here. The police will be here any minute and I don't want them to find that sonofabitch. We're taking him with us."

"What about de guys outside?"

"Fuck 'em."

The big man didn't move for a moment, until Ice Man shouted, "What the fuck are you standing here for! Get the fuck upstairs, and let's go!"

Brown, like a mini bulldozer, doubled-timed up the steps, then came back down, dragging Springer behind him, and the three of them left by the back door leading out to the yard. Ice Man considered killing Springer in the yard because he was holding them up; the barkeep had lost so much blood from his hand wound that he was weak and could barely walk. He knew Springer didn't have much time, but he also knew he couldn't kill him near the house, which would immediately make him the perpetrator. He'd have to kill him later on and dump the body.

"Pick him up, carry the motherfucker," he told Brown, and the big man snatched up the barkeep like he was the morning paper and stumbled through the debris and trash that cluttered the yard. Ice Man pulled open the gate, and they stepped out into the alley, where the street lamp was out. Without the light, the alley was dark, and they heard the police sirens approaching from a distance. Time was getting very short. They picked their way through the litter, fighting through the stench of tomcat urine. Ice Man had planned to exit the alley on Belmont Avenue, but just as they'd reached the outlet, they found the passageway blocked—someone had piled a huge amount rubbish at the entrance: old tables, broken chairs, rusted pipes, and every other imaginable piece of junk. They'd have to climb over it. "Put him down and clear us a path! Jesus Christ, man!"

Brown backed up a few steps, dropped Springer, then began to move an old tabletop from the pile of waste. Suddenly, a *pop* or a *piff*, like air being let out of a balloon, sounded, and Brown let out a groan, dropped the tabletop and fell backwards onto the pile of trash. Ice Man had his .45, but couldn't see what had happened.

"Ruby?" he hissed.

"I'm hit!" yelled Brown. "Shoulder." Another pop, and Brown groaned again. This time, he rolled over to lie face down in the muck and slime.

"Where the fuck are you, old man?"

"Here, motherfucker!" Kappernick yelled back, wearing

the night goggles Bittle had made a special trip to deliver. He could see Ice Man clearly, but he, himself, was hidden in a dark alcove only ten feet away.

"Where?" Ice Man fired some shots into the blackness, and they caromed off of some metal, ringing in his own ears.

Kappernick fired again, hitting the pimp in the shoulder. Ice Man fell back into a wooden fence, and the .45 dropped to the ground. Kappernick could have killed the sonofabitch, but he thought that could wait.

From out of a pouch attached to his belt, Kappernick extracted a flashlight, which he shined in Ice Man's face. The pimp's eyes were full of fury, a kind of wild hate mixed with fear, and he snarled like a cornered animal, trying to get to his feet but falling back down again.

"You like to fuck little girls, do you, Icy? Look at you, lying in a filthy alley, sniveling like a little baby. You dirty piece of shit. You're a nothing, nothing but a pussy, a faggot." Kappernick shoved the barrel of the silencer against Ice Man's head. "I want you to say you're sorry and that you'll never do it again."

"What?"

At that moment, Brown struggled to his feet, staggered a step or two and, clutching his chest, and again fell face-first into a pile of rubbish. Without taking the gun from Ice Man's head, Kappernick watched the huge man fall.

"Don't play with him, Mel," Springer groaned. "Kill the motherfucker!"

Kappernick had almost forgotten Springer was there, his adrenaline was so overwhelming, his hatred for Ice Man so intense.

"First things first, Jesse," he said, never taking his eyes off of his prey. Bewilderment sat on the pimp's face, all pomposity, all smugness gone, as if he couldn't believe this was happening to him. Then, right before Kappernick's eyes, the killer, the mobster, the pimp changed, and like Kafka's meta-morphosis, he became the druggist, the pharmacist. His voice changed, as well, higher in pitch, more womanish.

"Why are you trying to hurt me? What did I ever do to you? I'm a good, hardworking man."

"Really?"

"Yes, I am. I really am."

"Then, say you're sorry. Say you'll never do it again. Say it!"

"Will you let me get away if I do? I'll leave you be, I swear!"

Springer couldn't believe what he was hearing. "Jesus Christ, Mel, just kill the motherfucker."

"I want to give him a chance. Say it!"

Ice Man's face contorted. "I … I'm sorry," he whimpered, "I'll never do it again."

"I don't believe you, Icy. I think you're a fuckin' liar. I just wanted to hear you say it." Kappernick shoved the silencer at the Ice Man's groin. "I'm here to make sure you never do it again. Say goodbye to your balls," he said, and then fired. The pimp's screams split the night air.

"Let me kill him, Mel. Let me do it. Let me do it, let me finish him off." Springer struggled to his feet. "Please."

"No, my friend, this one's on me."

PART THREE

ARNOLD WEISMAN

ARNOLD WEISMAN PUSHED himself away from his desk, took a deep breath, removed his glasses, and wearily rubbed his eyes. He was exhausted; he was saddened. He liked Melvin Kappernick, and he knew from the beginning he did not want to defend this case. Losing was anathema to his very being; it hurt for a long time after the verdict was passed down—it refused to go away. And this case was so very losable. Like an Olympic athlete, you work, you train, you dream, and then you run the race. If you lose, it's all for naught. Even if you get paid, its excruciating. And this looked to be one of those insufferable loses.

Everyone had warned him about taking the case—his wife had begged him not to get involved, his legal associates had told him it wasn't worth the effort, and he himself knew what, in the end, would be taken out of him. But that, in fact, is what made law exciting. Most of the time it was provocative and stimulating; it forced you to read, to think, to contemplate. A long time ago, or so it seemed, one of his professors once said, "If you're not passionate about it, you shouldn't be doing it. Discover your passion, let it absorb you, and then let it loose." Weisman's passion was criminal law. For the first ten years of his career, he'd been on the other side of the fence, working for the city as a prosecutor. He put, as he would say, "the bad guys" away. But for the last thirty years, he was on the defense side, considered one of the best defense attorneys in the business. A reporter had once asked him how he felt about—here, he'd thrown Weisman's on words back at him—getting "the bad guys" off, and Weisman had answered, "I don't take on cases or clients I don't believe in."

He believed in Kappernick.

At first he didn't, though.

Initially, the papers had painted the accused, Melvin Kappernick, as something Weisman had come to know he was not. Kappernick was not a bigot, and because of that one editorial miscalculation, Weisman had reluctantly gotten involved. It'd all begun when Kappernick's son, Bruce, a former student at Penn Law where Weisman once taught criminal jurisprudence, came to him for help. Weisman liked Bruce, and the man had pled with his old professor to hear the whole story and help his father. Only … it'd been two o'clock in the morning when he called.

Weisman was an old-fashioned guy who still had an outdated landline on a night table next to his bed, which made his phone ring persistently and annoyingly. To be roused out of bed, jingly, happy tunes wouldn't do the trick for Weisman, and very few people had the emergency bedside number.

After groggily groping for the phone, he offered, "Hello?"

"Mr. Weisman?"

"Yeah, who the hell is this?" No polite reply was in order. Weisman didn't recognize the voice. For all he knew, it could have been a telemarketer.

"It's Bruce Kappernick."

"Bruce? Bruce, do you have any idea what time it is?"

"Yes, sir. I'm sorry, but this is an emergency."

"An emergency? What happened, did you kill somebody?"

"No, sir, but I think my father did."

"Aw, shit."

"Yes, exactly, that's what I said. . . ."

Actually, "Aw, shit" wasn't exactly what Bruce Kappernick had said when his father had called him and woken him up just forty-five minutes before:

"Dad?"

"Hi, boy. How you doing? Sorry to call you so late, but I had to before they make me give up my phone."

"They? What? Who? What's going on?"

"Son, I'm at the police station. I just confessed to killing Ice Man."

At that precise moment, trying to piece it all together had been a little too much for Bruce, but when he'd finally gotten the picture through the miasma of his wooziness, he'd begun to stammer. "Dad, Dad, Dad … are you out of your freakin', fuckin' mind?"

The phone clicked off.

Bruce stared at it and thought, *Well what did he expect me to say? Oh, that's nice?*

The outburst had made Barbara turn on the light next to her side of the bed and sit up.

"What's going on?" she'd mumbled.

"Dad just killed somebody."

"Oh, my God! What are you going to do?"

"Right now, I don' have the slightest freakin' idea. Give me a minute to think."

It'd taken two more phone calls to get to Weisman.

"All right, Bruce, now listen carefully," said the attorney. "In Philadelphia, they arraign everybody who's been booked that day at seven in the morning. When, exactly, did he call you?"

"Just after one thirty."

"He knows not to say anything, am I right?"

"Yeah, he knows it, but I can't promise he didn't."

They stayed on the phone for another five minutes, and in that short time, Weisman got the information he needed to make an important phone call. Upon hanging up, he called a friend who worked at the desk of the 36th Precinct, Joseph Bailey.

"Joe," he said, "I need a favor. Is there a guy down there named Melvin Kappernick?"

"Yeah, we got him."

"Has he been booked?"

"They're about to go in now. The guy confessed to killing someone, and the body was right where he'd said it would be."

"Shit." An official confession. A bad mistake. Weisman checked the clock: 2:20. "Joe, could they hold off booking him for five hours?"

A long silence followed. Weisman didn't usually ask for favors.

"Yeah," Bailey replied, "I think we can do that for you."

The next morning, Bruce showed up at Weisman's office, just after Weisman had arrived and argued his case. Bruce, who was no longer a kid, was so distraught, he could barely talk.

"Jesus, Bruce, you look terrible," Weisman said. "I guess you didn't get too much sleep last night." He'd seen Bruce just a month before at a Democratic fundraiser and had remarked to his wife how good and prosperous the young man looked, how confident and self-assured. Weisman, who prided himself on being an excellent judge of a man's body language, knew immediately this was a completely different man from the one he'd pointed out to his wife.

Weisman came out from behind his desk. "Lucky for us they booked him after seven, so it buys us a little time."

"And the charge?"

"Murder. First degree homicide."

Bruce pursed his lips and slowly shook his head.

"All right, here's what we'll do," said Weisman. "We have a little time. You go back to work and wait for my call. If you can, try to get some sleep. I'll clear my schedule sometime around eleven thirty and we'll go down together. There may not be anything I can do, but I'll get it started and handle it until we find someone."

Weisman noticed Bruce's expression lose hope. "Listen, you know I'll help you all I can," he said, "but right now, I don't know anything, and I'm not going to take on a project unless I know the whole story. So for now, do as I say: go to work, try to get some rest, and wait for my call. I'll at least take him through the bail process."

That afternoon, Bruce and Weisman went to the 36th Precinct to wait to see Kappernick. They all met in a gray room with nothing but four chairs and a table. Old man Kappernick hadn't gotten much sleep, either, and he didn't look well. Father and son embraced, then Bruce introduced Weisman.

"Dad, I want you to meet Arnold Weisman. He's the best criminal lawyer for miles and miles around."

Kappernick looked suspiciously at his son. "You mean, you're not going to defend me?"

Bruce held back his anger. As much as he loved his father, he was a true pain in the ass.

"Dad, I wouldn't defend you, even if I knew how. Truth is, I don't know how. I'm a corporate attorney. If I defended you, it'd be total incompetence on my part." Bruce stared at his father for a moment. "No, that's not right," he amended. "I am defending you. I'm defending you by bringing you the best criminal defense mind there is. I'm praying he'll take your case."

Kappernick forced a smile. "I understand."

"No, I don't think you do." First words Weisman had uttered. "I can tell by your body language—not only is your face expressing doubt, but your body also speaks volumes. You think because your son's a lawyer and went to Penn, that he can do anything when it comes to the law. Well, he's right about that. He can't. You're a smart man; you know he's right."

Weisman opened his briefcase and took out a legal pad, then gestured to a chair on the other side of the table. "And to be honest, I'm not sure that even I can help you. But I want to hear your story, to know what happened. I want to determine what your chances are and tell you what lies ahead for you, determine if you're worth the effort."

Again Kappernick smiled, and he held up a finger. "Truth is: I may not be worth it."

Weisman scowled. "Why don't you just sit down and let me decide." He waited for Kappernick to take a chair, then said, "Now, start from the beginning. Tell me everything, and don't hold back. Right now, I'm your attorney and anything you tell me I can't repeat."

It was hard telling the story without involving others, but Kappernick tried.

"I wanted to go live in my old neighborhood, but it had changed," he said. "I got into a fight with a drug dealer, who threatened me. It was either me or him, so I killed him. I tried to reason with him, but he wouldn't listen. He tried to kill me, so I killed him. To protect myself, I killed him."

Weisman removed his glasses and chewed the tip of the earpiece.

"How do you plead?"

The Honorable Alan P. Leebaum presided over the court, and he was as strict as his head was bald—nary a hair could be seen. Some called him "the hanging judge," though this name was a misnomer because they hadn't hung anybody in Pennsylvania since 1915. But, of the 1,068 executions since that time, Leebaum had two under his belt.

The *good* judge grimaced. "So, how do you plead, Mr. Kappernick?"

Kappernick looked over at Weisman, who stood to his right, then turned to Bruce seated in the gallery behind him and nodded. "Not guilty, Your Honor."

Judge Leebaum made to lift his gavel, when Weisman asked, "Your Honor, would you consider bail?"

Leebaum raised his eyebrows. "Bail?"

The Assistant District Attorney, an underling without much experience, immediately jumped into the discussion with a snort. "Ridiculous, Your Honor. The defendant killed two men in cold blood. Shot one twice—and that man eventually died of a heart attack. The other he shot three times— once in the shoulder, once in the testicles, and once in the brain. At least two others were wounded. The accused is fairly well-to-do, and he's definitely a flight risk."

"Flight risk?" Weisman said. "He's seventy-seven years old! Where's he going to go? He has no prior arrests; not even a traffic ticket. He's a decorated Vietnam vet. Release him under his own reconnaissance, Your Honor."

Leebaum pounded his gavel, then gave out a grunt. Talking directly to the Assistant DA, he said, "Mr. Weisman knows perfectly well that in Pennsylvania no bail is allowed in a capital offense."

"But this is a special situation, Your Honor."

"Is he sick? Is he dying?"

Kappernick, exhausted and unable to control himself, tentatively smiled.

Judge Leebaum slowly turned and, as if for the first time, studied the accused. "Do I see a smile on your face, sir? Do you think this proceeding is funny?"

"No, sir, Your Honor. It's not what you think. Sometimes when I'm nervous, I can't help it."

"Really."

"Your Honor, this man is a killer," said the Assistant DA. "A cold-blooded killer. He's a danger to the community."

"Please, Your Honor, the defendant's seventy-seven years old," Weisman countered. "He turned himself in. If he was going to run, he wouldn't have turned himself in. He would have simply left town."

"Is that so?" the judge replied with no concern. "He has the smile of a much younger man, and it looks to me like he's still spry enough to pull a trigger. I agree with the prosecution."

Weisman shook his head. "Being in the general population at Graterford will be hard on him, Your Honor."

"He should have thought of that before he pulled the trigger," answered Leebaum. "Remand is what it is. Bail is denied."

After Kappernick was taken away, Bruce whispered to Weisman, "That didn't go so well."

"Actually, we got lucky. At least Leebaum won't be the trial judge."

"Thank God for small favors, but—"

"No buts, Bruce. It's murder—murder!"

DAY 41

A LINE OF MEN waited to board the escort van that ferried prisoners from the courthouse to Graterford Prison: two Hispanic Americans, four African Americans, and Kappernick. Of the six, all were under forty, which made Kappernick older than the eldest by almost forty years.

In the van, prisoners sat on benches built into the body of the vehicle. One guy, trying to look like a Mohawk Indian, arms big enough to hold a thousand dark tattoos, sat directly across from Kappernick, eyeing him contemptuously. Apparently, the old white man looked like an easy mark.

"What you doin' here, pops?"

Kappernick didn't answer.

"Hey, motherfucker, I'm talking to you." Mohawk Man's voice held an edge Kappernick didn't like.

"What are you, a fucking attorney?"

The guy glared. "You crazy motherfucker. Nobody's gonna protect you where we're goin'. I'll kill your punk ass."

"Go ahead," said Kappernick, "you'll be doing me a favor."

Mohawk man glowered, but Kappernick ignored him.

In truth, he never thought he'd survive the confrontation with Ice Man, but things had gone so well, so precisely as planned that, incredibly, he'd emerged without a scratch.

And he'd been so intent on carrying out his mission, the consequences had never entered his mind … until it was all over. Thinking about the future would have interfered, and the old man wouldn't allow that to happen. He'd closed his mind to it. Only after Kappernick had terminated Ice Man did the weight of what he'd done fall upon him, and for a split second, he'd seriously thought about taking his own life. Physically exhausted, he'd momentarily stared at his pistol with that intent, but Springer had snapped him out of that dark thought: "Mel, let's get the fuck out of here!" he'd said, face contorted in pain. Kappernick had hesitated, looked down at the weapon in his hand one more time, then had gone to help his friend. "Come on man," he'd said, "let's go!"

Now, in the meat-wagon headed for Graterford, Mohawk Man smiled at the prisoner next him, whirling his finger by his own ear to indicate Kappernick was crazy. The other man gritted his teeth and nodded.

The gritted teeth reminded Kappernick of Springer after they'd climbed over the pile of crap he'd put there earlier. Cop cars had streamed down Girard Avenue toward 40th Street as he and Springer tried to walk nonchalantly up Viola Street toward Springer's car.

"Okay," Springer had said. "You got the son of a bitch." And he'd gritted his teeth, just like the guy sitting next to the wannabe Indian in the paddy wagon. "I'll be okay, but I can't be involved, Mel. Do you understand?" Kappernick had told him he'd understood, and Springer added, "What are you gonna do?"

"I'm gonna go back to my apartment and try to get a couple hours of sleep," Kappernick had whispered soberly. "And then I'm gonna turn myself in."

Springer winced. "What?"

"What else am I going to do, Jesse? Run? I'm an old man."

"They don't know it was you."

"Yes … yes, they do."

"If you can, leave me out of it?"

At this, Kappernick had nodded. "Not to worry," he'd replied. "I'll do my best."

DAY 42

WHEN KAPPERNICK WAS EIGHT, his father had given him a quarter to pay for a movie shown in the old Folkshul at the corner of 42nd and Viola Streets. The show started at 7 p.m. on a September evening and was a two-block walk to the tiny synagogue housed in a dreary brick building on the corner of 40th and Parkside. Kappernick could never quite remember the circumstances that made his father give him the money, but that's where he'd found himself.

The film was shown in the basement of the building, on an ancient clickity-clack, reel-to-reel projector, flickering black-and-white. The screen? An old sheet hanging from the wall. And the seats were wooden, fold-up chairs, with very few people in attendance. The place was already eerie, and the movie, *The Invisible Man,* starring Claude Rains was even spookier. Kappernick vividly remembered the movie scaring the living crap out of him, but even more terrifying was the walk home. He only had to go two blocks, but night had fallen and most of the lamplights on the tiny, twisting street had gone out. He wasn't used to the night noises of alley cats echoing back at him as if in deep, reverberating canyons, nor was he used to the intense odors that seemed magnified.

Instinctively, he'd walked down the middle of the street,

looking everywhere, readying himself to run if he had to. His imagination saw eyes watching from every feasible hiding place—telegraph poles, trash cans, porch furniture, cars ... they were everywhere!

Graterford Prison, in a lot of ways, was just like that night he'd walked down Viola Street as an eight-year-old. Eyes were everywhere, trained on him. He was new blood. At Graterford, he'd have to be very careful. He'd have to walk down the middle of the street.

TIFFANY

YOU CAN'T BE GOIN' AROUND *feelin' sorry for yourself. Things happen, and you gots to be strong. You gots to be brave. You got me now, and as long I'm breathin', I'm gonna protect you. But you need to be strong, too. You can't let those tears be fallin' and that chin be a-quiverin'.* Her hands were on her hips, her head bobbing as if in rhythm with her words. *If you're strong, you will prevail. You listen to your grammy: Ain't nothin' gonna hurt while I'm here! Humph!*

Tiffany could see her grammy standing there, saying those words in her own inimitable way. Yet she could also vaguely see her mother, her depressed, angry look, hear the yelling, the talking, the shadowy men passing through, looking at her strangely. She'd been so happy with her grandmother, but that had vanished as quickly as a car roaring down the street.

Then, she could see her aunt and Ice Man, feel the fear embodied in that house. She knew instinctively what would have happened had she not found Mr. Kapp, and now he … he was gone, too. The bedroom was larger than any room she'd ever slept in, with a comfortable queen-size bed, two bureaus, and a small TV. In the closet hung a series of new clothes Barbara had purchased the day after that terrible Sunday at the zoo. This was the room Kappy had stayed in when he lived at his son's house. At least that's what Barbara had told her when she first showed her where she'd be sleeping. Somehow, though, Tiffany had trouble seeing him there. It wasn't his kind of room. Seemed too girly for Mr. Kapp, but it was perfect for her. Ideal, really, with its light beige walls, bright white woodwork, sparkling mini blinds, and deep-piled carpet. She couldn't imagine a more delightful place, though under the present circumstances she had trouble appreciating it. Just hours before, she'd heard the devastating news that Mr. Kapp had been arrested. Now, she sat on the big bed and silently worried, fighting back tears, struggling to be brave.

A soft knock came at her door, and Barbara asked if she could come in.

"Yes," Tiffany answered.

Barbara entered, trying to be cheerful, though her expression immediately changed when she saw Tiffany. The young girl was suffering; she'd barely touched her dinner and had said little during the meal. She couldn't stop thinking about everything that had led up to the shooting and, as a result, Tiffany couldn't hide her fears.

Barbara sat next to her on the bed. "You okay?" she asked, and Tiffany looked down at the floor, biting her lower lip. Barbara wrapped her arm around her. "You want to talk about it?"

Tiffany merely shrugged.

"You can you know," Barbara said. "I know you're worried, but talking may help."

"I don't know what to say. It's everything."

"Are you unhappy here … is there—?"

"No. No. You and Mr. Bruce have been wonderful. But if they tried to kill Mr. Kapp, that means they're gonna want to kill me. I'm scared. I'm really scared." Tiffany silently whimpered, chin quivering, and Barbara pulled her closer. "And now … Mr. Kapp's been arrested. Why? What did he do?"

At these words, Barbara realized Tiffany had overheard her talking to Bruce about his father when Bruce had called after the bail hearing. Should she tell her the truth? How would she take it? How would she react? The truth held both good and bad—yes, the man who'd terrified her was now dead and could no longer hurt her, but the man who'd saved her, the one she'd come to admire and respect was likely to be in prison for a long time. Not knowing what to do, Barbara held Tiffany, stroking her hair.

Tiffany squeezed shut her eyes, still fighting back tears. "I'm so afraid. I'm afraid to lose Mr. Kapp. If he goes to jail, where … where will I go? Where could I go?"

Barbara had thought about that, too. She and Bruce had always wanted to have another child, a girl, but things hadn't worked out that way. Sometimes you didn't always get everything you wished for. The boys, being so close in age, had been more than a handful when they were babies, and while the joys had been more than numerous, the work for Barbara had been never-ending. So they'd decided to wait to try again, and the wait had proven to be the wrong decision. When they thought they were ready, trying to conceive again seemed impossible.

"You are a very brave little girl," Barbara said. "You've been through a lot. I can't even begin to imagine. I don't want you to worry. You can stay here with us for as long as you want. If I had a little girl, I'd want her to be just like you. I promise, you'll be safe here. This, if you want, could be your home.

MELVIN KAPPERNICK

AFTER HE WAS PROCESSED, Kappernick was assigned to a cell on Block D. The blocks radiated out from the guards' station like fingers, with each block containing twenty cells of ten by twelve chambers that slept four men. Each cell had two bunk beds, a toilet, and a sink.

Three other men, all black, were already there when Kappernick was let in. Two were lying in their bunks, one was on the toilet.

"Well, look what the fuck we got here," said the man on the commode. "Hey!" he yelled belligerently at the guard who'd escorted Kappernick to his new quarters. "What the fuck is this?"

"Shut up, meathead," the guard yelled back. "Gentlemen, this here is Kappernick." Then he backed out of the cell, slammed the door shut, and smiled. "Treat him with a little respect. He's in for murder."

The man on the lower bunk smoking a cigarette said, "I sure as hell hope you ain't prejudiced, brother. Murder, huh?" he added. "Guess you won't be with us long." He pointed up. "You're on top of me."

The man on the toilet quickly wiped his ass, yanked up his striped prison pants, and immediately jumped into

Kappernick's face, spitting as he cursed out a stream of profanities.

Kappernick, holding an armful of sheets and blankets, ran the sleeve of his free arm across his mouth. "Don't you think you should wash your hands?" he said, a remark that only drove Johnson into a greater rage and yet an another elongated list of profanities.

"Back off, Lonnie," shouted the man on the top bunk across from the cigarette smoker. Lonnie stopped cursing, though he circled the cell in a clenched-fisted rage.

The first man looked over at Kappernick. "Lonnie, here, has Tourette's. Sometimes when he gets going, he can't stop, you know what I mean? Name's Noles, but you can call me Zebbe. The guy that'll be sleepin' under you is Elroy Lamont. Lonnie you already met. Unlike you, we ain't murderers." Noles was young, light-complexed, with a pockmarked face. "We're all just a bunch of small-time thieves, but we look out for each other. We're a team, a cell, a unit. We gotta have each other's backs. You look out for us, we'll look out for you, you know what I mean? You help us, we'll help you. We gotta work together here as a unit, get it?" He stared at Kappernick, then asked, "You got any money?"

"Not a dime."

Noles curled his lip, "Don't bullshit me."

"What did I say?" said Kappernick, locking eyes with him. "Not a dime." Then he moved past, putting his clothes on the bunk above Lamont.

DAY 43

ON THE THIRD MORNING of his incarceration, Kappernick slid the plastic food tray down the stainless steel holder, took a plate of loosely cooked scrambled eggs from the server, then walked to an empty table, where he sat alone. His cellmates in line didn't sit with him. Instead, four other inmates, all dressed in prison greens and all African Americans, sat at his table, one to each side and two directly across. They began talking to each other as though he wasn't there.

"This fuckin' place is the worst," said the one to his right.

"This ain't no jail, man, it's a fuckin' prison."

"A bad fuckin' place."

"When was this fucker built?"

"Nineteen thirty, nineteen twenty-nine, somethin' like that."

"Yeah, it's creaky and buldgin' over-crowded."

"It's like a fuckin' city."

Every time somebody said something, somebody else had something to say in reply. Kappernick looked from one to the next as the conversation floated around. They never acknowledged him; they kept talking amongst themselves.

"Got thirty-five hundred motherfuckers in here."

"Too many by seven, eight hundred."

"It's like a goddamn city! It got everythin' a city got, and just as much crime."

"This here be one fuckin' hellhole. Any kinda shit can happen here."

Kappernick laid down his fork and stared at each of them.

"Largest, toughest motherfuckin' prison in the state."

"Shit, they got people bein' murdered in here, dyin' natural in here, goin' to school in here, gettin' stoned in here."

Still no one looked at the old man; they just talked around him.

Kappernick put ketchup on his eggs, planning to finish his food, when Mohawk Man from the paddy wagon walked over. Kappernick had seen him twice since the van had pulled through the main gate, and each time, Mohawk Man had made some threatening remarks—he was gonna get him, he was gonna fix him, all said with malice. Each time, Kappernick ignored him and moved away.

Now, the sonofabitch stood at the end of the food table, staring at him. Kappernick tensed, glaring back, and the four men stopped talking. Mohawk Man glanced at the inmates sitting around Kappernick, then spoke first.

"How you doin'?" His voice was different this time. Softer, calmer. "You got nothin' to worry about. You and me be okay. Okay?" Again he glanced at the other men, shuffling slightly from side to side. "Just wanted to let you know we okay, is all."

A short, dark-complexed man sitting at the table, his head full of kinky hair, jerked his chin at Mohawk Man, who backed away and left. Once he was gone, the four of them got up in unison and, without saying a word to Kappernick, began to leave. The curly-haired con who'd jerked his head at Mohawk Man leaned over to Kappernick and whispered, "Monroe took care of it."

Kappernick had no idea who Monroe was but whispered back, "Thank him," and the curly-haired guy nodded.

Next day, the same curly-haired man from the breakfast table came into the cell, calling for Kappernick by simply hooking his finger. No one, not even Johnson, said a word, just staring as Kappernick slowly walked over to the meet the guy.

When Kappernick was close enough, he said, "Monroe wants to see you. Come with me."

Kappernick hesitated. "I don't know no Monroe. What's he want?"

"Don't be stupid. Just come with me. You ain't got nothin' to worry about."

Kappernick reluctantly left his cell.

They walked past the guard at the lockdown and into the next tier.

Curtis Monroe had a cell as big as Kappernick's, though he was its only occupant. He sat behind a desk, where he wrote in a yellow-lined legal pad, and to his right stood a bookcase filled with volumes of law texts. Monroe wore wire-rimmed glasses and an accountant's visor, and sitting behind him was one of the talkers from the breakfast table the day before.

The curly-haired guy stood at Kappernick's side as they waited for Monroe to acknowledge them. Finally, Monroe stopped, put down his pen, and turned, removed his glasses, and studied the old man.

"Well, thank you for coming," he said, with neither playfulness nor sarcasm.

Kappernick took no chances. "Not to be disrespectful, but I don't think I had a choice." At this, Monroe smiled. "However," Kappernick added, "I am appreciative. Thank you for removing that impediment that initially wanted to do me harm."

"I'm here to help keep the peace," said Monroe. "That's one of the things I do, because of that I do have some privileges." He stood up to study Kappernick. Monroe was a big, physically imposing man in his early forties, taller than Kappernick by several inches and appearing fit. He had an ugly, jagged scar that ran from his left ear, across his cheek, and down to his chin. Bewilderment also seemed to sit in his eyes, as though not quite believing what he was seeing.

"So," he said, "you're the one who killed Ice Man. Huh. I'm surprised. Well done. They say Ice Man was one bad motherfucker."

Kappernick frowned, unable to tell if Monroe was being facetious or not. "Yeah, I'll go along with the motherfucker part, that's for sure. Right now, I'm hoping that that motherfucker wasn't a friend of yours."

"If he was, you wouldn't be here right now. No, I never liked the sonofabitch. Of course, I hadn't seen him in ten years." Monroe laughed grimly. "I never had much time for pimps."

"Can I ask why I'm here and why you helped me?"

"Fair enough." Monroe shrugged. "Why did I take time out of my busy day? First of all, I wanted to see you, size you up. I wanted to see what kind of white man you were. I wanted to see the sonofabitch who took out Ice Man. I would never have suspected you'd be as old as you are, and ... like Bruce Springsteen said in 'Dancing in the Dark': 'I'm tired of sittin' around here, tryin' to write this book.'" He looked down at the yellow pad he'd been writing on, and laughed.

Unable to control himself, Kappernick laughed, too—softly.

Then Monroe got serious. "More importantly, though, it seems people don't want you fucked up before or during your trial. After you're convicted, that'll all change, of course."

"People?"

"That's right—people. Me, personally, I don't give a shit. For me, it's just a business. I'm just doing a job, here." He clenched his teeth as if he'd just bitten something. "Just doin' a job. Well," he said, "that'll be all for now. Who knows? Maybe we'll talk again." With that, he went back to working on his book, and the curly-haired man took Kappernick back to his cell.

After Kappernick returned, Noles said, "Well, lookie here. You must be somebody! You meet with the big man?" Lamont saw Kappernick's concerned look and enlightened him. "Listen, cousin, in this place, if you wants something—anything, even somebody whacked—you go see Monroe. You want to smuggle something in? You gotta see Monroe. There's the warden"—he held out his arm, hand palm down, then raised it up over his head—"and then there's Monroe. Everything, and I mean everything, is under his control. See what I'm talkin' about?"

JESSE SPRINGER

EVEN THOUGH SPRINGER was a storyteller, he'd just lived through an experience he could never talk about. No one could ever know.

He thought about that crazy night.... Yeah, he'd have killed that sonofabitch, Ice Man, had Kappernick given him the gun. But the pain had been so intense that, after Kappernick had gotten him into the car, he could barely turn the key; just that action alone sent shots of torture through his body.

He'd wanted to go home to tell his wife, Cara, that he was okay. Instead, he'd gone to the hospital. The dirty spike that fuck had hammered into his hand had probably had so many germs on it Springer worried the doctors might have to amputate. He, Springer, who washed his hands twenty times a day, who rarely ever shook hands with anyone else, who suffered from a mild form of mysophobia, a fear of germs, had had his fucking hand nailed to a table! Spot Lite might have been old, but it was spotless; Jesse spent big money to make sure it was.

Yes, that spike might have been brutal, but being in that filthy alleyway with an open wound had been psychologically devastating. And crawling over all of that crap to get out of there? Worst of all. He'd had to use his injured hand to climb up that mountain of shit. Howling in pain, he'd managed to endure, though.

He'd thought of Cara. What would he tell her? He'd never imagined anything like this, had never been in trouble. He'd always walked the straight and narrow, and now it looked like everything was going to collapse. Jesus Christ, what had he been thinking? He wasn't a kid anymore. He had a wife, kids, grandkids. Kappernick had said he didn't want him involved, so why hadn't he just walked away? Why hadn't he said: "Okay, old buddy. You do what you gotta do, but I'm not going to be part of it." But he hadn't. Fear of disrespect had compelled him to be a part of it. Stupid fuck!

Thank God Kappernick had been there in the end. They would have killed him, for sure. Shoot his brains out. They'd grabbed him before Kappernick and that crazy Perkins guy had ever done anything. What had made him think they wouldn't? Who did he think he was, fucking Elliot Ness?

Springer had almost passed out from the pain when his car had bounced over a pothole. Leaving his vehicle in the drive-in circle at the hospital, he'd staggered into the emergency room, yelling for help. A nurse and intern had worked on him for an hour, and when the resident doctor saw his hand, he'd almost passed out.

"What the hell happened to you?" he'd asked, and Springer had told him he'd been working on a car.

"When did this happen?" asked the intern.

"Just a little while ago," Springer had replied.

The intern hadn't believed him. "Looks like this happened more than a *little* while ago."

"Yeah, I might have passed out from the pain," Springer had told them. "I don't remember. Do you have anything for the pain, doc?"

Springer had made it home by four in the morning, where Cara had been waiting up, both relived and pissed. Questions kept flying, and Springer had just wanted to go to bed, to be left alone. After forty-five years of marriage and working together, though, she wouldn't let him. Tomorrow, he'd pleaded. But it was no good. Finally, he'd said, "I passed out and fell on my head, unconscious, and lay for hours in an alley. A dirty, stinking alley! That's why I smell the way I do. My Hand? You want to know about my hand? A rat bit it! A big, fat fucking rat bit my fucking hand!"

Cara's mouth had dropped open. "Really?" she said tenderly, like: *Oh, you poor thing.* Then, moments later, her eyebrows had knitted as if she'd tried to sort out facts. Then she'd let out a quizzical, "Really?" She'd shoved her hands onto her hips and hissed out another, now disdainful, "Really!"

"Jesus H. Christ!" Springer had shouted. "What the fuck do you have to do? I can't talk about it now, all right? I need to get some sleep. I promise I'll tell you all about it tomorrow."

Cara had calmed down, though tears welled up in her eyes. "It's just that I was worried," she'd said. "Worried sick. And this the first time all these years you'd ever lied to me."

"All right," he'd said. "I'm sorry. Tomorrow. I'll tell you tomorrow, please. I promise."

❦

The next morning, Springer told Cara the whole story, and much to his amazement, she listened calmly and nodded.

He told her about Kappernick and how they'd met when they were kids; how Old Lady Teabloom had given him his first job, had trusted him, encouraged him to do the right thing. He related the events when Kappernick had first come into The Spot Lite, how he'd moved back into that terrible, broken-down street, and how they'd become friends again. And then, he told her about the night they'd taken him and what had occurred in the alley.

"Is he dead?" Cara asked.

"Oh, he's dead."

"Do you think this Mel will keep you out of it?"

A worried look ran across Springer's face. "I don't know."

"What do you plan to do?"

"Nothing. Hold my breath. Wait. See what happens."

"What about The Spot Lite?"

"Put a sign on the door saying we're on vacation."

"Do you think that's smart?" she asked. "Don't you think we ought to go on as usual, as if nothing happened, as if we're not involved?"

And that's what Springer loved about Cara. She'd always been his woman, and he'd always been her man. It was never just "him," it was always "we."

"I need time," he said. "I want to lie in bed for a week and see what happens."

A week later, they were back in business. Two weeks later, Perkins came into The Spot Lite and Springer bought him a beer. They exchanged looks, yet never said a word about Ice Man's death or Kappernick's incarceration.

SASHA RICHARDS

SASHA RICHARDS WAS EXCITED—her cell phone was blowing up! As acting executive director of the Philadelphia chapter of Black Lives Matter, she'd been besieged by several hundred text messages, and the news was all over Twitter Facebook. Everyone was talking about a White man having killed an influential African American male in West Philadelphia. Supposedly, the victim had been dragged into an alleyway and shot three times, and in Sasha's mind, this was almost like a lynching. Her job was to step up protests and to let important people know those who'd provoked these protests were irate. Nationally, young Black men were still being shot and beaten by the police—the armed, mostly White force who protected the elite, White middle class.

Sasha immediately called Reverend Joshua Clanton Miles to tell him that her BLM chapter was about to organize a march. Since the days of Selma, nothing had changed. Back then, the cause, the movement, and the tactics used against the establishment had been motivated by the elders, the leaders, and the church. No longer. Social media had created this transformation, and now inspiration for change came from the bottom up, instead of from the top down. Youth was now the driving force.

When Reverend Miles answered the phone, Sasha asked if he'd heard the news.

"News?" he said. "No. I didn't see the papers yet. I usually read it with my morning coffee. What news?"

"The newspapers are usually the last to know," she said.

"Really?"

Sasha ignored the reverend's apparent astonishment and instead related to him what had happened to the citizen in the alleyway not far from his parish. "This has to stop!" she yelled, her voice roaring through his phone as though she stood at the pulpit, sermonizing. "We must march! Protest! Let them know we won't tolerate that kind of thing here!" In essence, the reverend agreed. Even though blatant police brutality hadn't been happening lately in Philadelphia, decent citizens were still being harassed, stopped for no reason, searched without cause, and denied basic rights.

"What will the purpose of the march be?" he asked. "Seems to me our police are bending over backwards to do the right thing."

"Yes, but that won't last," she replied. "You and I both know that. We can't let things calm down, and we can't let them go to sleep. We can't let our White *brothers* forget we're watching them. A strong show of support is what's called for. Next time anything happens, anywhere—anywhere at all— we will march. We will protest! I'm just letting you know we need your support."

Reverend Miles nodded. Had she been praying for something like this to happen? Then he asked her to wait a minute as his assistant brought in the morning paper. He turned to the LOCAL section and scanned down to the right hand side of the paper where the headline read: White Man Kills Two African Americans in West Philadelphia Alley.

The reverend's lip curled. That son of a bitch shot two

Black brothers in an alley. Gunned them down. What the hell was a White man doing in a Black neighborhood? he wondered. What the hell was he doing in an alley? He'd basically lynched them. Maybe he was a cop? Hell, he must have been a cop. Is that purpose enough for you, Miles?

Normally, two Black men getting shot in a Black ghetto alleyway wouldn't make the front papers; it was almost non-news—it was, and always had been a daily occurrence for many, many years. Unfortunately, over that span of time, Blacks killing Blacks had made up the majority of the murder rate. In this year alone there'd been 247 homicides in the City of Brotherly Love, with still two months left to go! And even that staggering figure was, unbelievably, on a downward trend!

But this story had made the news. A White man killing two Black men had made the front page of the Philadelphia Inquirer's LOCAL section for one reason alone: because a White man had perpetrated the crime. And he hadn't even tried to hide it, almost arrogantly turning himself in. He'd confessed! Had he voluntarily turned himself in because he thought he might not be punished? That the police would go easy on him? That Black lives didn't matter?

Sasha was right—they needed to protest.

Reverend Miles circled the story in red with a magic marker. He had to give credit where credit was due. Sasha's organization had made this possible. By picketing, marching, sitting-in, badgering reporters and cursing elected officials—doing all of the necessary things to call attention to Black people being treated unfairly, and that Black lives did, in fact, matter.

Things changed so quickly these days, and it made his head spin. These days, young people like Sasha aroused the citizens enough to incite change. The reverend snickered at his own sarcasm. Being a man of God, he didn't want anyone to die, of course, but nothing put a charge in the African

American community like police violence or the murder of an African American by a White man.

Reverend Miles picked up his desk phone and, spinning his Rolodex, dialed the number of Calvin Michaels.

CALVIN MICHAELS

CALVIN P. MICHAELS had been the City of Philadelphia's District Attorney for three years. Having graduated from Temple University Law School in the early nineties, he was recruited by the city's Department of Justice immediately after he received his degree. Michaels worked hard and, by doing so, he'd made his way to the top echelon of his peers in handling major cases; he was considered one of the best prosecutors ever elected in Philadelphia—respected, hard-nosed, and dedicated. Michaels was a native Philadelphian, born in the West Philly section of the city, third son of hardworking parents—his mother cleaned houses, and his father worked as a cook in an all-night burger joint. He was the first in his family to graduate from college, which already made him a hero, and as if that wasn't enough, he became an attorney. When he signed on to be the city's prosecutor, he moved out of his old, decrepit neighborhood and into the posh section of Chestnut Hill.

When his secretary, Paige Parks, had entered the office to tell him that Reverend Miles was on the phone, Michaels had been studying a work chart, assigning new cases to his staff. He considered whether or not to take the call. When he was doing this particular chore, he didn't like taking calls and his secretary knew this. But the reverend was an important ally, albeit a pain-in-the-ass, though a pain-in-the-ass he needed. The reverend had helped him to get elected, and a new election was right around the corner.

He nodded to Ms. Parks, then picked up the phone.

DAY 44

OFFICER ELLISON, one of the day guards on Kappernick's block came to his cell one day and called out, "You got a visitor!" Kappernick assumed it was either his son, Bruce, or Weisman. Both had already been there twice—Weisman wanting to go over details and a strategy; Bruce, being the dutiful son, and not really knowing what to say, trying to support them. Kappernick was happy for any diversion from the utter, perpetual boredom of the four men in the twelve-by-twelve cell. Conversation, for the most part, was inane, and it seemed that when they weren't eating, they were crapping, and when they weren't crapping, they were listening to someone else trying to crap.

As he walked through the block in his baggy, orange prison jumpsuit, Kappernick wondered what was up. Both his attorney and his son had been there the day before, so he was totally surprised—no, shocked—when Linda Lansky was sitting at one of the visitor tables, waiting for him. Seeing her filled Kappernick with an unexpected pang of shame, and for a brief moment, he hesitated, lowered his eyes, and almost turned away. She didn't need to see him like this. Still, Kappernick took a deep breath, forced a smile, and gave her a half-wave. In the prison reception room's stark surroundings, she looked beautiful, wearing a soft, light beige cashmere sweater highlighted by a multi-colored silk scarf.

Kappernick walked over and sat down across from her. "Hi," he said, and she smiled. "What are you doing here?"

She blinked. "Well, I was just passing through, on my way to the supermarket, and I thought I'd stop by. What do you think I'm doing here? I came to see you."

But all he could think to say was, "Isn't there school today?"

"Yes. I haven't done it in years, but I took the day off."

"Really? Why?"

"To be honest, I've been thinking about you. Like you once said to me, you kinda got under my skin." Linda's gaze dropped to her hands. "You've been in my thoughts, Mel. I think about you every time I look at that big goofy dog you left on my porch."

"I'm sorry. I had no other place to leave him. I—"

"No, don't apologize. Truth is, I've grown to love him. I haven't the slightest idea why, but I do. And he loves me. It's a pure love. Totally unconditional. He makes me wonder why I never had a dog before." She laughed and, reaching across the table, touched the back of Kappernick's hand. "But I think he misses you. And … he's not alone."

At that moment, Kappernick wanted to hold her. Wanted to take her into his arms and just hold her—feel her body, touch her hair, kiss her lips. Instead, he ground his teeth and swallowed hard, at first looking at her with deep affection until his eyes glazed over in sadness.

"What is it?" she said.

"I think he'd better get used to missing me, because I don't think there's much of a chance of our getting together again."

They talked for the full allotment of thirty minutes. Most of the conversation was about Tiffany.

"She's such a good kid," Kappernick said. "I keep thinking, not about what happened at the zoo, but what happened before that a-hole tried to kill me. I keep thinking about how she wanted to be next to me for the picture. It was almost the perfect day, wasn't it? How's she doing?"

"I see her every day. Barbara brings her in and picks her up. When school lets out, Barbara's always waiting. I think your daughter-in-law's a fantastic lady. We've become good friends."

"You know, I was stupid. I never really appreciated her. Never gave her a chance."

The guard tapped his shoulder. "Kappernick. Time's up."

Kappernick stood. "I gotta go. I appreciate your coming, more than you'll ever know. Like I said before, you got under my skin, and nothing's changed. I wish things could have worked out differently."

"Can I come again?"

Kappernick shook his head, unable to quite word his thoughts. "No," he finally said. "Under the circumstances, I don't think that would be such a good idea. Thanks so much for coming today, though."

Linda Lansky watched him turn toward the prison door, and as the guard escorted him away, she whispered, "Goodbye."

TRIAL –DAY 1

THE CRIMINAL JUSTICE CENTER (CJC) at 1300 Filbert Street was a uniquely chaotic place with about twenty or more cases going on every day, many of which are filled with a lot of family members who often disrupted the proceedings. Homicide cases were usually more composed than drug cases, but the overall atmosphere was still pretty crazy.

Kappernick's trial opened on a Monday, three months after he'd been taken to Graterford. The proceedings began promptly at 9:00 a.m., and immediately the sides started with selecting a jury. The presiding judge, the Honorable Lawrence J. Harvey, had been on the bench for almost thirty years. A fair man who listened and who, for the most part, wasn't afraid to hand down stiff sentences. His courtroom was rarely ever chaotic; it simply wasn't tolerated. Right from the start, the gallery was crowded for the Kappernick trial, which initially surprised both the defense and the prosecution ... until DA Michaels spotted Sasha Richards sitting front and center. She'd made sure the courtroom was packed. Stacked the deck, so to speak. The case had only received moderate press coverage, and that had annoyed her, no doubt. And she knew, too, that her presence would keep Michaels on his toes.

The DA smiled briefly and confidently at her. No way would he lose this case; it was a no-brainer. From the corner of his eye he watched Sasha move over next to a reporter for the Philadelphia Inquirer. Michaels went back to his notes, though he couldn't stop thinking of Richards and how, in Sasha's mind, Blacks could kill Blacks, Blacks could kill Whites, but woe to the White man who killed a Black. She threw Caucasians and police into the same garbage can. Although he knew she'd never admit it, Sasha was of the opinion that law enforcement protect only the White community. She'd grown up in a small Georgian town where it'd been rumored (though never proven) that the sheriff's office had been part of some beatings and disappearances of some Black kids. Michaels remembered Sasha bellowing out at an event held at an African American church: "We are not ever going back to that again!" That night, she'd been a tough act to follow. Her passion had been explosive.

By the end of the trial's second day—at 3:15, to be exact—the jury had been chosen. The panel, broken down by race and ethnicity, consisted of seven African-Americans, four Caucasians, and one Latino. Weisman was neither delighted nor disappointed; he wasn't sure how the Black community would react to what Kappernick had done. As usual, it'd be up to him, Weisman, to convey the right message. Could he convince the jury that what the old man had done was not only in self-defense, but, in essence, also good for their community? That's how he planned to present his case. Given that seven African-Americans sat on the panel, would it have made a difference if he, Kappernick, had been black? Of course it would have.

Opening arguments began early on the third day. Weisman sat at the defense table, wearing a black pinstripe suit and a light gray tie. Kappernick sat next to him, dressed also in a dark suit and tie, and then Bruce, dressed in a light gray suit and dark tie, acted as second chair. Michaels sat in the first chair at the prosecution table, and next to him was his most trusted deputy, Assistant DA, William P. Meede. It was very unusual for both to be part of the same trial.

At nine thirty, Judge Harvey pounded his gavel and called on the DA to begin his opening statement. Michaels stood, checked his notes, then walked before the jury. "Ladies and Gentlemen, you are about to sit in judgment of a man who committed a vicious, cold-blooded crime. The state is asking that you return a verdict of first-degree murder, for that is what the defendant did. He murdered his victims without mercy. And there is no question he'd done it—he confessed, voluntarily—nor is there any question that it was heinous, despicable, and purely cold-blooded. The defense will try to tell you his client had no choice, how it was a case of self-defense. Don't you believe it. We will show you how he planned it—how every step, every move he made had been calculated; how he'd waited in the dark to kill these men.

"The first man, Ruby Brown, was shot twice. Brown was just left to die like a dog, then finally died of a heart attack while waiting for help. It must have been a slow, agonizing death. Then, he assassinated the second victim, Barton Berk, a pharmacist. First, he shot Berk in the arm, then almost, demonically, in the groin."

Michaels drew in a deep breath, sadly shaking his head for effect, then looked up at each juror whose eyes were glued on him. "And then finally, at close range," he went on, "he shot the victim in the head! He assassinated him. We are asking that you find this killer, this murderer, the defendant, Melvin Kappernick, guilty of murder in the first degree. Thank you."

When the DA took his seat, Weisman stood and walked over to the jury box. "The District Attorney is eloquent," he said to them. "He certainly does have a way with words. He almost described exactly how my client, the defendant, shot and killed Ruby Brown and Barton Berk, only … he left out the motive. Why did Melvin Kappernick do it? What was his motive? Why would a man who's never even had a traffic ticket; a war hero, a man who received the navy cross; a man who'd worked hard all his life, and who helped to raise a family, was married to the same woman for forty-five years, do such a thing! The motive, my friends, was self-defense. Mr. Kappernick had no alternative! I repeat, Mr. Kappernick had no alternative! And that's what we shall show.

"Now," he added, "let's talk about the place where this incident had occurred. It took place in a filthy, littered, junk-laden alley! And who exactly were these men? Well, for one, Mr. Ruby Brown had a prison record as long as his arm, and he was no stranger to violence. From the time he was twelve, he'd been arrested no less than twenty-two times, incarcerated four different times, and had spent time in major prisons for a total of eleven years. He'd been convicted of armed robbery, assault, and manslaughter, and when his body was found, he'd had a forty-five caliber revolver in his possession.

"The other man, Barton Berk, aka Ice Man, the real villain in this case, had indeed been a pharmacist by day, but he was also a pimp, a drug dealer, and a killer by night, and when his body was found, he'd had a forty-five caliber revolver in his possession, as well, one that had already fired off three shots. So, let's not think that the two slain men in this incident were upstanding citizens, because they were not. They were, in fact, vicious criminals.

"What Mr. Kappernick had done was, in fact, a service to the community. What Mr. Kappernick had done had saved the taxpayers thousands and thousands of dollars. Mr. Kappernick should, by all intents and purposes, be considered a hero."

TRIAL—DAY 4

THE DISTRICT ATTORNEY called Police Sargent Joseph Bailey to the stand. "Sargent Bailey," he said, "you are the desk Sargent at the thirty-fifth, is that correct?"

"Yes."

"You were on duty the night the defendant surrendered himself?"

"Yes, I was."

"Tell us, to the best of your memory, exactly what happened."

"Well, he simply entered the precinct and said, 'Excuse me, officer. My name is Melvin Kappernick and I just shot two men.' Well, I looked at him, and he's standing there as calm as a cucumber. 'Are those men dead?' I asked, and he tells me 'They are.' Then I asked where he perpetrated the crime, and he tells me, and I sent out two men. They found the bodies right where the defendant, there, said they were. Simple as that."

"Where was that?"

"In an alley behind Fortieth Street."

"And who were the dead men?"

"Ruby Brown and Barton Berk."

"Thank you. That will be all." He turned to Weisman. "Your witness."

Weisman stood and, leaning forward, placed his hands on the defendant's table. "Officer Bailey, how long have you been on the force?"

"It'll be seventeen years."

"At the desk?"

"Nearly fourteen years."

"I guess you've seen and heard just about everything."

"You could say that again."

"In all your years, how many times has someone come in and voluntarily confessed to shooting someone?"

"Just one. The defendant was the first."

"Did you ask him who he shot?"

"I did."

"And what did he say?"

"He said he didn't know one guy's name, but the other guy was a guy he called 'Ice Man.'"

"Ice man? Who was he? Was there a third guy?"

"No. Ice Man was a street name for Barton Berk."

"Objection, Your Honor!" Michaels called out. "What is the relevance? Nickname or no, the defendant killed Barton Berk."

"Overruled. I'll allow."

Weisman rubbed his chin. "Hmm ... So Berk was Ice Man and Ice Man was Barton Berk."

"Yes."

"Had you ever heard of Ice Man?"

"Yes. Over the years he'd been brought in for questioning several times. Never held."

"Objection!" Michaels called out again. "The fact that the deceased had another name is of little importance. He was killed in cold blood."

"Your Honor, please."

"Overruled."

"Do you know why he was questioned?"

"Objection! Conjecture!"

"Sustained."

"Well," Weisman said, "usually when people are brought in for questioning, it isn't as if they were running a charity bake sale, am I right?" He paused long enough to get the laugh, and just before the DA could object, he added, "No further questions."

Next, the DA called John Eckerson, the detective who'd headed the team that had entered the alley where the bodies had been found.

"Yes," he answered the DA's first question, "they were exactly where the defendant had said they'd be." To the next question, he replied, "Later that night, he reiterated he'd shot the two, Berk and Brown."

"Your witness," said Michaels.

Weisman stood, holding up a copy of the confession. "Detective Eckerson, this the strangest confession I've ever seen. What else did he say?"

"Not a thing."

"Didn't you ask him why, how?"

The detective snorted. "Of course we did. All we could get out of him was that he'd killed two men in the alley at approximately ten-fifteen. That's all he would say."

"How long was that session?"

"We gri … talked to him for three hours. I actually pleaded with him. I said, 'Since you're confessing, why not tell us why you did it?' Nothing worked. Then, we tried to use the decease's' real names, but he wouldn't sign that. He'd only sign it if we included the name Ice Man."

The next witness was a surprise to the defense.

The DA looked at Weisman as he said, "I call Darnell Perkins to the stand."

Perkins entered the courtroom, but before he passed the wooden rail separating the gallery from the trial floor, Weisman, after scanning the papers on the table, queried the judge. "Your Honor," he said in utter bewilderment, "I don't see this man's name on the list of proposed witnesses given to me by the prosecution."

Judge Harvey checked his own documents and agreed that Mr. Perkins' name was not on the list. He scowled up at the DA.

"Step forward, gentlemen," he said, and both Michaels and Weisman approached the bench.

"Your Honor," Michaels whispered, "this witness appeared at our offices yesterday after Your Honor had ended the session. I believe his testimony is essential and will further show the extent of just how premeditated this crime was. We could postpone for a few days to give the defense time to prepare, if that is your wish, but I now consider this witness's testimony of the utmost importance."

Judge Harvey ground his teeth. "This is highly unusual, Mr. Michaels. What say you, Mr. Weisman? Should we hold up the proceedings for twenty-four hours to give you time to depose?"

"If you please, Your Honor, that may not be necessary. Just give a few minutes to confer with my client."

Judge Harvey gave his consent, and Michaels returned to the defense table while Weisman conferred with Kappernick for several minutes. Then he returned to the bench.

"Your Honor, after conferring with my client, and to expedite things, we will consent to allow this surprise witness to testify today, on the condition that the prosecution allows me to call a surprise witness that is not on my list."

Michaels frowned. "Who would that be?"

Weisman smiled. "It's a surprise."

Judge Harvey let out a low laugh. "What say you, Mr. Michaels?"

Perturbed, Michaels reluctantly agreed.

Perkins, who'd been waiting at the rail for the question of his testimony to be resolved, held his head high. Kappernick, who, up until that point had been stoic to anything during the trial, turned to study Perkins. Darnell did not look at his old lieutenant; rather, he stared intently at the attorneys arguing in whispers at the bench. He wore an old, careworn army dress uniform, and his black military dress shoes were scuffed. His dress military cap had been folded in the epaulette of his left shoulder.

When the attorneys had returned to their respective benches, Perkins was called forward and sworn in. He took a seat in the witness box and smiled at the District Attorney, who approached him.

"Mr. Perkins, you know the defendant, Melvin Kappernick?"

"That is correct."

"You like him?"

"Yes, sir."

"How did you meet?"

"He was the officer assigned to the squad I was in in 'nam, Vietnam, sir. He saved my life—put me on his back when I was hit and carried me to safety."

"Would it be fair to say you are indebted to him, that you owe him?"

"That is correct."

"You understand that you're under oath."

"That is correct."

"You are here of your own free will?"

"That is correct."

"You voluntarily came into my office yesterday and told

me of your involvement in the case that is now on trial."

"That is correct."

"Did you shoot Martin Mobley and Timothy Savage outside of a building at ten twenty-one North Fortieth Street?"

"I don't know their names, but I did shoot two men outside of a building on Fortieth Street. Got 'em in the knees."

"Where were you when you shot them?"

"In an empty third-floor apartment across the street."

"How did you get there?"

"The captain showed me the way. We were lucky the place was empty."

"Captain? Who's the captain?"

"The Lieutenant"—Perkins pointed at Kappernick—"he showed me the way, through a back alley."

"The defendant."

"That is correct."

"Did he give you the rifle that you used to gun down those two men on Fortieth Street?"

"That is correct."

"Did he tell you to shoot those men?"

"That is correct."

"And you did it?"

"That is correct."

"So you conspired with the defendant to shoot those two men."

"You mean, did we talk about it prior to that night?"

"Yes."

"No, we did not."

"What? What do you mean? You just told me that the defendant told you to shoot those two men."

"That's right. But we didn't conspire. He told me to do it, and I did. He told me that night, about a half-hour before."

The DA whispered, cursing under his breath, not trying to hide his contempt, then turned to Weisman. "Your witness."

Weisman stood immediately at his table and smiled. "Mr. Perkins, you have testified that you are here of your own free will. But I'm a little puzzled." Weisman rubbed his chin. "Why would you come in here and, under oath, admit that you shot two men?"

"Well, originally, I'd wanted to help the captain," said Perkins. "But now I see I was wrong."

"I don't understand."

"I came here to tell it like it is."

"I'm listening."

"You see"—Perkins turned to the jury—"we was at war. I'm talking about 'nam. We took fire, and we gave it back. We ran into some rotten people in 'nam. Bad people. People who killed people, forced them to do things they didn't want to do. If they wasn't mean and bad, why else would we have been there?"

Weisman remained silent. Michaels tried to interject, but the judge waved him off.

"Well, we're still at war," Perkins said, "right here in the old U.S. of A., but no one admits it. And no, it's not a race thing; it's not White against Black or Black on Black. It's about good on bad. Why is there so much killing in the ghetto? Because no one is shooting the bad guys. And when they do shoot a bad guy, everybody's bitchin' and yellin'! Captain Kappernick is one of the good guys! Ice Man, he—"

"Objection!"

"Overruled. I want to hear this."

"He's an Uncle Tom!" someone yelled out from the gallery, followed by several other shouts that repeated the same reference to the old slave who saved little Eva in the novel *Uncle Tom's Cabin.*

Judge Harvey banged his gavel. "Order! Order, in the court! If I hear any more of that, I will clear this courtroom!"

"No, sir, I ain't no Uncle Tom," Perkins said directly to the man who'd yelled at him from the gallery. "If I was an Uncle Tom, I'd be like you—just yellin' and doin' nothin'. But I'm just tellin' it like it is. It's like the Wild West out there—if somebody tries to kill you, wants to kill you, swears to kill you, you gotta defend yourself."

"Did the defendant ask you to kill those two men?"

"No. He said he just wanted me to shoot them in the legs, make it so they couldn't walk. He was adamant about that."

"Didn't the defendant tell you that he didn't want your help, that he didn't want you to get involved?"

"That is correct. But I demanded that I go along. I felt I had an obligation."

"To Kappernick?"

"No. To the community! I'm no Bill Cosby."

"Bill Cosby?"

"Yeah, he goes around tellin' people to give back to the community, but he, himself, don't. This was my way of givin' back."

Weisman nodded. "No further questions."

The DA jumped to his feet. "Your Honor, may I?"

"Do it."

"Why didn't you call the police?" Michaels asked, and Perkins started to laugh.

"That's funny," he said.

Incensed, Michaels glared at Perkins. "You think it's funny?"

"That is correct. What're they gonna do? Just last week, the tenants in the building I live in heard something in the basement. Sounded like someone was prowling around down there. We called the police, and about three hours later, the boys in blue showed up to look down the dark cellar stairs from the top of the landing. The bulb must've blown out, because it was *real* dark down there. 'Ain'tcha goin' down?' the guy who lived on the second floor asked, and the biggest cop said, 'Hell no, I ain't goin' down there!' then they left. They never did go down."

Perkins giggled, then fell silent, thoughtful. "There was a time when a beat cop might have helped, but those days are long gone."

"I didn't ask for your *learned* opinion," Michaels snapped sarcastically.

"Oh, excuse me, I thought you did," said Perkins with such genuine sincerity on his face, the gallery laughed loudly.

"Your Honor," Weisman said, "the DA seems to be badgering his own surprise witness." And this remark provoked more laughter.

The judge, however, was not amused. He banged his gavel, demanding silence.

Annoyed, Michaels spat out at Perkins, "Have you ever been arrested?"

"No, I have not," Perkins replied.

"Really?" The DA curled his lip, unable to help himself, well aware that an emotional display would work against the prosecution. But his guts were churning. He'd made a stupid mistake, not thoroughly vetting Perkins before calling him. Perkins had been the key in proving that Kappernick's act was premeditated, so much so, that he, Michaels, had rushed in. And now he hated himself for it. "Well," he now said to Perkins, "all that is about to change. Are you ready to go to jail? Do you know you just confessed to a crime?"

Perkins nodded. "That is correct. But you'd promised me immunity if I came in today and told my story. That's what you said."

Once again the gallery snickered, while Meede leaned over and whispered into Michaels' ear. Michaels smiled. "Mr. Perkins," he said, "what do you do? How do you make a living?"

"Well, I do get some Social Security. I'm old enough."

"How do you make extra money?"

Perkins shrugged as if, at last, he'd been caught, as if the truth was finally being revealed. "I steal things," he said. "I'm a petty thief."

"What kind of things do you steal?"

"Suitcases from bus stations."

"So you admit it."

Perkins blinked, seeming offended. "That is correct. I'm a thief, not a liar."

The DA turned to the defense table in dismay, and then immediately turned back to Perkins. "Did the defense counselor put you up to this? Did you meet with him before you came to my office? Did you ever meet him before today?"

"No, sir."

"No more questions."

Judge Harvey spoke up. "Let's have a psychological done on this man before we charge Mr. Perkins." After Perkins left the witness stand, he stopped at the defense table to salute Kappernick. Kappernick nodded and smiled.

So far, the trial proved unusual. No depositions were ever taken—the police had done nothing wrong, so no reason to get them on record; and Kappernick had given himself up, signed a weird confession without any details. Initially, the DA thought the case would be cut and dried. A cakewalk. Now, that was no longer so. And Michaels had been more than a little surprised when Weisman proceeded to go directly to trial. Normally, a defense attorney would waiver the forty-five days required for criminal cases to go to court, because they needed more time to prepare. But Weisman had been ready to go and hadn't asked for an extension. Now, the prosecution rested its case, and the judge ended the day's proceedings. "We'll start with witnesses for the defense first thing tomorrow morning."

TRIAL – DAY 4

WEISMAN ROSE AND LOOKED over at the bench where the District Attorney sat. "I call Calvin Patrick Michaels."

Michaels stared back at Weisman, gave a short laugh, then whispered under his breath, "You're crazy."

Judge Harvey raised his eyebrows. "You're calling the District Attorney?"

"Your Honor, please," moaned the DA in disgust. "This is ridiculous. He's calling me as a defense witness? How could I help his case?"

"I just want to ask you a few questions," Weisman said. "It might indeed hurt my case, but as long as you answer truthfully, I'll take my chances."

"I can't talk about the information that the department has—"

"This has nothing to do with department information. I'd just like to get your perspective, as an African American. I mean, I certainly could bring in a series of people to develop a picture, but that would take days, and we could do away with all of that in just a matter of minutes, if you agree."

Reluctantly, Michaels took the stand.

Weisman smiled. "Trust me, this won't hurt."

Michaels laughed. "Do I have your word on that?"

"Now, you're originally from Philadelphia and, as a matter of fact, were born close to Parkside Avenue, am I correct?" asked Weisman. "Not far from the murder scene?"

"Yes, I was. I was born at 4014 Wyalussing Street, about five blocks away."

"Did you live there for a long time?"

"My family lived in that house until I was seventeen."

"Let's see, you're forty-five now, so that's twenty-eight years ago."

"That's about right."

"Did you enjoy growing up on Wyalussing Street?"

"Your Honor …"

"Get to it, Mr. Weisman, please," said the judge.

"Just a couple more questions, Your Honor." Weisman turned back to Michaels. "Did you like your old neighborhood, Mr. Michaels?"

The DA gave an annoyed response. "Yes, I did. The park was close by. I had a lot of friends. I liked my school."

"Why did your parents move away?"

Michaels saw where Weisman was going. "I don't know, you'll have to ask them. I think they wanted a new house."

"Now, you say you liked growing up there, had a lot of friends there. After you moved away, how often did you go back to your old neighborhood, go see your old friends?"

"I don't know."

"Other than this case, when was the last time you were back there?"

The DA glared but remained silent.

Weisman answered for him. "That long, eh? Did you ever think about buying a house and living there?"

"Are you trying to be funny?"

"I'll take that as a 'no.' One last question: Has the neighborhood changed since you were a kid?"

"Yes."

"Drastically?"

"Yes."

"Would you not live there now because it's become dangerous; so dangerous, in fact, that you would fear for your family and your kids?"

Weisman's opening argument was all about alternatives. His client, Melvin Kappernick, a man who wanted to live in peace, a man who'd never been arrested, an honored war veteran, was not guilty because he had no alternative. He killed—no, assassinated—Ice Man, aka Barton Berk, because he had no alternative. He killed Berk in self-defense. Berk, Ice Man, had tried to kill him and failed, and his client had feared for the lives of his family and his loved ones.

On that first meeting in the stark room of the 36th Precinct, as Kappernick talked, Weisman started to hear it. Started to hear how he'd tell it to the jury, and for the next six weeks, it streamed through his head.

The old man's story would become Weisman's story; he'd tell it over and over again, like a mantra—driving to and from work, eating lunch, watching television; it would always be with him. He had to know it so cold, so perfectly, that he'd be able to recite it like a poem he'd memorized. And his delivery had to be impeccable, for he'd learned early on that his job was to mesmerize the jury, to entice them in such a cunning and interesting way, they'd want to listen, want to think. The words, no matter how important, no matter how succinct, weren't as important as the delivery. Weisman was a great actor as well as a superb attorney, but he first and foremost considered himself a storyteller. Every innuendo, every nod, every wink of the eye, every outrage had been planned for the benefit of the jury. So when Weisman stood in front of them, his whole focus was on winning.

Now, after six grueling days of the trial, Weisman studied the man sitting next to him at the defense table, regretting the promise he'd made at their first meeting. Just after twenty minutes at that first meeting, Weisman had looked at Kappernick in disgust, putting his pen down on the legal pad. "Look, Mr. Kappernick," he'd said, "I'm here as a favor to your son, but please don't bullshit me. I don't buy it. I can't defend you unless you tell me the whole story. Why would this guy you call Ice Man want to kill you? What did you do to him?"

"I can't tell you."

"Then I'm out of here."

"Dad, please."

Kappernick looked at his son. "What the hell's going on here, Bruce?"

"Dad. Tell him. Tell him why. If you don't, I will."

"I don't want her involved. It would ruin her life."

"Is this about a woman?" Weisman asked.

"No. No. It's about a girl, a little girl. But you have to promise me you won't get her involved. She's a good kid, and she's in a good place right now."

Weisman had suddenly become fascinated. "Why don't you just tell me the whole damn story, then?"

So, after hearing Kappernick's story, he'd made the promise he was now regretting. He'd sworn not to involve her, because he thought for sure the prosecution would ask the same "why" questions and find her. Once they'd found her, it'd be them who'd involve her, not him, and he, Weisman, would then have to come to her defense, making his promise null and void.

But the prosecution hadn't done their job. They didn't care why Kappernick had done it. They didn't want to know why. They were so sure of a conviction, and they didn't want to soil Barton Berk, so they mistakenly hadn't done their homework.

So Weisman had gone about his own business, methodically building his case. He'd established who Kappernick was—a peaceful man who just wanted to live in his boyhood home. He'd shown the jury that Ruby Brown and Barton Berk were basically hoodlums who'd been in the alley with weapons and had fired shots; they'd wanted to kill Kappernick. He'd called the two men that Perkins had shot to establish that they were part of Ice Man's gang, and that the house they'd been coming out of was basically a whorehouse. He'd been hoping to get them to reveal more, to mention Springer and the girl, but they hadn't, and that frustrated Weisman. He'd also called Bruce Kappernick to the stand to talk about what had happened at the zoo. After that, he'd called Roger Reese and his employee, Harry Frye, who'd testified that a car belonging to one of the men Perkins had shot had passed by Bruce's house several times in the wee hours of the morning.

By the time he'd done all of those things, Weisman realized he had a real chance of saving his client. Only one thing was lacking—the jury needed something else to solidify what they felt. He sensed that they, like himself at that first meeting with his client, wanted to know why Ice Man had wanted Kappernick dead. Why had he tried to kill the old man? What had Kappernick done? Was he secretly a drug dealer trying to take over Ice Man's turf? Was it blackmail? What did Kappernick know, what was he hiding, and why shouldn't they send him to death row?

Now, they were at a crossroads. At this point, Weisman

could rest his case, or call his client to testify, or he could …

Judge Harvey thought he was taking too long and coughed a couple of times. "Counselor?"

"Your Honor," Weisman said, "could we have a fifteen-minute recess so I could talk to my client?"

ARNOLD WEISMAN

THE DEFENSE GATHERED in a room five doors down from the trial courtroom. They were escorted there by a guard who unlocked the windowless chamber, allowed them to enter, then stood outside waiting for them to conclude their business. The room consisted of six oaken armchairs and a mahogany conference table. They all sat, and the two Kappernicks studied Weisman.

"Melvin," Weisman began, "do you want to spend the rest of your life in prison?"

"Does it look that bad?"

"No. Actually, it doesn't. And truth is, I think we could win this case, if you'd let me do my job."

"You promised …"

Weisman held up his hand. "I know, and so far I've kept my promise. But let me tell you why I'd made that promise in the first place—I'd made it because I honestly thought it would come out without my ever saying anything or introducing it. I believed it would come out that the girl was involved, and that once it was revealed, you would allow me to proceed to defend you."

"But it hasn't come out."

"No. To my absolute amazement, it has not. In fact, I'm

more than somewhat astounded that it has not. I'm in awe that Tiffany has been living at your son's house for more than three months without notice, without anybody asking questions. I don't know why the papers haven't jumped all over it."

"That's good."

"No, that's bad. That can't last. Sooner or later, people are going to ask what's she doing there, how she got there, who she is. I mean, after all, she is African American."

"What are you suggesting?"

"Look, I know juries, I know people. That panel is asking the same questions I did when we first met: Why was Ice Man trying to kill you? Let me do my job!"

Kappernick put his hands to his face. "I don't know ... I just don't know."

"Do you want to spend the rest of your life in prison?"

"Dad, please."

"But what will happen to her?" Kappernick asked. "Won't Child Welfare Services take her away? What will happen to Bruce and Barbara, and Linda Lansky? Isn't it a crime not to report child abuse?"

"We can take care of all of that. It's all diddly compared to what will happen to you. Melvin, let me do my job. I think we can win it."

TRIAL—DAY 7

"**DOCTOR, IS IT TRUE THAT,** every day, every single day, on average, twenty veterans who have seen military action overseas commit suicide?"

"Objection! Relevance. Is the defense now claiming insanity as a defense?" Michaels asked.

"Mr. Weisman?"

"No, Your Honor, not entirely. But it does go to cause, and if you give me a little leeway, I think it will all become clear."

Judge Harvey briefly considered this. He looked at Kappernick, then he looked at Bruce. "I'll give you a little leeway. Proceed."

Michaels tossed his hands. "Oh, for Christ's sake!"

"What was that, Mr. Michaels?"

"Your Honor—"

"Don't 'Your Honor' me. Honor me by keeping those comments to yourself. I'm allowing it. Proceed, Mr. Weisman."

"Doctor," Weisman asked again, "is it true that every day, every single day, twenty veterans commit suicide?"

"Yes, unfortunately that is true."

"What do you believe, as a trained psychiatrist, is the major cause of those deaths?"

The doctor was quick to answer. "Remorse."

"Remorse?"

"Yes. Everyone—every single, thinking person—anyone who has any smattering of sensitivity—has experienced remorse. No one is perfect. At some point in their lives, everyone has done something that makes them feel guilt or shame. The degree of the remorse is determined by how often the incident comes back to plague them, eat at them, haunt them. These regretful incidences vary from person to person. It may be the way he or she treated a lover, a friend, a parent. Maybe they humiliated someone they really cared for, or had betrayed a close friend, showed cowardice, didn't do the honorable thing."

"So, let me make sure I understand. You're saying that because the defendant did, or had failed to do, something in the past, his guilt or remorse may have compelled him to act. And in this case, to execute Ice Man."

"That is exactly what I'm saying."

"Objection!"

"Overruled."

"Dr. Morton," Weisman said, "when did you first meet the defendant?"

"I met him in 1968 in Vietnam."

"What were the circumstances?"

"We spent several hours talking about a tragic incident that left him feeling as though he let his people down."

"Can you tell us the details?"

"Yes. I remember our sessions vividly. A young girl, strapped with explosives, had killed herself and a man in his squad. What I made the defendant see was that someone had forced her to do it."

"Your Honor, may I approach?" Weisman asked.

Judge Harvey waved him forward, and both DAs joined him at the bench.

"Your Honor, my next witness is Tiffany Hall, a young lady who is only eleven."

The judge raised his eyebrows. "What is the purpose of her testimony?"

"She is the reason Ice Man … Barton Berk … wanted to kill Mr. Kappernick."

"In my chambers," said Judge Harvey. "Bring her in through the office next to my mine. I don't want this to turn into a sideshow yet."

Tiffany wore a blue skirt, a white blouse, and a dark blue scarf. Her hair had been pulled into a ponytail that trailed down between her shoulders. She sat in a chair before the judge, back straight and chin high. She smiled as he studied her. Then he smiled.

"Young lady, may I call you Tiffany?"

"Yes, sir, that would be fine."

"Well, Tiffany, I wanted to meet with you to determine if you will be able to testify. I want to find out if you're competent. Do you understand?"

"Yes, sir. I think I'll pass the test. I've done very well in school, and I believe you'll find me very competent."

Judge Harvey laughed. "Yes, I think I will. What do you think, Mr. Michaels?"

Michaels frowned. "Young lady, if I said I was wearing a purple hat, would that be true?"

Tiffany laughed. "No. You're not wearing a hat."

"How would you describe that statement? True or false?"

"False."

"Do you believe that the Vice President of the United States, John Schmidt, will run for president?"

"Do you mean Mr. Biden?"

"That's enough," said the judge. "I believe this young lady is competent. How old are you, Tiffany?"

Tiffany smiled proudly. "I'll be twelve in three months."

Judge Harvey, in turn, smiled profusely. "Wow," he said to her, and then said to the waiting attorneys, "Okay, let's go."

When the court reconvened, Weisman called Tiffany to the stand. She'd been sitting next to Barbara Kappernick in the back of the gallery. A sudden murmur rose up as she walked forward and was sworn in. People were impressed by how poised she appeared, but Barbara knew she was nervous.

She sat in the witness chair, hands folded in her lap, and looked straight ahead. Barbara had told her to take deep breaths and to focus on an object in the court if she became uncomfortable. She saw Barbara in the back, and tentatively smiled.

After asking permission, Weisman approached. "Tiffany, how are you doing?"

The girl forced a smile. "I'm doing fine, just fine." She looked down at her hands.

"How old are you?"

"I'll be twelve in three months."

Judge Harvey leaned forward on his elbow and smiled.

Weisman's voice was very gentle. "I'm going to ask you some tough questions. I want you to take your time and answer as truthfully as you can, okay?"

Tiffany laid her hands on the arms of the chair. "Okay."

"How did you come to meet Mr. Kappernick?"

"Well, when my grandmother got killed, and my aunt came to get me to live with her—"

"Your aunt came to get you? Where were your mother and father?"

"I never met my father; my grandmother said he left before I was actually born. And…" She bit her upper lip in hesitation, then said, "My mother was arrested when I was five. She's in prison. I haven't seen her in six years."

"How did your grandmother die?"

"She was hit by a car. The driver just ran her over and disappeared."

You could hear a pin drop in the gallery. One woman in the jury had tears running down her face.

"So you went to live with your aunt. What was that like?"

"Well, it wasn't good. My aunt really didn't care. She didn't know what to do with me. She didn't enroll me in school, and she was busy with all of the men. They were always coming and going. She just wanted me to stay in my room and be quiet, but I found me a bike and started riding."

"Just riding around?"

"That's right. I'd ride around all day, then return late in the afternoon. Renee, my aunt, never even knew I was gone. She didn't care. All she cared about was Ice Man."

"Ice Man? You mean Barton Berk?"

Tiffany shrugged. "No, I mean Ice Man."

"Was Ice Man living in the house?"

"No, he came at night and bossed people around. He was the boss."

"Go on."

"Well, the trouble started when Ice Man started coming into my room and doing things, things I didn't like." Tiffany stopped, rubbing her hands together.

Weisman spoke very softly. "Sexual things?"

"Yes, but I didn't want it. I told him 'no,' but he wouldn't stop. And then he hit me. My grandma told me about men like him, so I decided to run away."

"Where did you go?"

294 \ TED FINK

"Well"—she took several deep breaths—"when I was biking around, I saw a tree that had fallen in the backyard of a building. I climbed it and found a trapdoor that led to what I thought was an abandoned building. There was a room on the third floor, and I started sleeping there."

Weisman looked at the jury, who held its collective breath. Several jaws had fallen open. "Was there a bed there?"

"No, it was just a dirty, empty room. I got me a broom and swept it up, and carried some blankets up there. I even had some candles for the night."

"So, let me get this straight: In order to escape Ice Man—who, by way, is also known as Barton Berk—you climbed a tree to the third floor of a building every day and kinda made it your home."

"Yep. I slept there at night, and went back to Renee's during the day to clean up and eat."

"You slept in an empty building?"

"Yep. But I was wrong about the building; it wasn't empty at all. Kappy—" She slapped her hand over her mouth and, looking at Kappernick, let out a little laugh. "I mean, Mr. Kapp, was living on the second floor, and he caught me livin' there. He tried to tell me to leave, but I pleaded with him to let me stay."

"And he did."

"Yes, but only on certain conditions."

"What were they?"

"Well, I had to make dinner once a week. I had to keep my room clean. I had to go to school. He enrolled me in school, and I had to do my homework."

"You liked Mr. Kappernick."

"Oh, yes. I felt safe with him. He was like my grandmother. He walked me to school every day, and would be waitin' there when it let out. He taught me how to play chess.

Like my grandmother…" Suddenly, her chin quivered and tears rolled down her face. She wiped them away with the back of her hand. "He was like my father, wanting nothing from me but to do good."

"Tiffany, you're a smart girl, and a brave one. When Ice Man started doing those bad things, why didn't you go to the police?"

"The police were always there, in the house, you know, messin' with the girls. If I had told them, they would have told Ice Man, and Ice Man would've beat me. I was afraid. I was so afraid."

As a hardened defense attorney, Weisman had seen a lot in his day, but even he had to fight to keep from misting up. He swallowed hard. "Thank you, Tiffany. Thank you so very much. I don't have any more questions for you, but Mr. Michaels might. Your witness."

Michaels stood at his table and glanced over at the jury. Several of the women shot him looks that would have killed a normal man, and at that moment, he could have killed both the good Reverend Miles and Sasha Richards.

He hadn't seen her leave, but when Weisman had finished his examination of Tiffany, Sasha Richards had left the courtroom. Michaels knew why. She didn't want to hear what his cross-examination would be. What could he say?

He was trapped.

He shook his head. "I have no questions for this young lady."

TRIAL—DAY 8

JUST AS THE DAY'S PROCEEDINGS were about to begin, Judge Harvey was called away and he was forced to order an additional short recess. Weisman took advantage of the time out and left the courtroom to walk the crowded halls of the courthouse. In a lot of ways, he likened those corridors to a rush-hour subway platform; people milling around waiting for the train to come in or, in this case waiting for a decision to be made or a trial to resume. For most people the stirrings would have been disconcerting, but not for Weisman. For some reason he possessed the ability to ignore the clamor and think, and sometimes being in the fray helped frame his thoughts. He had to make another major decision, one with which he had been struggling. Should he call Melvin Kappernick to the stand? If Kappernick didn't testify in his own defense, the jury would think he had something to hide, even though he'd confessed to the crime! Weisman understood juries; he knew Kappernick's jury wanted the defendant to testify, wanted to hear his voice, needed an emotional connection. He thought about Michaels, whose air had all gone out of him with Tiffany's incredible testimony. Could that be enough? Calling Kappernick to the stand could open a lot of doors. Still ... what did he have to lose?

"I call Melvin Kappernick."

Kappernick hadn't fared well while being incarcerated. He was gaunt and pale, and had lost several pounds. Not that he'd been abused or threatened while in prison. The stress and fear of a possible attack, and his constantly being on alert had taken its toll. In all the time of his incarceration he never had a moment when he felt completely relaxed. He'd told himself all of that would change, but it hadn't. His weight loss was due to nothing more than the food; if a restaurant served what Graterford was offering, he doubted they'd last even a month. It was horrendous, but there was no alternative; you ate to survive.

Now, as he walked down the aisle to be sworn in and sat in the witness chair, Kappernick seemed haggard and old. Despite his standing tall and proud, his own suit, the one brought to him from the second floor of the old Teabloom store, seemed too big.

Weisman worked the timeline of facts perfectly: his client's growing up in the old neighborhood, his college experiences, his marriage, his son and grandchildren, and the death of his wife. He skillfully introduced Kappernick's living with his son's family, then moving back to the old neighborhood. Through Kappernick, Weisman captured the beauty, freedom, and joy children feel before they have to face adult pressures. That's what Kappernick wanted to recapture. And why not? Didn't a seventy-seven-year-old man have the right? Hadn't he paid his dues? Then, Weisman introduced Tiffany, and for the jury, he reconstructed the bond between the two, after which he took Kappernick back in time to Vietnam.

"You see, my job, my main job, was to keep my guys alive," said Kappernick. "That's how I looked at it. Now, just days before, we'd seen some heavy action. We'd been dropped behind enemy lines, had done what we had to do, and then, as we were trying to get out, we got caught in a heavy barrage of enemy fire. But we made it out of there—got back, mind you—without so much as a scratch.

"I gotta tell you, I was feeling pretty good that day. Felt I could do no wrong. My only problem was a PFC named Malley. It wasn't that he was a goof-off … he was … as it turned out … a pacifist.… He just didn't care. He wasn't gonna kill anybody. What the hell was he doing there? I mean, when we were under that intense fire, he never once fired a round.

"Later, when we got back to base, I tried to talk to him, tried to tell him how everyone's life depended on everybody pulling his own weight. But it was like he wasn't listening; just nodding his head and smiling. Unbelievably, he'd become a flower child! Then, we got what I thought was this easy assignment. A village was having a problem, though nothing heavy. It was friendly and close by, not even a day's march. A piece of cake. So I got this idea of how to straighten out Malley. I'd put him on point; I'd make him responsible for all of us."

"What exactly is 'point'?"

"Point—the lead position in the column. You're maybe twenty feet ahead of the second guy in line; you've got to see everything. Your eyes are all over the place. Not only is your own life dependent upon how observant you are, but also the lives of every man in the squad.

"So, we leave at six a.m.," Kappernick said, "and we hit the village about noon. Malley was doing good. I could see just by the way he was moving that he was conscious of everything. He wasn't just flaking off, smelling the daisies. I figured, maybe this was what he'd needed. He knew we were all depending on him.

"He stopped moving when we hit the village. I was to his right, about twenty-five feet away, and I started walking toward him. I was almost to him, when this little girl came out of a hut, tears running down her face. She was wearing this ragged dress, and I can see Malley's face. He relaxed, smiled. He wanted to hug her. She was crying big tears, only I saw what was making her cry."

Kappernick lowered his head, "It was strapped to her back," he told them. "I saw it, the rest of the guys saw it, so why didn't Malley see it? He kind of put out his arms to her; the big bear just wanted to comfort the scared little cub. Then … it all went crazy. Next thing I knew, her body parts were flying all over the place, and Malley was dead. Somehow, I'd come to believe his death was my fault. I should have known he wasn't ready. I should have yelled. I should have killed her myself … but I didn't. Initially, it tortured me to the point where I'd thought about eating my gun. I couldn't think, I couldn't lead. Finally, I spoke to the shrink, and he made me look at it differently, helped me to see that it wasn't the little girl, but the sonofabitch who'd strapped the shit on her back and made her walk toward us. I accepted that explanation."

"Didn't you later receive the Navy Cross? Didn't you save a couple of your men under intense fire?"

Kappernick reluctantly said rather grimly, "I did. That helped. It helped me, in my own mind, to hide my mistake."

"You mean, the mistake of putting Malley on point?"

"Yes. For years I'd shoved the incident to the back of my mind. When I mustered out of the service, I devoted myself to my wife, to making a living, to raising my son. But after my wife died, I started to think about it again—about all of the mistakes I'd made, about all of the things I regretted. But Malley and that little girl … it flashed through my mind every day. Sometimes for seconds; sometimes for minutes.

You know, a man reaches a point in his life when he starts to think about what he's done and all he can see are the mistakes."

"And then ... this girl appeared. Not in my nightmares, but in the present. A brave kid, a gutsy kid. A kid who climbed a tree to escape the bastard who was trying to make her do something she knew was wrong, something she felt was wrong. Turned out, Ice Man was like the Cong, in 'nam, in that village—the one who strapped that shit to the little girl's back. All he wanted to do was use her. It was like I had a second chance—I could save this little girl, could give her a life. I could redeem myself."

"How did you know that Ice Man, Barton Berk, wanted to use her, make her a prostitute?"

"She told me, and ... he told me. He actually came into my house and told me I was interfering with his business plans for her. He said, as if he were discussing a business deal, that people ... sick people—pedophiles, he said—would pay small fortunes to be with her."

"He actually came into your house?"

"That's right." Kappernick nodded once. "I told him, asked him, to just leave us alone, leave the girl alone." He sighed heavily. "But he wouldn't. He didn't care. He discounted me, thought I was too old to defend myself. So he got physical, slapped me in the face, like he thought he was untouchable. Then, he tried to have me beaten up, offered to pay one of his men to kill me. The guy who tried to shoot me at the zoo was one of his men. Right in front of my entire family, he fired a shot! That's when I decided that he, Ice Man, had to go, and that it was my job to do it."

"Once again, why didn't you call the police?"

"Look, I believed Ice Man was crazy and ... I didn't trust the system to remove him from society before he hurt a lot more people."

Weisman nodded. "Your witness."

Michaels jumped to his feet. "So, you decided to be judge and jury."

"Yes."

"And executioner."

"Yes."

"Because you thought Barton Berk, the pharmacist who worked every day for an established national firm for over twenty years without ever missing a day—the man you called Ice Man—was really corrupt; a killer, a pimp, a crazy. Is that what you want us to believe?"

"That's the way it was."

"You want us to believe a lot. You want us to believe the man whom you killed, the one who worked in a pharmacy every day, was really a pimp in disguise."

"Yes."

"You want us to believe that this man came into your house and *told* you he was a pimp, that he was going to make the girl involved his sex slave. Don't you think that's a bit over the top? A bit ridiculous?"

"I can't explain it."

"Why would he do it?" Michaels said. "And even more importantly, why would we believe such a cock-and-bull story?"

The recording he'd made that day Ice Man had come to his place flashed through Kappernick's mind. If only he hadn't lost that recording. "That's the way it was," he said. "That's the way it happened. He swore he would kill me if he didn't get Tiffany back. He was crazy."

"Are you a psychiatrist?"

"No."

"Yet you determined this man to be crazy. Are you a judge?"

"No."

"Yet you determine this man to be guilty. Are you in law enforcement?"

"No."

"Yet you decided that he must be executed."

"That's right."

"Seems everything you do is against the way the world, the way society works."

"Objection!" Weisman called out.

"Sustained," said the judge. "Questions, not preaching, Mr. Michaels."

"Your Honor, I'm speechless at this man's incredible audacity."

"Does that mean you have no further questions for the defendant?"

"No, I have a few more." Michaels turned back to Kappernick. "So, you were burdened with guilt over something that happened in 1968, and you thought the way to redeem yourself was to kill someone?"

"No. Not just someone, not just anyone," Kappernick said. "I sought to eliminate Ice Man before he killed someone I loved!"

"Eliminate. Eliminate! What about the other man? What about Ruby Brown? Did you plan to eliminate him, as well?"

"No, actually, I'm sorry he passed. From what I understand, it was actually a heart attack that killed him, not any of the bullets that I'd fired. My mission was to take out Ice Man. That's who I was after."

The DA could not hide his rage; his face fairly radiated with the heat of his wrath. And then, catching himself, he said, almost in a whisper, "So you, using your own words, had decided to eliminate him. Tell me, did you get any satisfaction out of killing him?" At this, Kappernick did not respond.

"Did you relish the moment?"

Judge Harvey pushed for a reply. "Answer the question, Mr. Kappernick."

"I might have," Kappernick said. "At this time, I really can't be sure."

"Oh, really? You can't be sure. Then why, after you shot Barton Berk in the arm, and before you put a bullet in his head, did you blow his male parts to smithereens?" And then he added sarcastically, "Didn't that make you feel good?" He put his hand up to his ear. "Well, didn't it? I have no further questions for this killer."

Judge Harvey called an end to the day's proceedings. "We will begin with closing arguments first thing tomorrow morning."

Kappernick was taken to a holding room, where he exchanged his dark suit, tie, and shirt for his orange prison jumpsuit. He was then handcuffed and taken back to Graterford.

That night, he lay in his bunk and tried to sleep. With his eyes shut, he listened to the collective sounds of over a hundred men sleeping—a persistent, low droning. Suddenly, he was aware of a confrontation. From a few cells down from his came the start of a whispered struggle, as though a young newbie tried to fight off an older prisoner forcing him do something repulsive. Kappernick had seen the kid two days before, knew he'd have trouble protecting himself. The kid tried to walk tall, though it was obvious he wasn't a fighter. To make matters worse, the kid had been put into a cell with thugs who wouldn't hesitate to use and abuse him. Once broken, the kid would become the property of some brutal bastard who passed him around for favors.

Kappernick heard the muted punches, the muffled cries of pain, the agonizing moans, the pleading, and then the final submission. But he was the only one who'd heard it; no one said anything, no one yelled anything as the block's collective murmur continued, uninterrupted. Everyone knew what was happening, and no one cared. They'd heard it all before. This wasn't the first time, and it certainly wouldn't be the last. In the short time Kappernick had been incarcerated, two other similar incidents had occurred.

Now, as he lay in his bunk, he thought of Bruce and Barbara, his wife, Linda Lansky, his grandkids, and Tiffany. Only they mattered in his dismal life. The grandkids would soon forget about him; they'd shake off what he'd done, or convince themselves he'd done it to save them. In all likelihood, he'd never see them again, since he'd probably die in prison. If he was lucky, it wouldn't be all that long. He had another ten years, at most. Probably less. Then he thought of Soldier, and before he fell asleep, Kappernick smiled. He had no regrets.

TRIAL—DAY

DISTRICT ATTORNEY MICHAELS stood before the jury and studied the panel. "Ladies and gentlemen," he said, "you have an obligation under the law, an obligation that makes up the cornerstone of our society. It is your job to tell people, to tell the world, that a person cannot take a life without being punished. You must find the defendant guilty of first-degree murder. "The burden of proof lies with the prosecution, and we proved our case. You heard the defendant admit he committed this heinous, first-degree murder. First-degree murder means that the killing of a human being was premeditated. The law is very clear on this point. This was no crime of passion, no irresistible impulse, no mock insanity. This was pure, premeditated murder; it was planned, and the victims were viciously gunned down, murdered in a dirty, stinking alley. It doesn't matter if the victims were bad or good, they deserved a fair trial. Civilized people do not take the law into their own hands; they trust the police to do the right thing, and the courts to decide who is and who is not guilty.

"The defendant, Melvin Kappernick, took the law into his own hands. He'd planned the murder for days. Had enlisted his old Marine buddy to help. Took Darnell Perkins to an empty apartment and gave him a high-caliber, scoped rifle, told him to shoot the first two men who emerged. Then he waited for Barton Berk and Ruby Brown to escape out the back. When they came out, as he planned, he gunned them down, viciously assassinated them.

"There is no question that he shot them. He signed a confession! You heard him take the stand and reiterate it. You heard him say he'd murdered Barton Berk and poor Ruby Brown. You have an obligation to the good people of this city, an obligation to your community, and an obligation to yourselves to find Melvin Kappernick guilty of murder in the first degree. For the welfare of all concerned, do what you know is the right thing. Find Melvin Kappernick guilty of murder in the first degree. Thank you."

Several moments passed before Judge Harvey called on Arnold Weisman to address the jury with the defense's summation and their final comments.

Weisman stood and walked toward the jury, studied them and allowed them to focus on him. "The District Attorney asked you to do the right thing," he said. "I am also asking you to do the right thing, though the DA and I have two different concepts of what that thing is. I am asking you to look into your hearts and see the truth. I want you to take a look at Melvin Kappernick. Before this, he'd never even had a traffic ticket. He'd joined the Marines, became an officer, led a squadron of men in Vietnam, was sent many times with that squadron behind enemy lines, distinguished himself, earned the Navy Cross awarded to members of *the* U.S. Marine Corps for heroism and distinguished service. Yes, of course his tours of duty had left scars. But despite everything he'd been through, everything he'd endured when he came home, he'd always done the right thing. He always honored his wife, saw that his son went to college, worked the same job for over forty years. And then, in the sunset of his life, he did something he always wanted to do: returned to the place that, in his mind, represented his youth. The neighborhood in which he'd grown up. But that place he remembered had changed. And then, he met this brave little girl. A little girl that some brutal bastard wanted to turn into a prostitute. She's eleven years old! And when Melvin Kappernick tried to protect her, the bastard who wanted to force her to do things anathema to her basic instincts tried to have him killed. What was he supposed to do, up against a gang of killers? Go to the police? You heard Tiffany Hall, heard her say that the police hung out at the whorehouse the gang controlled!"

Weisman paused, looked each juror in the eye, and then, almost jumping off the ground, he shouted, "This case shouldn't have even come before a jury! This case should have been dismissed! This defendant, who has spent the last three-and-a-half months in prison for defending himself against a gang of killers, rapists, pimps, and child predators should be set free and given another medal! He did the community a service!"

Breathing heavily, Weisman had to take a moment to contain himself. "So," he went on, "I am asking you to do the right thing. I am asking you to look into your hearts and find Melvin Kappernick innocent of all charges and return this good man to his loved ones. Thank you."

Weisman finished his summation at noon, and Judge Harvey ordered the jury to retire and consider a verdict.

Kappernick was escorted to a holding cell, while both Weisman and Bruce went to their respective offices.

In less than three hours, the jury was out and everyone had reassembled by 4:15.

Judge Harvey asked the panel if they'd reached a verdict. They had. He asked for their decision. The bailiff took the written verdict and handed it to Judge Harvey, who read it, folded it, and handed it back. Then he asked the jury foreman to stand, and asked Kappernick to do the same and face the jury foreman. Weisman and Bruce stood on each side of the defendant.

"Mr. Foreman ... how do you find the defendant?"

"Your Honor, we find the defendant, Melvin Kappernick..."

LINDA LANSKY

LINDA LANSKY LEFT Leidy School twenty minutes after the day's final bell had rung. Always one to last leave the building, Linda was a meticulous person who had to make sure everything had been put away and was ready for the following morning.

Using colorful thumb tacks, she'd pinned a couple of excellent spelling tests to the corkboard at the front of the room, along with a couple of chalk drawings. With that done, she shut out the lights, closed the door, and walked to her car.

Soon, it would all be over, and then what would she do? She hadn't really planned or thought about what lay ahead. She'd probably travel, since there were still so many places she wanted to see. But what would she do with the big dog, that wonderful galoot that Kappernick had left her. Soldier would be lost without her, and she'd be lost without him—a special case of true love. Of course, thinking of Soldier made her think of that other big galoot, Kappernick, and she sighed. What would happen to Melvin?

Sitting behind the steering wheel of her car, Linda began to tear up. She pulled over and breathed heavily. No two ways about it, she would miss Melvin Kappernick. She couldn't put him out of her mind.

Linda felt a deep affection for the man. What was wrong

with her? Was she crazy? He'd killed somebody!

She dried her eyes and got back on the road. Was it just that she was just lonely? Again, with the deep sighs. She never realized just how lonely she was. Yes, she was attracted to Melvin, but it wasn't a purely sexual thing. Pure sex. Ha, ha! Those days were long gone. But something about him made her feel safe, made her feel good. His calls, when he called, made her feel young again. She loved the way he touched her hand, laughed at her, and admired her.

"Damn you, Melvin Kappernick, for doing this!" she said aloud. "We could have had such great fun together."

Linda pulled into the driveway and started walking up to the house. She put down her papers and searched for her key. Hearing her come up the porch steps, Soldier ran to the door and whined, spinning around, excited to see her.

"Take it easy," she yelled. "Don't scratch up the floor. I'm looking for my key."

Finally, she unlocked the door, and the big dog ran right past her, sprinting around the corner of the house. And that's when she heard it. Not exactly Frank Sinatra, but definitely a version of his song. It was loud, and it was clear, and it was almost in tune: "I've got you under my skin … I've got you deep in the heart of me … so deep…"

THE END

ABOUT TED

Ted Fink received a BA in creative writing and a Master Degree in Educational Administration. He is a nationally recognized professional story artist and has performed his original adult tales at many important venues including The Kimmel Center, the Philadelphia Art Museum, the National Storytelling Conference, and the Philadelphia Folk Festival.

After teaching for ten years in the Philadelphia School system Ted became involved in a variety of business ventures, from creating restaurants, to exporting sea food. For 5 years, from 1977 to 1981, Ted co-owned a business which was the largest exporter of Anguilla Rostrata in America, shipping millions of pounds of eels to Europe and Japan. Up and down the coast, he was known as, "the Eelman".

Ted's fiction has appeared in the Philadelphia Inquirer and the literary magazine, Chapman. His latest book, The Tales I've Told is a special multi-media collection of his short stories.

Ted is married, has two children, and two grandchildren. He lives in a modern glass house that he himself built 1983.

OTHER BOOKS
BY THE AUTHOR

The Tales I've Told
In Search of Joel Gomez
Game of the Gods

Made in the USA
Columbia, SC
08 December 2020